Darke

First Edition 2024
Yorkie-Montague Books
Devon

Darkest Dartmoor

Andrew McAuley

Contents

Introduction

This collection is inspired by the landscape, myths and superstitions of Dartmoor. Many of the stories are based around actual Dartmoor locations, others are loosely based on existing folk tales. Most of these tales appear here in print for the first time and have been written specifically for this anthology. The afterword of this book reflects further on the origins of the stories – a difficult thing to delve into in the introduction without spoiling surprises. Each of the thirteen tales are intended to give the reader 'the creeps' rather than to simply horrify with slayings and gore. Incidences of violence in these pages are mostly muted, as is the language. That which lurks in the shadows, remaining unseen and beyond comprehension, is much more terrifying than the masked psychopath butchering teens with a chainsaw – and so it is hoped that these thirteen stories will haunt rather than repulse: very much in the tradition of good old fashioned ghost stories.

As most of the legends of Dartmoor are firmly set in the past, this book has been divided into two sections: the first half consists of seven short stories which take place roughly between the 16th century and the first half of the 20th century, whereas the second part contains five short stories and one novella-length tale set in modern times.

The stories of the past do not specifically state within the tales which year they are set in (*except The Whaler*), but the rough timeframe should be apparent within the first couple of paragraphs. For clarification – *The White* is set in the 1850's, *Cursed Earth* takes place around the middle of the 19th century, *Wolf at the Door* is set in the 1830's, *Ordeal* takes place somewhere between 1500 and 1600, *Devil's Cauldron* is the

1830's, *Legend of Vixana* is toward the end of the 19th century, and *The Whaler* states the year as 1951. The stories in *Part I* are not arranged chronologically – instead having been placed so as to have the most appropriate neighbouring tale.

If one should decide to venture out onto the moor to explore some of the locations where these stories are set (specific places are given in the afterword), it is suggested that attention be given to the weather forecast; dress for all weathers as Dartmoor pays little heed to the seasons, take a map, compass, torch, waterproof boots, and most of all be prepared to be absorbed into a landscape of mists and myth where the rules of world beyond the moor don't always apply.

Part I: Stories of the Past

The White

Corporal Parsons rubbed his trembling hands in front of the fireplace. The knuckles were sore and swollen, purple and bloodied. Strong-scented pipe smoke from one of the inn patrons overpowered the smell of burning logs, reminding him of home. A bawdy song about Queen Victoria's underskirts failed to rile the weather-weary solider who could only sit on the creaking stool and stare into the dancing flames, thinking of Mary.

The window shutters were closed against what little midday sun filtered through the white haze outside, casting the corners of the tavern which candlelight failed to reach into gloomy crevasses. Occasionally, the wind would pick up and rattle the shutters against the frames: little did this disturb the handful of patrons from their chatter until the February snowstorm blasted into the tavern as the door was thrust open, scattering white flakes like shrapnel and causing the fire in the hearth to recoil from the frosty gust that battered it.

'Shut the bloody door!' Two voices from the far side of the sparsely populated tavern shouted as one. The singing trailed off as the few pub regulars who had braved the cold turned their attention to the strangers.

Parsons shivered as the fire recovered from the wind's assault. Hearing footsteps trudge from the doorway toward the fireplace, he hugged his shoulders and lowered his gaze to the small puddle between his feet where the snow had melted off his boots.

'Parsons? That you?' a loud, cockney voice enquired.

Parsons turned on his stool so that he could peer at the newcomer with one eye.

Two young men stood side-by-side in frost encrusted greatcoats with frozen haversacks at their sides and their grey woollen blanket rolls fashioned into makeshift hoods over their crumpled shakos.

'That's Corporal Parsons to you, Ryder.'

'Yes, Corp,' Ryder said, exchanging a sideways glance with his neighbour.

Parsons stood, stroking his moustache as he inspected the pair of dishevelled and wind beaten privates. He saw one of the soldiers wince at the sight of his red knuckles and so he concealed them in the sleeves of his overlong greatcoat. 'Well then, Privates. You kept me waiting here long enough. I suppose you've some tale about the train into Dousland being delayed by weather. Now, are we to stand here all day or shall we return to our station, as is our duty?'

The soldiers looked at each other and back to the corporal.

'Leave now, Corporal?' Private Foster, the younger of the two men, stammered. 'We got proper frosted in the three-minute tramp from train to here.'

'You've been loitering on leave a fortnight and now you want to laze at a tavern some more afore returning to your post?' Parsons sneered, glaring at the two men, ready to pounce on any indication of insubordination.

'You're not going out in that!' the innkeeper called out, pausing from wiping a misty glass. A pub patron nodded his agreement from the bar, scrutinizing the frozen soldiers through a cloud of pipe smoke. Singing and chatter ceased as the half dozen patrons turned their attention to the three soldiers.

'Please, Corporal,' Foster said, his large eyes pleading. 'It were labour enough trekking from train station. It's four mile of moorland to Princetown.'

'Snowdrifts up to your armpits,' the innkeeper added, returning to cleaning his glass.

'Duty is duty!' Parsons growled. 'I'm to escort these here two men back to barracks, not to watch them get drunk.' He dug a pair of coppers out of his purse in payment for the gritty ale he'd left half-drank. He tossed the coins purposefully short of the bar and marched to the door, swinging it open. Swirling winds spewed into the bar, drowning out the sound of the spinning coppers.

'Shut the bloody door!' The chorus chanted.

Parsons leant into the wind. Each footstep sank into three inches of white and was marked by a muffled crunch. The cold instantly penetrated old leather and threadbare wool. He turned to check that the two soldiers followed, waved at them to hurry on, and braced against the blustering wind which stung nose and cheeks.

The sky was a haze of white and grey through which the sun only occasionally glinted, teasing the memory of warmth. The wind blew with such force that it was impossible to be certain if the snowflakes carried upon the gusts were falling fresh or merely blown up from the ground. A line of skeletal trees along what was once the road faded into oblivion at the tenth trunk.

'Keep up!' Parsons shouted over his shoulder, trusting the wind to carry his voice. 'Don't stop walking: that's when the cold gets you! My orders are to fetch two privates from Dousland and I don't mean to turn up short – but don't think I'll carry ya! Two hours, lads, and you can complain in your bunks with a flask of grog.'

Parson's toes soon began to hurt. Waiting for the privates at the Dousland Inn had done little to prepare him for returning to the cold, but he could not delay: Tomorrow was Sunday, and after the church service he could see to poor Mary, who was waiting for him back at the cottage. 'I'm coming home to you Mary,' Parsons muttered. 'Worry not: I shall be there to take care o' ya soon enough.'

'What's that, Corp?' Ryder shouted, holding his shako and the wildly flapping makeshift hood to his head with one hand.

Parsons scowled. He hadn't realised Ryder had caught up. He pointed ahead with his sleeve bunched up in his fist. 'Keep the trees to this side of us 'til we reach the gully, then it's over the hill and we're home and dry.'

'It's bloody freezing, Corp. I can't walk that far.'

Parsons snorted and marched on. Sharp wind made his eyes water and froze the tears to his cheeks. He clamped his teeth tight to stop them rattling and thought of Mary waiting at the cottage. He had to get back to her: to look upon her sweet face, apologise for having to leave so suddenly, and see her safely on her way before someone found her in his billet and reported the indiscretion.

'Help!'

Parsons turned to see Foster laying in the snow with his hand outstretched toward his companions, begging for assistance. Although only twenty paces behind, his form was already starting to dissolve into the white.

Ryder rushed to his comrade, kicking up a dust of snow and stumbling himself before reaching the fallen soldier. He helped Foster to his feet and let the younger man lean into him for support.

'Hurry it up you two!' Parsons roared.

Ryder shouted something but it was lost on the wind. The two men waded toward their corporal, clinging to each other, their free arms swaying to aid balance.

'He's getting frost bitten!' Ryder shouted over the wailing wind. 'We've not even come a quarter mile. We must go back!'

'I can't feel me toes, Corporal,' Foster added, his teeth chattering as he spoke. Cloudy vapour from his breath obscured his reddened cheeks.

'Stomp your feet like a proper soldier when you walk – that'll keep 'em warm,' Parsons snarled and turned his back on the men.

'You just want to get back to that bloody baker maid you're always chasing, Corp. What's her name? Mary?'

Parsons kept walking. He wasn't going to waste energy arguing in a blizzard; he would file charges against Ryder once they were back at barracks.

'Corp, you're a bloody-minded, two-penny, officer's boot licker. How far do you think you'll get? We can't stay out here: we'll bloody freeze!'

Parsons wondered if Mary was cold in his one-room cottage. It wouldn't do to keep her waiting. He tried to increase his pace

14

as the wind and the deepening snow conspired to try to drive him back the way he'd come.

'She's not even interested in you, you old fool!' Ryder yelled. 'We're going back! To hell with you!'

Parsons fixated on the horizon and kept moving, mumbling the step: 'Left, right, left, right.' He continued to announce the step even when his shaking legs were three paces behind his murmured commands.

Glimpses of a black shape blinked into view through the flurry: at first Parsons thought it was a small tree, but it appeared to move. He squinted, making out what looked like the figure of a person – visible one moment and obscured by swirls of snowflakes the next. He shook his head, unsure if it was tiredness conjuring phantoms out of the white, but the figure remained and became momentarily clearer: it was Mary. Dressed in her pinafore with her brown hair hung in an unkempt tangle. She seemed to be saying something, but the sound was carried off on the gale.

'Mary? Is that you? How are you here?'

Mary beckoned. She didn't seem to be moving, but even as Parsons rushed through the snow she remained just at the edge of visibility with the flurry constantly threatening to swallow her.

'Wait!' Parsons yelled. Each step became more difficult until the drift reached knee-height and he had to wade through its freezing wet thickness which seeped through his twill trousers and down into his boots. He could no longer feel his toes and he couldn't stop shivering. He halted, looking for the line of trees or any other landmark but seeing only a white-grey haze. He turned back to Mary and saw that the blizzard had almost devoured her.

'I'm coming, Mary!' Parsons shrieked. Tightly packed snow pulled at his boots as he flailed through the thigh-high drift. The greatcoat was heavy with frost, slowing progress. He fumbled with the brass buttons and shrugged off the heavy coat. Parsons surged forward and fell, flailing in the snow, calling out for Mary.

Mary beckoned still. Silently mouthing encouragement for him to follow.

Parsons couldn't make his legs move and couldn't even feel them below the knees. He pawed at the snow with numb fingers, trying to drag himself toward his love. He saw his bloody and swollen knuckles and remembered.

Mary had moved near enough that he could see her bruised neck and cheek, and the thin line of blood that had come from her nose when he threw her against the table in his cottage.

'Why?' Mary mouthed.

'I'm sorry, Mary!' Parsons reached a trembling hand out to her. 'I didn't mean to. You shouldn't have refused me!'

A blast of snow enveloped Mary, whisking her away.

Parsons called out, but the screaming wind stole his voice. Frosted fingers were wet, swollen, reddened, and no longer obeyed the Corporal's will. It took the last available strength to turn his head, looking for Mary, but all that could be seen was the white.

Cursed Earth

'There's something odd going on over there,' Beth said, pursing her lips in disapproval.

John wiped sweat from his forehead and leaned on his hoe. He followed his wife's gaze upstream toward the dilapidated cottage of their neighbour. Gaps showed in the thatch, once white walls weather stained and sagging, and the field around it untilled and strewn with weeds.

'Something very odd indeed,' Beth said, squinting at the hovel as if her scrutiny might squeeze secrets from the decaying wattle-and-daub structure.

'Why do you say that?' John shrugged, holding his hoe ready to return to his work.

'Her fields are spoiled and unattended since before last season. Not a bud will break through that clod.' The wind snatched a stray lock of blonde hair loose from Beth's bun to whip it around her cheeks. She licked her weather-cracked lips, but her granite-grey eyes remained fixed on the neighbour's plot.

'Aye. Shame about them fields,' John said. 'It be back-breaking toil for us at three score years, let alone an old crone like Myrtle.' John returned to his labour, breaking up the frost-hardened ground and turning over the softer soil underneath. The earth strenuously resisted John's efforts and he was soon panting for breath, with sweat stinging his eyes despite the cold March morning. He paused work again, realising his efforts weren't accompanied by the familiar sound of his wife's hoe scraping the crusted ground. He looked back at Beth: she hadn't moved, remaining transfixed on the ramshackle cottage.

'Not since her son was carried off has she worked a day on that field,' Beth said. 'How can she remain here with no yield and naught to eat?'

John removed his cap used it to dab his forehead. 'Aye. I'd be of a mind to lend aid if I could, but we'll starve too if we don't get our field properly broken up for sowing.'

Beth sighed and put her hoe to the soil, grimacing as she bent into the work and grunting with each churn of toughened earth. With each stab of the hoe she exhaled a short trail of vapour that evaporated on the cold wind. She glanced sideways at John, who had been watching her with a concerned frown, prompting him to rejoin the labour.

At the end of the furlong the couple sagged into each other. John's lips brushed Beth's forehead and she ran her fingertips over his sore and calloused palms. The meagre field had worked against them, but they had overcome it in the dying rays of the day.

'The land here hates us,' Beth said as they retreated toward their clay-walled cottage. The setting sun had stained the horizon blood red and the hills surrounding the twin farms began to darken, drowning the valley in shade.

'Wasn't always so,' John said, feeling his cheeks flush.

'I don't mean it that way. I don't blame you for our life here. Not anymore.' Beth's weather-beaten features softened into a sorrowful smile. She squeezed John's hand and paused at the doorway to pick up and light the gas lantern.

John looked to Myrtle's cottage, noticing a dim light around the edges of the crumpled window shutters.

Beth caught his gaze and her expression hardened again. 'It can only be some unholy compact that lets her thrive while we struggle.'

'Thrive, does she? I think not, dearest.' John said, forcing a smile.

Beth let out a weary sigh. She gently pushed her husband inside their ancient and diminutive dwelling.

The floor of the cottage was made of compacted dirt and, like longhouses of days gone by, there were no interior rooms. A stone channel ran down the centre to serve as a drain for animal effluent, yet there had been no beasts in the cottage for many years other than pests which lived in the rafters and the thatch, stealing such morsels as they could. Tottering chairs flanked a chipped table near the fireplace. In one corner lay a bed with a mattress of straw; above it an iron crucifix stood guard, slightly askew. Beside the bed lay a deflated sack of barley seeds. There were no possessions beyond those the couple deemed essential to life. John lit the fireplace while Beth prepared their late dinner. The stew was weaker than usual: a mere broth flavoured with nuts, browned cabbage, and pieces of wild mushroom which forlornly bobbed in the boiling pot like pieces of driftwood in a rough sea. They ate in silence at the fireside.

'That's the last scraps,' Beth said when they had finished. 'I didn't want to say before lest it ruin your meal.'

John nodded, not knowing what to say.

'Tomorrow I'll go over the hills to seek more mushrooms while you dig the furrows.'

'You'd be lucky,' John said. 'They'll be picked clean.'

Beth bowed her head and gulped.

John patted his wife's hand and looked over at the sack of seeds which they would soon sow. It would need to be a bumper crop if they were not to starve come winter; the spring was late in coming, endangering everyone's livelihood after a poor harvest the previous season.

'How does she survive?' Beth said, her voice scratchy and hoarse with stifled emotion.

John lit his pipe, inhaling as he regarded the hessian sack upon which so much relied. The taste of bark shavings mixed with dried grass was no substitute for tobacco, but he'd become accustomed to the taste and the rough aroma masked the faint scent of damp and decay that permeated their home.

'Could she have stored food left over from last August's harvest?' Beth stared into the fireplace, frowning in thought.

John sagged in his chair and grunted. 'We should get abed before the fire burns out.'

John watched his wife's diminishing figure ascend a gorse-covered hillside. She moved in a crooked fashion – more like a wilting crone than a woman of thirty. She didn't turn to wave farewell, but John waited until Beth disappeared from view before starting work on scraping narrow furrows in the ground. The newly turned soil was full of slugs and snails which he flicked aside with his hoe. A strident cackling announced the presence of crows waiting in ambush from their hideouts among windswept hawthorns: their dark eyes studying his labour, anticipating the sowing which must follow.

Movement upstream caught John's eye; Myrtle emerged from her cottage in a tattered brown homespun dress. She skulked bent-backed about her desolate field as if searching for something. John shook his head: the poor old lass was likely starving and desperate for any miracle growth of grain. He watched her drop to her knees and begin digging, seemingly with bare hands. John was about to call to her that she would rake her fingers raw, but curiosity compelled him to watch.

Myrtle, perhaps suddenly aware of her neighbour's scrutiny, jolted and looked around at John. She scrambled to conceal whatever she had found among the dirt into the folds of her dress and then scampered back into her hovel as hastily as frail legs would permit.

John was chopping logs when Beth returned with hunched shoulders and the corners of her mouth sagging. She didn't meet his gaze. He did her the small honour of not glancing into her empty basket or enquiring if there had been any success.

'Tomorrow, after we've sown the seeds, I'll go into the village and see if I can't do some odd jobs,' John said.

Beth nodded. They retreated inside and, with the setting of the sun, went to bed hungry. John lay staring into the black. He could tell by Beth's breathing that she lay awake too. Neither spoke.

In the morning they put out the wooden cross that served as their scarecrow. Beth dressed it in an old coat. John sacrificed his cap to the cross. The couple silently went about their work, dripping seeds along the furrows and then lightly covering them with earth, nurturing the earth like it were a sickly child. Finally, they stood together in the corner of the field, surveying their handiwork. John put his arm around Beth's shoulder. They remained together in silence until the groans and complaints from John's stomach forced them apart out of shame of their predicament.

'I'll head into the village,' John said, raising a hand to straighten his cap before remembering he no longer possessed the hat.

'I'll come. Might be something I can do for a loaf of bread. Perchance even some cheese.'

The mention of food made John's mouth fill with saliva, although all he could taste was mud. He caught a glimpse of movement from Myrtle's field.

Myrtle was lurching toward her cottage, cradling something which she kept wrapped in the front of her dress. She glanced at her neighbours and went inside without returning the faint wave John hailed her with.

'She's losing her mind,' Beth said. 'This cursed land will do for us all.' A suppressed tear glistened in the corner of her eye.

'Yesterday, I saw her digging,' John said. 'I almost fancied she'd some buried treasure or hidden food, but you're right: hunger is driving her wild. If we do get cheese maybe we can spare her some.'

'How does she live?' Beth said. 'Truly, the land is cursed.' A sudden gust made her shiver and rub her arms for warmth.

'I'll fish the river,' John said, breaking the sullen silence as they neared their farm upon returning empty-handed from the village.

Beth nodded.

John was grateful that she refrained from pointing out that the river hadn't yielded fish since the surviving salmon swam back downstream in November. Their ramshackle homestead came into view as they rounded a grassy mound which had been the spoil heap of some predecessor's fruitless effort at tin exploration.

'No!' Beth cried, breaking into a run.

John startled, expecting to see the cottage aflame or the roof blown off. The danger was worse: crows circled the field, cawing and swooping. John ran to the cottage, pausing only long enough to snatch up his hoe. He charged the birds, swinging the farming implement and yelling with the fury of a berserker.

Beth wailed and screamed, flailing uselessly at the crows who taunted her with mocking cries as they swarmed safely out of reach.

John chased the birds until, exhausted, he dropped to his knees, panting. Only then the dark things tired of their cruel game and returned to their hawthorn watchtowers. John collapsed into the dirt, breathing in granules of musty earth that choked him. He felt Beth's hands on his shoulders and her cheek resting on the back of his neck.

'Why are we forsaken?' John croaked. 'Is the land truly cursed?'

'It is. Cursed by a witch.'

John sat up. The scarecrow had collapsed. The fallen guardian's hat blown to the edge of the field. John looked toward Myrtle's cottage. No crow stood sentinel over her field. The ground lay dried and grey, yet somehow yielded the owner some secret reward.

'Those crows must be her familiars,' Beth whispered.

A dark bird screeched in answer to the accusation: whether in affirmation or rebuttal, John didn't know. A red sunset descended behind Myrtle's cottage, casting the abode into a mishappen silhouette framed by charcoal clouds.

'What does she hide in the earth?' Beth said.

John's argument caught in his throat: perhaps there was something to his wife's misgivings. He shivered. His stomach groaned. 'We'll find out. After dark when she's asleep.'

Beth helped John to his feet. He recovered his cap and together they pulled a bucket of brown water from the well. Beth boiled it three times and they sat together in silence by the fireplace, sipping their bitter, earthy brew.

'I'll go outside to see if the witch is abed,' Beth finally said. Her chair creaked as she rose and reached for the gas lamp.

John put his hand over hers. 'We'll check together.'

They went outside into the night. There was no glow of life from Myrtle's cottage. The couple exchanged a nod in the lamplight. John picked up his hoe and they trudged side-by-side to the neighbouring field.

Beth held the lamp low as they searched the cracked and dried ground. Here and there were shallow holes clawed out by hand. John rummaged through the disturbed soil, discovering nothing but slugs and stones. He pierced the crust with his hoe, creating a small exploratory hole; then a second, and a third. Still the field refused to reveal its secrets.

'This cursed earth yields naught but to the Devil's servant,' Beth said, her voice quavering.

Myrtle's den remained dark. Beth's hand on John's elbow stirred him into motion. He gripped the hoe with both hands like it was a halberd and advanced on the lair of the witch with Beth marching at his side. He paused at the doorway, unsure whether to knock or smash through the brittle walls with his weapon.

Beth turned the iron door ring. The lever squealed and the door groaned when pushed open a few inches. Beth held the door ajar, turning her ear to the gap. Her eyes met John's and they exchanged a nod.

John moved past Beth, pushing the door wide, and stepped over the threshold. He held the hoe ready for whatever might assail them. Light from Beth's Gaslamp washed over John's shoulder, casting his shadow across the room like that of a giant. A dusty table stood laden with jars, urns, and pots. Cobwebs hung in giant curtains from the ceiling and shrouded the walls. A stench of rot assaulted eyes and lungs alike.

Beth gasped at a sudden movement in a corner. She directed the light, illuminating the witch.

Myrtle sat up in her bed, shielding her grey face with a filthy palm. 'Who goes there?' she wailed.

'It's us: your neighbours whom you torment daily whilst you sit here supping your fill from Satan's teat,' Beth spat.

Myrtle peered through her fingers with a dark eye. She grimaced. Yellowed teeth bore the evidence of her last meal: tiny clumps of brown matter between crooked canines and a silky film staining her lower lip.

'Leave me be! I've done naught to you,' the crone whimpered.

John kept his weapon levelled at her chest – unsure if her fear was a feint and that she might fly from the bed in rage or spew bewitching words.

Beth circumnavigated the room, searching in the lamplight. She stopped at the table, eyeing the variously sized clay jars – each covered with a cloth top tied off with string.

'Here!' Beth cried triumphantly. 'There must be supplies enough to see the year out.'

'Please no – my shame!' Myrtle cried. She moved as if to rush from the bed but was restrained by the threat of the hoe.

'What's in them?' John said, dividing his attention between wife and witch.

Beth set the lamp down and tugged at the string binding the largest jar.

'Please, no!' Myrtle shrieked, tearing from her bed and past the edge of the hoe before John could react, charging Beth with clawed hands outstretched.

Beth screamed, recoiling, sending lamp and jars smashing to the floor.

John swung the hoe in an arc. The corner bit into skull, pitching Myrtle sideways and over a stool where she crumpled to the ground. John dropped the hoe and rushed to his wife.

A flare of light was followed by a crackling and the scent of searing wood as flame from the shattered lamp climbed the table leg.

'The food!' Beth cried, shrugging John's hand off her shoulder. She snatched one of the remaining jars. 'Quickly, save the food!'

John looked from the table of provisions to Myrtle's crumpled form which looked little more than a pile of rags.

'Leave her! Save the food first!' Beth screeched, rushing to the door with two jars of provisions.

John picked up two more clay containers and hurried after his wife. They set the jars down a safe distance outside and hurried back inside to grab two more each. Smoke filled the small cottage. Fire consumed the table. The clay jars burned to the touch, nearby glass vessels popped and shattered under the heat. Flame encircled Myrtle, tickling the edge of her rags.

Beth pulled on John's arm and, with a last forlorn look at his unmoving neighbour, he followed Beth outside.

They stood together, watching the farm implode. Only when the flame began to abate did Beth open the first of the jars. She tilted the vessel toward the light of the fire and peered inside. She recoiled, dropping the jar and covering her mouth and nose with a trembling palm.

John snatched up the pot. He peered at the contents and emptied them onto the ground: The vessel spewed forth a mass of oily slugs and shrivelled snails. He tore open the tops of the other pots – each contained a multitude of the creatures: some dried out, some fresh, others pickled. He fell to his knees and retched.

'By God, she *was* mad,' John gulped. He looked up to see Beth shovelling handfuls of the spilt beasts back into the jar; her face pale and grim, eyes red-rimmed and watery.

'What are you doing?' John breathed.

'We must eat,' Beth whimpered.

Wolf at the Door

Joseph extinguished the lantern beside the cottage door and cast a look around the vast landscape of varying shades of blackness. The only movements were those of bare branches buffeted by the wind, waving and creaking in protest of their rough treatment. The wind ruffled Joseph's coat and made him shiver. He went inside and barred the door.

Ingrid removed her shawl, folding it and greeting her husband with a smile before leaning toward the fireplace to stoke the coals.

'Cloudless night,' Joseph grunted, easing into the rocking chair by the fire. He huffed with the effort of pulling off each of his encrusted work boots, ignoring the clods of brown that dropped to the floorboards and the disdainful glower and sigh from his wife.

'Boots off at the door next time,' Ingrid said, pursing her lips for effect.

A baby's cry from upstairs brought Joseph to his feet, but he was stopped by Ingrid's hand on his arm.

'Stay there and warm yourself beside the fire: you've been out all day.'

Joseph did as he was bade and watched Ingrid rush up the stairs, holding up her skirts so she wouldn't trip. He heard her gentle cooing noises as she tried to calm their newborn son. Joseph put his clay pipe to his lips and looked around for his tobacco, feeling the pockets of his homespun waistcoat, realising with a deflated sigh that he'd smoked the last of his meagre supply earlier that afternoon.

Ingrid came downstairs with baby Christian rolled up in a bundle. A tiny fist escaped the woollen cocoon and shook in frustration. Ingrid sat and began to feed the boy, upon which the wailing immediately morphed into a satisfied murmur as the child suckled.

'I shall have to go into village in the morn,' Joseph said, smiling at his young family. 'We need tobacco. And cheese.'

'We have cheese,' Ingrid said, not taking her eyes off month-old Christian.

'Ah,' Joseph said.

'Oh!' Ingrid suddenly looked up from their child, her big blue eyes wide. 'You could pop into church and confirm the date for the christening.'

'I'll do that,' Joseph said with a quick smile, pleased that his wife had provided a reason for him to go on an otherwise selfish errand. He revelled in the visage of Ingrid's smooth and serene features bathed in warm orange light from the fireplace, contemplating – as he often had – how he, a simple farmer, had managed to win the hand of the prettiest girl for miles.

A howl from outside stirred the family from their reverie. Ingrid frowned and looked questioningly to Joseph before returning her attention to the child, who screamed his dissent at the long, drawn-out canine wail.

Joseph lurched from the chair and strode to the window, leaving the chair rocking to and fro in his wake. He flung the ageing wooden shutter open. The howl had already subsided as he winced into the black and shivered at the sudden gust that blew over him.

'Shut the window!' Ingrid squealed, hugging the babe close.

Joseph did as instructed, muttering a curse at his own foolishness for subjecting their precious newborn to the winter elements that claims so many babes.

'Was that a wolf?' Ingrid said, her voice tinged with worry.

'Ain't been wolves hereabout for two hundred year. Likely it were a hound got lost out on moor.'

Ingrid made a sour face. 'Let us drink some warm milk and put ourselves abed.'

Joseph shook his head. He took his seat and began pulling his heavy boots back on. 'If there be a dog loose it'll go for the sheep. Best I see to it lest there be sorrows in the morn.'

'In this gale?'

'Sooner brave the wind than dead livestock. Shan't be long.' Joseph fetched his woollen cap and double-breasted greatcoat from the stand beside the door and took one of the two muskets that rested against a cabinet nearby. He jerked open a drawer and filled a pocket with percussion caps and handful of waxy cartridges then marched to the door, unbolted it and paused, turning to his wife and child.

Ingrid held Christian defensively to her chest and silently watched her husband with a sorrowful expression.

'Keep the door barred 'til I return.' Joseph said, then went out into the dark. He took the lantern from beside the doorway and relit it with some difficulty – only succeeding in doing so by using his body as a windbreak. He touched the horseshoe on the door for luck and marched resolutely to his errand, holding the lamp out at arm's length while keeping the musket in the nook of his other arm.

It was difficult to hear anything over the wind, which would have had Joseph's hat away had it not been a tight fit about his head. He began to wonder if the howling had been a trick of nature: a gust blowing through a hollowed log or some other natural perforation that acted as a whistle. The lanternlight illuminated the edges of the nearest chickencoop. The door was ajar. Joseph knew he had closed it and doubted the wind would have loosed the latch. He rushed toward the small wooden hut.

White feathers were scattered about the ground outside the coop, blowing over the grass and swirling like a light snow. Inside, the coop was a mess: blood, feathers and clumps of raw meat everywhere. Of twenty chickens, not one remained alive.

Joseph rushed to the next coop and found a similar scene. The door of the final coop swung open and shut with the wind. He reached for the three-foot high door to prop it open so he could inspect inside when he was stopped by a glimpse of movement just inside the coop and the recognition of an unnatural silhouette emerging from the hutch.

A slavering mouth amid a mass of a black fur slowly extended from the doorway. Blazing red bloodthirsty eyes fixed on Joseph with a malevolence matched only by the gleaming dagger-like jaws which dripped bloody saliva. The creature's snarl carried on the wind as it moved slowly and purposefully from the chicken house.

Joseph quickly set the lantern down by his foot and dug into the pocket of his coat for a cartridge, cursing himself for not loading the weapon before he ventured outside. He walked backwards to put a little distance between himself and foe, biting off the end of the cartridge as he retreated, pouring powder down the musket barrel with a shaking hand and spilling much of the black powder.

The wolf – for Joseph could see now that was what it was – emerged fully from the coop and raised itself to full height. The beast was huge: as tall as a wolfhound but wider and with a ragged jet-black coat.

Joseph dropped cartridges and brass percussion caps in his haste to prime the weapon. To quicken the dispersal of powder down the barrel he merely thumped the musket's butt on ground instead of using the ramrod. His trembling fingers pulled back the hammer and put a percussion cap in place.

The wolfs eyes narrowed. The hair on its shoulders bristled, then the beast turned and bolted for the nearest hedgerow.

Joseph brought the butt of the musket up to his shoulder to take aim but could see only black. He pointed the barrel in the approximate direction the wolf had fled and squeezed the trigger. The muzzle flash caused momentary blindness. The explosion of black powder stung his eyes in the moment before the wisps of smoke were dispersed on the wind, leaving only a metallic taste on the tongue.

Joseph fumbled in his pocket to for ammunition, reloading as quickly as he could before retrieving the lantern and giving chase.

For half an hour Joseph stalked the giant black predator, finding a sheep with its throat torn out, but of the wolf there was no trail. Finally, he decided to return to the cottage, resolving to set snares in the morning and warn his neighbours that such a beast was on the prowl. He trudged back with shoulders slumped in defeat while his tired eyes remained vigilant, watching the hedgerows for movement and scanning the ground for prints.

Christian's frustrated cries emanated from the small farmhouse. As Joseph went to hang the lantern in its place, the lamplight illuminated deep scratches in the door: a flurry of gouges a quarter of an inch deep had almost carved their way through.

A cry of desperate alarm escaped Joseph as he frantically thumped the door and called his wife's name, fearing some dire fate throughout the long moments before he heard the bolt being lifted. The door opened to reveal Ingrid with tear-streaked cheeks and the child clutched protectively to her chest. They embraced. Ingrid's body shuddered as Joseph kissed her fair hair and murmured words of assurance which were lost between the gale and the sobbing of mother and child.

'It was terrible,' Ingrid said as she sat by the fireside with Christian sleeping soundly in her arms. 'No sooner had you gone then there was a terrible howling was at the door. Oh! The scratching and snarling.' She shook at the memory.

'That can't be,' Joseph said, frowning and placing a reassuring hand on her shoulder. 'I cornered the beast at the coop and gave chase. Are you sure it came so soon after I departed?'

Ingrid looked up at him with pink puffy eyes and a dripping red nose. 'Certain as can be. I took the babe and fled upstairs. The monster attacked the door until moments before your return.'

Joseph hummed and scratched his stubble. 'Then there be two of them.'

There was no sleep for husband or wife that night. Joseph went out at first light with his musket, leaving instructions for the door to remain barred and the windows shuttered. Returning to the chickens, he found no discernible tracks. He walked to the barn, intending to use his sheepdogs to pick up the scent, but found both dead with their throats torn out. A patrol of his land turned up a half-dozen dead sheep – all with bloodied necks – yet no sign of the wolves having fed on their prey.

Joseph trudged across along the lane to his neighbour's farm where he found the fields clear of carcases and with no sign of disturbance; highland cows passively watched him approach the farmhouse and three dogs ran out to bark and snap at his heels. Joseph told his neighbour what had passed the night before. The older farmer listened without interrupting but maintained an eyebrow arched in incredulity throughout the tale.

'Ain't been wolves hereabouts since afore me great-grandfather's time,' the farmer said. 'Must be a wolfhound gone wild.'

'I know the look of a wolfhound, and it wasn't one.'

The neighbour allowed a curt nod and said he would set snares about his property and pass the news of a wild dog along to the next farm.

Joseph returned home and spent much of the day setting his own old iron traps around the farmhouse and making crude caltrops out of long nails. He saw to the cows and made sure their enclosure was secure: the wolves would have to scramble over a five-foot drystone wall to get at the cattle; recalling the size of the dark beast, he wondered if they might leap the gate.

At dusk he built a bonfire a dozen yards from the cottage: close enough to ward off ravaging canines, but far enough to not threaten the thatch with fire. He lit the pile of branches and old fenceposts as darkness set in, then went inside and propped his two loaded muskets by the window.

'Do you think they'll return?' Ingrid breathed into Joseph's ear as she hugged him from behind.

'Aye. They know there's easy prey here. They'll keep coming until there's no more feed.'

Ingrid kissed his neck and sighed.

'Go upstairs, dear, and remain with Christian until I say it's safe. Sleep if you can. I'll keep watch.'

'When will you sleep?'

'When I've two wolf pets stretched out to dry.'

Joseph awoke with a fright. He was sat in the rocking chair which he had moved to the window. He wasn't sure what had awoken him: a dream, a sound, or a sense of danger. He stood and pressed his nose to the glass.

The bonfire had died down to embers. There was no wind. The only sounds were his own breathing and the occasional groans of fitful slumber from Christian's cot in the room above.

Motion beyond the bonfire stopped Joseph from retaking his seat. He squinted, wondering if what he had seen was just part of the charred woodpile collapsing, but as his vision adjusted to the dark, he could make out the pair of fire-red eyes glaring with hatred.

Joseph snatched up the musket and flung the window open. He took aim and was just about the squeeze the trigger when peripheral vision caught the glow of a second pair of red eyes to his right, just beside the cottage door.

The wolf leapt, drooling jaws snapping.

Joseph fell back, landing in the rocking chair with a yelp. The wolf's hot fetid breath warmed his cheek in testament to how close he had come to having his own throat torn out.

Claws scrambled at the window ledge. Jaws gnashed as the beast thrashed, shattering the fragile windowpane as the wolf tried to climb inside.

Joseph clambered to his feet, sending the chair skidding backward. He looked along his barrel, the gunsights bearing directly between the red eyes. He squeezed the trigger: nothing happened. He cursed, realising that in his haste he hadn't pulled the hammer back. In the heartbeat that it took to ready the musket to shoot, the wolf had gone. Joseph reached out and slammed the wooden window shutter.

Claws scraped the door with such ferocity that the bolt rattled and dust fell from the overhead beams, but the door remained firm. Ingrid and Christian both wailed in the bedroom. The wolves howled.

Joseph remained focused on the door, holding his weapon ready to fire should the hinges be worked loose. His bladder felt painfully full. Sweat stung his eyes and greased his palms.

The baby cried. Ingrid chanted the Lord's Prayer. The wolf at the door snarled. The other monster circled the cottage, howling.

'What do you want?' Joseph roared: it made no sense for the beasts to seek prey secure in the cottage when the farmyard still contained livestock and the hills were dotted with sheep.

After what seemed a long time, the howling ceased and the assault stopped as suddenly as it had begun. All was quiet save the muffled crying of the baby against his mother's breast and her cooing to sooth the child.

Joseph remained poised to shoot; his arms ached from the weight of the weapon. It was several minutes before he dared inch toward the door and reach a cautious and trembling hand to the bolt. He unlocked the door and jumped back, holding the musket at the ready, expecting a wolf to launch its full weight at the door. Nothing. He crept to the door and opened it by a few inches, then flung it wide, brandishing his weapon at the darkness. He held his breath and waited.

Heavy grey clouds blocked out most of the moonlight. Hedgerows and trees were black silhouettes against charcoal sky. The crackling remains of the bonfire did nothing to illuminate the night, but the glow from the embers were enough to prevent Joseph's sight from fully adjusting to the night.

Joseph squinted at the nearest hedgerow, making out two red pinpricks. A wisp of grey fog marked the wolf's breath as the outline of the dark beast became apparent – a mere hundred yards from the house – on the very edge of effective musketry. Joseph pulled back the hammer and took aim. His finger quivered on the trigger: the chance of hitting the beast at this range was slight – especially at night. The wolf could easily cover twice the distance between them in less time than it would take to reload.

'Ok, you devil,' Joseph muttered. He put a boot over the threshold, deciding that if he kept the wolf in his sight he could advance to a good range. If the beast charged, he would hold his fire until the last moment. He took another step.

Wait, Joseph thought. *Where is the other one?* He glanced left and then right. Seeing nothing, he took a step back, inwardly scolding himself for his rashness. Then he caught a glimpse of movement in his peripheral vision. He spun; hearing paws beat the earth as the second wolf bounded toward him. There was no time to aim. Joseph lurched through the doorway and swung the door shut a moment before the weight of the wolf impacted the door. He pulled the latch across as the beasts snarled and raked the wood.

Joseph fell onto his back in his desperation to get away from the battered door which quaked with each assault. He held the musket poised and remained unmoving on the floor, fixated on the door, until the wolves gave up their attack and slunk away into the night.

Shrill cries of terrified and livestock carried across the hills. The howling continued until near dawn, daring the farmer to come out and protect his livelihood, but Joseph refused to be drawn out, maintaining his vigil until sunlight showed through the cracks around the door. Satisfied that the farmhouse was safe for now, Joseph went upstairs to comfort Ingrid, finding her sat shivering on the bed with the sleeping babe in her arms.

'What will we do?' Ingrid sobbed. Her complexion was too pale and her eyes too red.

Joseph stroked her cheek. 'Rest while the babe is quiet. I'll tramp over to George Crook's farm and see if we can get together a hunting party.'

Ingrid snatched Joseph's wrist as he made to leave the bedroom. 'Don't go.'

Joseph sighed. 'You'll be safe here 'til my return. I'll not be made a prisoner in me own home: if we don't deal with those… things, they'll keep coming back.'

Ingrid let her hand drop but regarded her husband with a wounded expression. 'We should eat. A few eggs and some bread at least before you go.' She set the baby down in his tiny wicker cot.

Joseph nodded his assent and lumbered downstairs. He wasn't sure he could stomach any food; he was desperate to get out and inspect the damage the wolves had done and track down their lair before they could strike again, but he wanted to give his wife a sense of normality so she wouldn't worry once he left. They ate in silence, startling on hearing voices outside shortly followed by three loud thumps on the door.

'It's George Crook,' a grizzled voice growled.

'Look here at the state of the door!' another exclaimed.

Joseph patted his wife's hand, stood, and went to the door, finding himself faced with three neighbouring farmers and a half dozen of their labourers; each carried a firearm and wore grim expressions under their caps.

'They heard the carnage down in the village,' Crook said. A wiry grey beard concealed his lips even as he spoke. A bushy brow pressed down over his eyes in a permanent squint, making it impossible to read any emotion from his weather-beaten features. 'Took the liberty of gathering a hunt afore venturing up here. What in the Lord's name has happened?'

Joseph shrugged and leant against the doorframe, attempting to appear nonchalant. 'Wolves. A pair. Killed me hens, me dogs, and several sheep the night before last. I've yet to inspect last night's toll. Did they not strike at your farm?'

'They did not,' George sniffed. 'Joe, you have not a beast left alive on your farm. Every cow, goat, and sheep we saw had its throat torn out.'

Ingrid cried from the table out and covered her mouth. 'Oh, what shall we do?'

George took off his cap and nodded a greeting in Ingrid's direction. 'Morning, Ingrid. We'll fetch dogs up and track them wild hounds down. They won't be coming back: don't you worry.'

'The damage is done,' Ingrid said in a voice cracked voice. 'We could replace an animal or two, but all? We're ruined.' She put her face in her palms, shoulders shaking as she sobbed.

George cleared his throat. 'I'm sure the church will hold a collection for you, but first we need to exterminate those wild dogs.'

Joseph patted his wife's shoulder and said a quick farewell before snatching up his musket and joining his neighbours outside, waiting until he heard the door bolted behind him before moving on.

Several dogs were brought up from neighbouring farms, but they were distracted by the dead livestock; the only one who seemed to be able to sniff out any kind of trail soon fell back cowering with tail curled between hind legs, refusing to proceed much beyond the boundary of Joseph's farm. The dogs proved more of a hindrance than help, so they were sent back. The farmers found no tracks or any indication of which direction the wolves had gone; none of the traps had been sprung and the few bits of bait left out had been ignored.

Some of the labourers were overheard whispering doubts about there being any wolves: they were long extinct in England, they said, musing that Joseph had murdered his own animals in a fit of rage, or that he was guilty of some heinous sacrilegious practice that caused such an evil to plague his farm while the neighbours went unmolested. George Crook overheard their chatter and angrily ordered the gossipers back, leaving just a half-dozen farmers. They scoured hills and gullies for miles around the farm with no success. Sheep, cattle, and hill ponies grazed the common land, seemingly untouched by the marauding beasts.

'It's true they've only desolated your stock,' George said as he scanned the horizon, purposefully not looking at Joseph. 'Any idea why it might be so?'

Joseph shook his head.

George turned sharply toward Joseph, roughly grasping his shoulder and peering into his eyes. 'What ain't you telling me? We're out here helping you when we could be tending our own stock.'

Joseph released a long breath. 'It's just… there's no tracks… and they have blazing eyes: red like fire. They were after us, not the animals. They only went for the livestock when they couldn't get into the house.'

George studied him for a long moment before grunting. 'I'm sure it seemed that way.' His gaze turned to the other farmers, who all bore dark expressions that did little to hide their misgivings about the venture or their doubts about Joseph's tale. 'It'll be getting dark in a couple hours. We should head back and see what the night brings. I don't think they'll be back to your farm tonight, but they might hunt at one of ours, so everyone should stand guard. If there's any howling, we'll gather at the crossroads and go together to the relief of the afflicted farm.'

The farmers nodded their agreement and slunk off in the direction of their holdings.

George clapped a hand on Joseph's shoulder while his beard quirked in suggestion of a curtained smile. 'Don't worry, Joe. We'll see them off.'

Ingrid threw her arms around Joseph's neck as he stepped through the doorway. 'Is it over?' she asked, drawing back to examine his face when he didn't answer right away.

'Shall be soon enough.'

Ingrid's face dropped. She collapsed onto her chair and ran her palms over her face and tugged at her hair. 'I can't stand this.'

'I'm sorry,' Joseph said, setting the musket down. 'If it's not done by tomorrow, I'll send you to stay with your sister and come fetch you once it's safe.'

Ingrid hugged her shoulders. Her usually smooth skin was blotchy and the bags under her eyes were swollen from sobbing, making her appear much older than her twenty-two years.

'Did you sleep?' Joseph said.

She shook her head no and rubbed her temples. 'I'll sleep when they're gone.'

Joseph nodded. 'Stay upstairs with Christian until morn unless I call for you.' He boiled the kettle and poured tea for his wife before seeing her to the bedchamber.

There was little time to make preparations before dusk. Joseph checked that all the windows were secure and lit a lantern for upstairs and another one to keep nearby. He turned the heavy dining table on its side and pushed it to the door to act as a barricade and placed a pitchfork within reach – in case it came down to a melee – then he sat in the rocking chair, facing the shuttered window with the fireplace warming his back.

The first howl came shortly after dark. It was distant but threatened slaughter to come. A few short minutes later the sound of ragged breathing passed by the window and then the door – not even pausing to test the wood for weakness. Light padding footfalls circled the house: only stopping occasionally as the wolves sniffed, growled, and then continued their macabre patrol.

The baby began to cry, as if he could detect the evil that stalked outside. Ingrid hummed a lullaby but could do little to quiet the child. The outburst of sound stirred the wolves into action: snapping, yelping and scratching at the cob plaster on the walls and howling their rage at the impenetrable granite underneath.

Joseph remained silently seated, not even priming his weapon to shoot, waiting for his neighbours to come to his relief, worrying that many might prefer to remain in defence of their own farmsteads instead of coming to his aid.

Eventually the wolves ceased probing the walls and their paws beat the ground as they retreated. Moments later the distant sound of human voices called out, whistles blew, and hounds barked.

Joseph got to his feet but waited until the voices were near before unbolting the door. The glow of flaming torches and lanterns illuminated the same faces as had come to his aid in the day. George Crook was at their head, armed with a carbine and a hatchet. Hounds pulled at their master's ropes; at first Joseph thought they were eager to get after the wolves, but realised the yapping and whimpering creatures were scrambling to get away.

'C'mon!' George yelled, hoisting his short-barrelled carbine aloft. 'We've got them on the run!'

'Bar the door!' Joseph yelled over his shoulder as he followed the posse which had already begun to make after the wolves, leaving behind two men to try to control the panicked dogs who desperately pulled on their leads in a forlorn effort to scramble back to their farms.

In his haste, Joseph had left his weapon beside the rocking chair. He followed close behind George. The lead men waved their lanterns, searching for tracks, gesticulating and shouting. Within a short distance from the farm, each man had a different idea about which way the wolves had gone.

'Stop it!' George snapped. 'Halt and bloody and listen. They can't be far.'

The group of men stood on the hillside, hearing only their own breathing. They had lost the two dog handlers and one other man who failed to keep up the pace. They caught their breath and peered into the darkness.

The distant white walls of Joseph's farmhouse were illuminated in moonlight. Further along the valley pricks of light showed the location of the other farms; the rest of the landscape stood in varying shades of charcoal and black.

'Surely their lair isn't on this hill,' one of the farmers sniffed. 'They'd be down by the river in some nook.'

Joseph squinted at his farmhouse. He detected no movement, but a sudden fear gripped him. 'They've not run to any lair. They've led us away so they can circle back to the farm.' He charged back down the hillside without waiting for the others to follow.

'Don't be absurd!' George scoffed. 'They're animals.'

Shouts, howling and cries came from the direction of the farm: not the sounds of wolves, but those of terrified men and dogs. The rest of the hunting group rushed after Joseph, but he raced ahead, running without haste for the terrain, charging past the corpses of hounds and sheepdogs and a firearm discarded by the farmhouse door.

'Ingrid! Christian!' Joseph shrieked, trying to shoulder his way in through the door but finding it bolted. He hammered on the wood until it swung open to reveal the pale and frightened faces of the two dog handlers and the farmer who had failed to keep up. 'Where's my wife and child?' Joseph panted.

'Here!' Ingrid said, standing from where she had taken refuge behind the upturned table with Christian.

Pounding boots announced the arrival of the other farmers, huffing with the effort of the frantic marathon. George's eyes were wide as he surveyed the scene of slaughtered hounds.

'Inside!' urged one of the dog handlers. 'They're still out there!'

Snarling confirmed the wolves' proximity. Firey eyes descended on the party from two directions. The group hurried for the door with panicked cries as they struggled to press through to sanctuary. Only George stood fast for a moment until the frightened entreaties of his comrades urged him into motion. The door was shut and bolted a moment before one of the beasts slammed into the wood.

'Good God!' someone cried.

George Crook ordered the farmers into a ragged defensive line. The men muttered prayers and brandished their weapons, expecting the beasts to find a point of entry at any moment as the wolves ravaged the door, window shutters and walls.

'They're twice the size of any wolf,' George said, his forehead beaded with sweat.

'Devil-dogs!' one of the former dog handlers wailed.

George hissed at the man to be quiet, but they all had seen the demon-red eyes. Nobody dared risk opening door or window to try a shot. It was near dawn when the assault ceased and the wolves retreated to wherever they had come from. The assembled men shuffled nervously and muttered that they needed to return to their own farms.

'We'll call on the yeomanry,' George said to Joseph without making eye contact.

One by one the men filed out of the farmhouse without any promise to return. Joseph shut the door behind the last of them and collapsed into his chair.

'Are we on our own?' Ingrid said in a hoarse whisper.

'We'll pack up what we can and I'll torch the farm and outbuildings. We'll stay with your sister until I can find labour.'

Ingrid nodded and carried Christian up to his cot.

Their only horse had been killed, and so only a handcart could be packed with such clothes, provisions and tools as were thought essential. Joseph climbed onto the roof and spread oil over the thatch and was about to get down to light it when he sighted a lone figure walking through the gate at the southern end of the farmyard. He hailed the man, who waved in response. Joseph climbed down and went to greet the stranger.

The man wore a wide brimmed hat like that of a cavalier of olden days, and had a moustache and thin pointed beard in the same style. He bore a pleasant smile on this narrow face and his long hair was cut to shoulder length. His brown leather greatcoat was so long it brushed the grass, and an old flintlock pistol was tucked into his belt beside a glinting buckle. The long-barrelled rifle of a marksman was slung over a shoulder. If he carried any personal effects, they were stowed in the small haversack at his side.

'What brings thee, stranger?' Joseph said as the man neared.

The man chuckled and stopped a few metres away, looking beyond Joseph toward his wife child and then to the farmhouse. 'Going away, are you?'

Joseph looked at his wife and then back to the stranger. 'That I am. Forgive me for saying so, but I see not what concern it be to you, nor why you're on my land.'

The man gave a thin smile and pointed at the thatch. 'Looked like you were about to fire the place. Does this not mean the demesne is, or soon shall be, vacant?'

'Now look here!' Joseph rolled up his shirtsleeves for effect. 'State your business plainly or move on, stranger.'

The man bowed his head and touched the rim of his hat. 'Forgive my dry humour. My name is Nick Jackson: a huntsman of some repute. Perhaps you have heard my name?'

Joseph shook his head.

'Oh,' Nick frowned, sucked his lip then shrugged. 'Well, it matters little. I have long been on the trail of two dark and wild beasts of vile repute. I was newly arrived in the village yonder this morn when all the talk was of dire wolves which, as talk would have it, consumed every living thing on your farm.

However, I see you and your family are in health so perhaps I am misinformed.'

'There be wolves alright. My entire livestock is what they slew but not one did they eat for their hunger is for my family and I. If you've come to kill 'em, then you are my most welcome guest.' Joseph kept his tone firm and unwelcoming, suspecting some ulterior motive from the stranger, whose gaze kept wandering toward Ingrid.

'It is the chase I enjoy. The kill is but bittersweet victory. Yet, such a pestilence on your farm should be vanquished and I, Nick Jackson, am your saviour.' The man showed his big, straight white teeth in a wide grin that only a travelling merchant or confidence trickster could perfect.

Joseph took a step to the right to better block Nick's view of Ingrid and crossed his arms, unsure how to respond to the marksman's boast.

'Perhaps if you can stay the burning of your homestead a short time, we might go inside and discuss terms over a cup of tea?' Nick said, moving a step to his left.

Nick's smile was slightly mocking and a little too superior for Joseph's liking, but he nodded his agreement. He led Nick to the cottage without introducing his wife. Ingrid followed the pair inside with the babe in her arms and stood by the fireplace, staring at the peculiar visitor.

'A pleasure to meet you, my good lady,' Nick said, removing his hat with a flourishing bow.

Joseph and Ingrid exchanged a look.

'Nick here claims he can rid us of the wolves,' Joseph said, reaching for the kettle and finding it empty. He handed the vessel to his wife. 'Be a dear and go fill this from the pump so our guest may have tea.'

Ingrid nodded, put Christian in his cot and went outside with the kettle.

Nick unslung his rifle and took to the rocking chair without waiting for invitation. He looked around the cottage, humming as he took in the rustic contents. 'Nice place. Shame to condemn it to flame.'

'What payment do you want for ridding us of the wolves?' Joseph snapped.

Nick's eyebrows quirked and he grinned as he stroked his moustache with a gloved hand. 'Straight to business, eh? You seem like a nice family, and I want to help, so why not say… if you promise me such goods as I might desire from your farm which I can carry away with me, then we have a compact.'

'Like my wife?' Joseph said, balling his hands into fists.

Nick tipped his head back, laughing in a high pitch that bordered on hysterical.

Joseph ground his teeth and gave thought to throwing the man out of his home – only staying his hand out of the desperate hope that the arrogant stranger might prove true to his boasts.

'Oh dear,' Nick said, as wiped an imaginary tear from his eye. 'I haven't laughed like that since… well, I don't know when. Your wife is safe from me. I can see that she is a slight and pretty thing, but I don't think I could carry her far. I promise to only take such possessions or trinkets as can fill my haversack.' He gestured at the deflated canvas bag at his side which was barely large enough to hold two loaves of bread.

Joseph felt his cheeks warm in embarrassment; whatever the stranger could fill his bag with was sure to be outweighed by the service done in killing the wolves, and Joseph reasoned that if Nick should fail and be slain in the process of hunting the wolves, then they were no worse off than before.

'Do we have a compact?' Nick said, the superior grin playing on his lips.

'Aye.' Joseph decided against mentioning the wolves' fiery eyes or lack of tracks for fear that Nick's resolve might fail and he would change his mind about hunting such a prey, or would demand a higher price for doing so. He extended his hand and Nick rose from the chair to shake it just as Ingrid returned with the kettle filled.

Ingrid frowned at their handshake as if worried at what manner of deal had been struck. Joseph quickly explained what had transpired and Ingrid gave a weak smile. She boiled the kettle for tea and blushed under the stranger's gaze.

They toasted Nick's hunt, clanking their metal teacups together.

'You will remain here tonight?' Nick said over the rim of his cup, an eyebrow arched questioningly.

'Aye. I suppose one night won't hurt,' Joseph said. 'If you fail, we can pack again in the morn and be on our way.'

Nick nodded. 'Good. I shall leave momentarily. I am sure the wolves will come at nightfall and so I shall return then. Whatever you do, both of you are to remain down here where they can smell you but not get at you. Once you hear my second shot, my part of the bargain will be done.'

Joseph and Ingrid wished Nick luck in sombre tones. Joseph didn't expect the man to succeed – especially not to slay the animals with one shot each. Nick refused the offer of a lantern, saying he could see as well at night as day, then went on his way.

The handcart was unpacked and the belongings piled inside the house where they could be easily reloaded onto the cart in the morning. Ingrid made a stew and together they secured the cottage windows and doors. Christian fell asleep after nursing and so Ingrid carried him up to his cot where she remained for several minutes.

'Ingrid!' Joseph called up the stairs, 'you must come back down. The huntsman bade us both remain here. I don't want him finding we didn't stick to the letter of his agreement and thus declaring it void.'

Ingrid descended the stairs, casting a worried look behind her.

'If he cries, we'll fetch him down,' Joseph said to placate his wife's worry.

They sat hand in hand, facing the door, each with a musket resting between their knees. Shortly after dark a howl announced the approach of the wolves – soon followed by growls and snarls around the perimeter as the beasts searched for any new sign of weakness in the defences.

Ingrid's grip tightened on Joseph's hand. He gave a gentle reassuring squeeze back, but neither of them moved from their chairs.

A shot sounded. A whimper. A growl.

'Did he hit one?' Ingrid gasped, rising from her chair.

'Might be he did,' Joseph said, moving to the window. He reached out to crack it open, but Ingrid slapped his hand down.

'Not yet!' she hissed. 'They could still get inside.'

A second shot blasted out – the report louder than any rifle Joseph had heard. A wolf howled in pain, yapped, and was then silent. Ingrid and Joseph held their breath. Joseph heard Ingrid gulp at the sound of footsteps approaching the cottage.

'That is the second shot, Joseph!' Nick called out. 'It's safe to come out now, my little lambs.'

Ingrid and Joseph exchanged a look of disbelief. They rushed to the door together. Ingrid unbolted it, but Joseph kept his weapon in hand as the door was opened in case there was some life remaining in the vicious creatures.

The wolves lay next to each other not far from the door. Their bodies looked desiccated, as if they had been dead a long time. Smoke – perhaps from gunpowder – arose from both bodies. The once blazing eyes had become tiny, shrivelled coals and their mangy pelts stank of charred flesh.

'A shot a piece, as promised.' Nick smiled and touched the rim of his hat in salute.

Joseph stared agape at the twin corpses, which seemed to melt away to nothing before his eyes.

Nick slung the rifle upside down over his shoulder, the long barrel almost touching the floor. He winked and turned, walking away from the farmhouse.

'Wait!' Joseph called out. 'What of your prize?'

Nick turned back toward the young couple and patted the now bulging haversack at his side. 'Oh, not to worry. I've helped myself.'

Joseph frowned, wondering what the strange fellow meant. He looked again at the dead wolves who were now only vague scorched shapes on the grass.

Ingrid gasped and ran back inside, letting the door slam shut behind her.

Joseph turned and rushed after her, dropping his weapon in his haste.

'No!' Came an anguished cry from the bedroom.

Joseph burst into the bedroom to see his wife clutching the empty bundle of wool which once wrapped their child. He knew before he looked that the cot was empty.

'Get him back!' Ingrid screamed.

Joseph ran back downstairs and out into the night, snatching up his musket. He called out and ran in the direction the huntsman had headed, finding only a trail of cloven hoofs which vanished at the farm's perimeter. He called out again, but of Old Nick, his hellhounds, and Joshua's un-christened son there was no trace.

Ordeal

The accused wife stumbled, falling onto hands and knees in the long yellow grass. She wailed, raking tear-streaked cheeks with fingers blackened from moorland peat. Stains from the earth soiled the once white shift which covered her slender form from neck to calves. Red-ringed eyes begged her husband for mercy as she pulled the linen coif from her head, revealing unkempt blonde hair roughly tied into a bun.

The husband stood a few metres off, at the head of a group of four men. He observed the piteous figure with clenched fists and his jaw, hitherto set firm in resolution, trembled as he gulped back some exclamation.

Jan, the village headman, scrutinized the husband through narrowed eyes. Perceiving weakness in the man, he stepped forward and clapped a hand on the husband's shoulder, feeling him twitch at the touch.

'Don't ye be tempted to pity yore wretch,' Jan snarled, spittle flecking his white whiskers and cracked lips. He advanced on the young woman, navigating around a muddy patch that might soil his gown. Jan nudged the unfaithful wife with the butt of his staff and made such sharp sounds as one might use to encourage a draft horse to motion.

The husband blinked away a tear and silently relented to the authority of the headman with a shaky nod of surrender before closing his eyes and biting his lip.

'Don't ye turn yourn cheek on this good work!' Jan hissed at the husband as he continued to prod the wife as he had done to many faithless wives before along the same stretch of wild terrain toward their place of judgement.

At a signal from Jan, his two burly henchmen: sour-faced blacksmith brothers in leather jerkins, positioned themselves either side of the husband: ready to subdue him should he show weakness in his spouse's ordeal.

'Cover yourn hair if you truly be penitent or keep it loose like a whore's if it be thy nature!' Jan snarled in a raspy voice.

The wife, her forlorn cries reduced to sobbing, replaced her coif and struggled to rise as the headman's staff jabbed her ribs and threatened to push her off-balance. She lurched onward with bare feet dirty and bleeding, remaining wary of Jan's staff – ever ready to prod her like livestock into the right direction, or strike her like an unruly dog should she slow.

The grim procession continued across desolate moorland, following cattle trails through thick straw-like grass, heading ever closer to Cranmere Pool. The summer evening breeze that gently combed the grass soon evolved into a gust which whipped the unfastened coif from the wife's head, sending it flittering back toward the distant village and causing her long golden hair to trail like a resplendent pennant while shards of granite gnawed her feet and the chill of the wind bit through the thin fabric of her shift.

The group ascended the crest of a hill whereupon the head of the West Okemont River came into view below. Tufts of reeds stood as islands among a thin layer of emerald, covering unknown depths of stinking bog water. A brown trail down the hillside marked the safe path around the marshy head and up the next hillside toward Cranmere Pool.

'Move on, damn ye!' Jan snapped, using the staff to prod the girl in the small of her back.

She cried out and stumbled a few steps down the slope, managing to regain balance and turning with a wincing scowl at her snaggle-toothed oppressor.

'Move!' Jan spat, trying to close the gap between them so he could give another push, but the accused's gait had increased so that Jan was reluctant to rush after her on his spindly and arthritic limbs lest he should suffer the indignity of falling himself. Instead, he made an impatient gesture at one of the smithies to catch up to the young girl.

A dark-bearded henchman left his spot at the husband's flank and wove a trail through long grass to snatch up the wife's wrist like a ferret snaring a rabbit. The blacksmith seemed unsure what else he was supposed to do and looked back to the headman for guidance, receiving an irritated brushing gesture directing him to move on in the direction of the pool.

The calm waters of Cranmere Pool came into sight atop the next rise. The shallow pool reflected the dark blue, cloud-filled, sky. As the party neared, clouds veiled the sun, turning the water black and causing the wife to sob anew as if this change was a portent of her fate.

With the four men at her back, the wife was made to kneel at the edge of the pool and say the Lord's prayer. Despite her predicament, she sang the prayer out in a strong, honeyed voice, full of new confidence and apparent fervour. At the conclusion, her head remained bowed in penitence and hands clasped under her chin.

Jan suppressed increasing rage, tightening his grip on the wooden shaft until his knuckles hurt. He struck the young woman on the backside with the staff, eliciting a yelp from his victim.

The accused knew what was to happen next: everyone knew the ritual. She rose, keeping her head bowed, and sank a foot in the pool with a whimper and shudder at the temperature. The young wife proceeded into the dark pool; the edges of her shift blossomed out on the water's surface as she cautiously waded further until reaching waist-deep blackness near the centre of the pool. She knelt, just as she had at the water's edge, then pinched her nose and submerged her head, remaining underwater for several seconds before rising for a few breaths then bowing again, repeating until she had sunk herself into the pool three times. She then stood and waited for Jan's command, whereupon she emerged, shivering. The water had done little to clean the soiled shift and the fabric now clung to the wife's thin form, forcing her to cover her vanity with shaking and goose pimpled arms.

Jan wrinkled his nose at the obscene visage and jerked his head, indicating the new direction of travel: toward the ancient stone circle, and place of final judgement. He waved the husband back as the man made to remove his coat: no doubt intending to offer it to his shivering wife. Jan shook his head in dismay at the pathetic man, wondering how it was any surprise to the weak village men that so many of their womenfolk felt free to disgrace themselves with lewd language, immodest dress, and barely concealed lascivious intentions.

The girl led the way: there was little need to direct her, as all the women took pilgrimages to the strange place to pray for the souls of those proven guilty by ordeal and to implore to the ring of ancient stones for protection should they one day be plucked from the fragile safety of their homestead to face the dreaded trial.

Jan knew the women spoke in hushed voices among themselves about a curse on the village: none had survived the ordeal since before Jan's time as headman. He was sure that the females' superstitions only served to prove their leanings toward sin. He himself had many times paused for rest by the shutters of this wife's cottage and overheard her gossiping with other village women. Jan knew that such women needed to be kept under careful observation; when he saw her venturing into the woods, he was certain that she was either cavorting with pixies or up to some other misdeed. When rumours were heard that she had been seen in the woods with a man who was not her husband, Jan was the first to accuse her.

The men walked in single file behind the wife, following her past an old cairn which marked some boundary in ancient times and aligned with another cairn on nearby Watern Hill, the alignment indicating the way toward the venerable ring near Gidleigh.

The sun dipped low in the sky when the circle came into sight. Jan tightened the collar of his old woollen gown with fingers half-numb from the evening chill and blew into cupped hands for warmth, letting out a growl of irritation when he noticed the wife had pushed on ahead, marching with the determination of Joan toward judgement.

'Get on!' Jan snarled at the men as they pursued their quarry, only catching up with her once she had already entered the circle and knelt in front of one of the great stones.

Of the three dozen stones in the circle, near to one-third lay recumbent: each collapsed column represented the judgement of a fallen woman. Every stone was at least the height of a man, and each separated by several paces, making a rough circle of more than fifty paces across. The thick granite pillars may have once pointed heavenwards, but over time even those which remained standing had come to bend like crooked fingers, tilting at varying degrees and eroded by thousands of years of rainfall.

The wife knelt by one of the standing stones, murmuring words of prayer. Despite the long walk from the pool, the cold breeze had done little to aid the drying of her clothes and the fabric still clung to her waif-like body.

A pair of wild horses, one white and one dark grey, stood some distance outside the circle, watching the blonde girl with apparent interest. Jan thought to shoo them away but realised with growing horror that the judgement was in danger of proceeding incorrectly.

'Get up from there!' Jan shrieked, waving his staff as he lurched toward the wife.

The penitent woman didn't move but continued praying. The blacksmith brothers rushed ahead of their superior, halting awkward and idle by the accused's side, reluctant to intrude on her prayer.

'Get away!' Jan snarled, jabbing with his wood when he was in range, striking the woman on the arm and knocking her onto her side.

'I shalt tell thee which stone to pray at, wench!' Jan stomped past the wife, ignoring exchanged glances and shrugs between the blacksmith brothers. He walked the perimeter of the circle, touching each of the ancient monoliths and making a show of examining them for some mystical quality before arriving at his preordained stone.

The huge granite stood at more than two metres, tilting some ten degrees toward the centre of the circle. Earth around this stone showed sign of recent disturbance around the base and a slither of black shadow betrayed a hollow gap under the stone but was only perceptible from outside the circle.

Jan patted the old granite and stood back from it, nodding. 'This one: tis a good, righteous rock.'

The blacksmiths hoisted up the accused, taking one arm each, and brought her before her judgement stone. The husband followed close behind with his forehead creased in worry as he chewed his lip and fidgeted.

'Take strength!' Jan cried. 'Have faith in yourn wife – if thou wills it. Should what has been spoken of her be untruth and she be truly without sin, the stone shall harm her not and you may give thanks unto The Lord. If she be guilty, it shall be God's will that the stone should crush her and send her cursed soul to hell.'

The men nodded. The blacksmiths released their prisoner, who instantly fell into a praying posture.

'Now, pray for absolution, faithless whore!' Jan salivated and rubbed his hands on the grain of his staff. 'Now, you men: bow your heads in prayer. Pray for her innocence and for her soul, and spare nary a glance upwards until the ritual be done. Keep your eyes closed there, I say!'

Jan watched, ensuring that all heads were bowed in mumbled prayer. He scowled at the horses and made a stabbing gesture with his staff which did nothing to deter their impassive observation.

The accused wife retained her composure, praying quietly in a voice that no longer quavered with fear. The tears were long dried on her cheeks, and she did not even shudder from the cold.

Jan quaked with suppressed fury at the arrogant confidence of the woman. All the other accused women had cried and pleaded to the last: did this one truly think herself guiltless? He had seen her himself, walking into the woods, returning hours later with a basket of flowers: surely, nobody could believe she spent all that time picking wildflowers. He was certain that she had a clandestine meeting with someone from outside the village and he made sure the right chinwags heard as much. Jan walked around the kneeling people, making sure that all kept their heads down and eyes closed.

The three men knelt several metres behind the woman: safe from sharing her fate should she be found guilty. The husband sobbed as he prayed, begging that his wife be proven innocent, declaring that he could not bear the thought of her having been with another man. The blacksmiths kept their rough hands cupped together, but they made no sound.

Satisfied that all were deep in prayer, Jan made his way back to his chosen granite pillar. Moving around the back of it, he slipped the butt of his staff into the crack below the base which he had dug out the day before. He gripped the staff with both hands and held his breath as he heaved, levering the stone.

The tall column groaned. Jan peered around it, hoping that none of those assembled had heard the sound. He put all his strength into the effort; the grain of the staff burning his palms. The stone wouldn't budge. Jan cursed. He pushed with both hands to no effect: it remained entrenched in its foundation. With growing dismay, Jan realised the rock was not going to topple.

The wife ceased her praying, looking up just as Jan emerged from behind the menhir. She smiled and released a long sigh. Standing on wobbling legs, the young woman looked skywards and mouthed her thanks at the darkening sky, then turned to her husband who moved to embrace her with his arms outstretched. She pushed him away and looked set to scold the cowering and pleading fellow, but instead spat on the ground near his feet and turned away, walking back toward the village with him rushing behind and calling her name like a yapping dog begging for attention.

'No!' Jan seethed, snapping out of a self-absorbed incredulity. He reached out a thin arm as if he might be able to snatch the diminishing figure of the woman back to face judgement again. 'She's not innocent! They're never innocent! They're all the same! Get after her!'

53

The blacksmith brothers were looking at the judgement stone, frowning and stroking their beards. They glared at Jan and shook their heads.

It was only then Jan noticed the absence of the familiar feeling of the staff in his grip. The long shaft still jutted at an angle from the base of the granite column. He gaped at the brothers, his mouth working wordlessly as he tried to formulate an explanation which would appeal to the two men.

The blacksmiths turned and silently followed husband and wife back toward the village, marching in a slow and solemn step.

Enraged, Jan strode to the menhir and snatched his staff, yanking it loose. He shook the staff and shrieked insults and threats after the brothers, his ire then turning on the horses when he noticed they had moved nearer the circle.

The white horse, a mare, trotted into the circle and stood motionless at the centre. Jan advanced on her with the staff raised high. As he neared, the horse moved off at a leisurely trot and left the circle. The stallion seemed to be attempting to enter the ring but each time he tried to pass between two stones he shied away, only to try again at another spot with the same result.

Jan rushed the stallion, intending to land a blow on the beast's nose as it stood at the circle's perimeter. He swung the staff in an angry arc. As the wood breached the edge of the circle it rebounded, as if from a solid but invisible force, and struck Jan on the forehead. He stumbled back, landing on his backside and gaping in shock.

The dark horse shook its head and trotted away to rejoin the mare.

Jan stood, brushing strands of grass from his trews. He walked to the perimeter of the circle with a hand cautiously extended, feeling an invisible force prick his digits and make the hairs on his bony hand rise. A sharp shock knocked his hand back when it would have breached the circle, leaving the skin of his fingertips and palm a sunburnt shade of red.

Jan walked around the interior of circle, exploring with his good hand, but feeling a similar charge in the air between the stones throughout the entire circumference: there was no way out.

He called after the blacksmith brothers who had already disappeared over the next hill. He rushed from one stone to the next, frantically swiping at the invisible barrier: each time his hand was slapped away with a stinging fury. Finally, he turned his desperate rage on the stones themselves. He kicked one, hurting his toe but receiving no shock. He explored the edges of the monolith, feeling crackling energy around both sides and the top, jolting his fingers if he dared to reach to the far edge. Then he remembered the pillar he had loosened: if it could be toppled, perhaps his prison could be breached.

He hurried to the compromised stone and braced himself, pushing it with both hands. He heaved and strained, putting all his meagre bodyweight into the effort. The mighty boulder refused to budge. Jan pressed his face to the cold surface, sobbing. He sank, crumpling to the foot of the pillar.

'Oh, why good God? Why doth thou punish thy servant so?'

A loud groan answered from the earth beneath the stone, jolting Jan to attention. He looked up at the ancient rock and opened his mouth to cry out just as the shadow of the listing monolith enveloped him in black an instant before the cold, dispassionate granite thumped down to smother him in judgement.

Devil's Cauldron

Constable Christian Hare yanked on the reins of his Chestnut mare, bringing her to a stop. He lifted the rim of his stovepipe hat to better survey the landscape: shrubs, branches, and long grass swayed with the breeze in suggestion of possible human movement, diverting his attention from one spot to the next, discovering only disappointment each time. Undulating hills thick with late-summer undergrowth provided many places for fugitives to hide.

The thump of boots on earth announced the approach of the posse. More than a dozen local men, some mounted, most on foot, were armed with various farming implements and one or two muskets. They were strung out in a ragged formation, reminding Christian of a screen of skirmishers such as he recalled from his service in the Peninsular War in his late teens, more than three decades ago.

'Must've gone yonder,' a barrel-chested older man in a straw hat growled as he neared, pointing at the next rise. 'Down into the gorge where they got their den.'

Christian narrowed his eyes as he scanned the summit of the slope, then unfastened a leather pouch on his horse's flank and withdrew a small brass Lookingglass. He extended the implement and brought it to his eye, inspecting various distant granite lumps that were each large enough to conceal a man, expecting to discover the distant pale face of the fugitives' rear guard keeping watch for pursuers. He observed nothing of note and collapsed the telescope with a deliberate press of the palm on the eyepiece. He pursed his lips in frustration and scratched his implacably brushed mutton-chop cheek with his hairy knuckles.

'Shan't we go back Lydford and raise more men?' the older man asked. His red-face and heaving chest belying his efforts to appear unaffected by the labour of his half-mile run across open country.

'More men?' Christian snapped, putting his telescope away. 'Nay, Mister Smithers. Most of the able-bodied men are already among us. Aside from which, I don't believe the Gupney gang hideout to be located in the gorge, which has been searched more than once. I suspect they've swung north-east and headed back to one hamlets or farms outside Lydford where someone is concealing them. Tis there we shall locate those vagabonds.'

'Back t'Lydford!' Smithers roared, waving his arm in a circular motion as if wielding a flag to rally fleeing troops.

There were muted cheers and words of assent among the amassed men – Christian knew this was not arising from appreciation of his command decision, but rather out of relief that the men would not need to descend the treacherous slopes of the gorge in what was increasingly seeming to be a lost pursuit – the Gupney gang had gotten away again, leaving a bloodied merchant from Tavistock horseless, penniless, and with much of the grain he was transporting spilt over the road as the ruffians had searched his sacks for hidden treasures. The man was lucky to have been left with his life, as only days before a farmer had been murdered on the same road, and his young wife stolen away by the gang.

Christian and his followers trudged back toward their village. Residents of the small cluster of homes surrounding a ruinous keep had, over the last year, been regularly preyed upon by the Gupney gang. These footpads were especially active around harvest and market times: hiding in hedgerows to waylay travellers, farmers and merchants on the road between Tavistock and Okehampton. More than one of the thieves had ended up swaying in a cage on nearby gibbet hill, but none could be convinced to give up the location of their hideout before they were hung, and not one member of the gang had been caught in months despite a sharp increase in the frequency and violence of their crimes.

Constable Hare knew that returning to Lydford empty-handed again would serve to provide sustenance to the rumours of his ineptness and inability to protect the village, and so the constable turned his attention to the nearest farm: one of the few which had not suffered at the hand of the Gupneys. The farmer and his family were brought outside while the house, barn, outbuildings, and hedgerows were ransacked. No evidence of contraband or concealed criminals were discovered, and the constable silently endured the vicious tongue of the farmer's wife while the disenchanted posse, made up largely of neighbouring farmers, reluctantly stabbed haybales with their pitchforks while wearing expressions of distaste and embarrassment.

Even the young men, recently eager for adventure at the start of the pursuit, began to lose interest when the search failed to yield result. Christian caught two of them stuffing eggs into their coat pockets and was intent on arresting them, but glowers and murmurs of dissent from the other men made the constable decide to send the two youths home with a warning. As the group marched out on the short road back to Lydford, the constable noted that a few men seemed to have slunk off during the search of the farm.

'Shoulda gone into the gorge,' Smithers said.

Christian turned in the saddle and looked down at the burly farmer, noting that only a few men walked with them; others could be heard talking further down the track, while plumes of pipe smoke wafted over the hedgerows that lined the lane as the posse dispersed into groups of friends and neighbours at each split in the track.

'A Hare!' a teenage lad near Smithers declared, swiping the cap off his head as he erupted into pursuit of the animal which had bounded off down the lane before disappearing into the bocage. The boy scrambled after it, hurdling a gate to pursue his quarry across a fallow field and disappearing from the constable's sight.

'Shan't he catch it?' Christian said, wondering how the boy hoped to snare such a fleet creature on open ground.

'Not likely without a dog,' Smithers grunted. 'Yet the Hare might lead him to his den, so the lad can return later and catch the whole down. Course, a big-town peeler's man not yet two year on the moor won't know nothing about catchin' hares, namesake or not.'

The constable dug his heels into the flanks of his horse and trotted on ahead, hoping that his mutton chops masked his flushed cheeks. He startled at the sudden high-pitched sound of the hue and cry. Christian stood in his stirrups and looked over the hedgerow toward the wailing sound.

The boy was running back toward him, waving his arms and crying out. Two bare-headed men in dirty white shirts were in pursuit. The lad glanced behind at his chasers, tripped, and scrambled to his feet with a desperate cry as the nearest man closed to within grasping distance, his expectant hand grasping at air as the fleet boy escaped out of reach.

Christian snatched at the handle of the pistol tucked into his belt and began loading it, using the small flask of powder hanging from the saddle.

The remaining vigilantes, all on foot, couldn't see the robbers that assailed the boy, but craned their necks or jumped to try to see over the hedgerow. Smithers jogged toward the gate, his sway betraying an old hip injury. The other few members of the posse followed his lead, shouting their outrage when they saw the highwaymen giving chase to the village boy.

Both pursuers stopped, only now seeing the danger they were in, and turned, fleeing back the way they came.

'Damnable fools!' Christian seethed, fumbling with his powder in his outrage and spilling much of it his dark blue trouser leg. 'A few moments more and the boy would've led them into our grasp!'

The five or six men jumped the gate and gave chase. Smithers paused long enough to cast a narrow-eyed look of disapproval at the constable before he clambered over the gate with a wince as he hoisted his right leg over. Smithers went straight to the boy, clasping him by the shoulders and conversed with him briefly, gesturing for the lad to leave the field by the gate.

Christian dismounted and beckoned the lad. He handed the reins of his horse to the boy before joining the pursuit, holding his now loaded pistol barrel skywards like a duellist. He overtook Smithers and caught up with the rest of the group, who wisely had not plunged headlong after the fugitives and instead maintained a cohesive distance between themselves; no doubt, Christian thought, out of pack mentality and sense of security rather than military discipline, which they showed no evidence of.

The criminals, both wide-shouldered men, barefoot and skulking, seemed to know where the gaps in the hedgerows were and led the chase through one field to the next before the sloping fields gave way to bracken-covered hillsides and tangles of jagged hawthorns. The villains expertly ducked under spiny branches, leading the chase further and further downhill.

'They's going into the gorge!' one of the farmers shouted, pointing with his club.

'Git after 'em!' Christian seethed, regretting his earlier declaration on the feasibility of the gorge as a hideout.

The fleeing men vanished in ever-thickening undergrowth, but their direction of travel had been constant and, as the terrain became increasingly steep and rocky, the ground served to funnel the chase in a singular, inevitably downward, route. The gradient was such that the pursuers were forced to slow and put out steadying hands on rocks or grasp trunks and branches for support. Stones slid from underfoot, clattering down the winding trail. The men moved in silence despite the certainty that the noise of their descent alerted their quarry.

The trail led all the way down to the River Lyd, which flowed through the gorge. Torrents foamed and splashed against rocks as it twisted through the narrow valley. Riverbanks were overgrown with tangles of bushes and nettles; rumours of bandit camps had kept local people out of the pass for the last two summers and nature had smothered the old trails.

The track opened up into an area of sodden ground which released an odour of decaying vegetation whenever a boot sank too far in. A criss-crossing of older prints indicated that Christian was still on the right path. The track narrowed again, following the path of the river with a towering wall of smooth rock on the land side, forcing the party into single file. The rush of water grew louder as the group neared the waterfall, which was glimpsed on the far side of the river: a long narrow stream cascading down a sheer rockface that the posse barely glanced at in the heat of their pursuit.

Hare and his men followed the path until it twisted away from the river, winding uphill and seemingly out of the gorge. A new track on the far side of the river continued on through the pass.

'It's fordable here,' Smithers said, grimacing at the waist-deep river; it was clear to all that although it could be crossed, a misstep could mean being carried off by the current.

Christian looked for tracks: shoe prints and bare prints of various sizes marked the ground in many places without any seeming pattern of direction or indication of age. The constable removed his hat, setting it on the ground, and dabbed at his brow with a handkerchief, feeling his pulse pound in his chest as the assembled men, perspiring, tired, and now more fearful than vengeful, looked at him expectantly.

'We shan't split up, shall we Constable Hare?' one of the men said, his voice tinged with worry.

'No,' Christian snapped, setting his hat back upon his head. 'That won't do at all.' His bicep ached from holding the pistol above shoulder height, but he kept it elevated lest the ball roll out when he might have need of it. 'They've followed the river.' Christian gestured with the pistol. 'We'll cross together.' He spoke with the conviction of an experienced NCO and the men followed him without question or comment, forming a human chain as they went into the river.

Christian led. Water filled his boots and soaked through his trews – it was shockingly cold. His smooth-soled boots threatened to slip on slimy rocks, but the firm grip of the next man steadied him. The entire group was soon on the far side, pouring icy water out of their boots and shoes. Christian bade them hurry on, but no sooner had they started off than he began to wonder if he'd chosen the correct route: nothing other than a vague intuition led him.

The pathway became narrow again, forcing the men to scrape their shoulders against wet rock and tread with care over water-soaked stones above a fifteen-foot drop into the frothy torrent below. The water was at its fiercest at this point, indicating that they had drawn close to Devil's Cauldron: a swirling circular pool of water enclosed on all sides by sheer rock. If the villains had come this way, they would be trapped unless they dared to jump into to water to be drowned or dashed against boulders.

Christian edged his way down to the cauldron. Water spray showered his tunic with a layer of tiny sparkling rivulets. One of the men cried out as he slipped on slick water-smoothed rocks, the man behind grabbed the falling man, but one of them dropped their weapon – a club or staff – which clattered against rocks before being swallowed by the rage of water crashing through the narrow defile.

The path came to a dead end. There was no sign of any robbers and no way through. Christian closed his eyes, dreading having to turn to his men and admit failure, losing any last respect they had for him as constable of the newly formed police force. He opened his eyes again, casting his gaze around in the forlorn hope of spotting some clue. A flicker of motion caught his attention. A brush of green movement among the lichen and thick rocks that suggested some disturbance. The path to it was difficult: a slither of soaked rock with only a glistening smooth rockface to hold onto. It was that or failure.

Christian tucked the pistol back into his belt and edged around the ledge, which narrowed to no wider than the sole of his boot. The frothing, roaring white below threatened to consume him should he fall. The rest of the men held back; Christian felt their eyes on him but dared not divert his attention from navigating the narrow pass as he sidestepped along, back to the rock, palms gliding over the sleek surface, searching without success for purchase. Christian felt himself nudged by a small outcrop of rock against his back, eliciting a sudden flash of alarm in which a cry escaped his throat. He somehow steadied himself and held his breath for a few moments, waiting for a wave of vertigo brought on by the sudden shock to pass.

He continued, inching along and expecting every moment for the narrow causeway to collapse under his boots. Finally, Christian reached the moss-covered section of rockface and felt around it, sinking his hand into deep spongy wetness. He found some purchase and was able to turn and face the rock, pawing out moss and muck like a dog digging in dirt.

Lichen fell away, revealing a hollow which had apparently been stuffed with the material to conceal an entrance wide enough to crawl through. Christian beckoned to his men and removed his hat so he might crawl through the passage, hoping that no ruffian waited on the far side to deliver a fatal blow as his head emerged.

The constable slid out from the split in the rock as if it had given birth to him, falling from the narrow gap onto muck and rock. His frock coat and trousers covered in wet dirt from scraping against soiled rocks in the short tunnel. He panted, finding himself in another narrow pass – this time between two sheer rockfaces. The route led down a steep path littered with rocks of various sizes, having long ago tumbled from the heights above.

Christian looked back through the cleared-out tunnel. Smithers and the others stared back at him with furrowed brows and jaws jutting in reluctant determination. Smithers shook his head and turned away. One by one the men followed.

Christian shouted through the tunnel, questioning the honour of the men in no uncertain terms, then collapsed back against the rock and took deep breaths as he steadied himself to plunge further into this unknown realm. He did not blame the men for not following him: it was only luck which had saved him from falling to a watery demise. They would surely have lost at least one life had they all tried to pass.

Christian checked the pistol, finding the powder as damp as he'd expected it to be. He tutted and scolded himself for not wrapping the weapon, then spent a few moments cleaning out the wet powder and doing his best to dry the weapon. He tucked it back into his belt, deciding to let the firearm dry before reloading.

The path wound around several sharp bends before the granite walls gradually gave way to a thick tangle of hawthorns. The trunks were close together that the twisting branches knotted with those of their neighbouring trees, creating an impenetrable wall through which nothing much larger than a hare might have hope to traverse without being scratched by barbs from the trees. This unnaturally dense forest blocked out most of the sunlight, creating the likeness of dusk. The higher branches of the trees formed a canopy over the pass and forced the constable to stoop and then to crawl. Twigs snagged on his clothing at every movement and leaves, damp with dew, brushed across his face and obscured vision beyond arm's reach.

Throughout the effort, evidence of recent human activity encouraged the constable: disturbed earth where others had crawled the same way, a discarded button, a glint of silver from coins dropped by the thieves in their hurry to return to their lair, and strange marks on the trunks which Christian likened to witches' marks found on old rural houses to ward off evil.

Gradually, the narrow route widened enough that the constable could stand, only stooping occasionally under low hanging branches. Natural corridors of brown and green opened new pathways to his left and right, providing consternation as the soil showed footprints on both new paths, and trunks and branches bore markings like those he'd already seen. Snapped twigs had been placed on the ground to form crude arrows which seemed to point in every possible direction. It was a labyrinth, Christian realised, and one which even the thieves had trouble navigating.

The constable added his own markings to the myriad of crude designs, using a long twig, he drew an arrow in the dirt at each decision point, marking his direction of travel. He advanced with caution, pausing only to load the pistol, hoping the weapon was dry enough to not spoil the powder.

A scent of burning warned of the proximity of his quarry. Deep in the valley and submerged in such dense foliage there was no breeze to carry the smell, so he knew the camp was close.

A rustle of undergrowth and crack of twigs announced movement nearby. Christian remained silent, not daring to put down the foot he had been about to step with. He squinted at the sound of crunching sticks just yards away. There was no clear path to where this other person was walking, and the sound passed. Christian felt certain that he remained undetected.

At the next branch in the trail, one route widened into a circular clearance where the remains of a small campfire smouldered and two piles of rags and furs marked bedding either side of the fire. Trinkets of gold and silver adorned the branches nearby, glinting like Christmas decorations, while three plates of greasy animal bones lay discarded by the fire. Christian approached the camp and knelt, putting a hand to the rocks lining the edge of the firepit to check how recent the fire was.

Movement from the makeshift bed to the left caught the constable's attention. The pile of furs erupted, sending forth a cascading mass of shrieking hair and thrashing limbs. Christian fell back, dropping his weapon and raising his forearm defensively as the wild shape that emerged flailed and screeched. Remembering the pistol, Christian's right hand searched the ground while he prepared to bat off any assault with his left.

The crazed thing before him was a woman, Christian realised once the initial moment of shock had passed: the pitch of the screaming was unquestionably female, while the wiry form was too slight for all but the most malnourished men. The wild woman was dressed in soiled rags, which Christian had taken for bedding, and her long black hair was tangled, masking much of her face. Long dirty nails swiped at the air, more defensive than offensive, creating a swirling mass of raking claws about her. She frothed at the mouth like a berserker.

Christian regained his footing and swung a fist, smashing into the woman's temple. She flopped back onto the furs and dirt, moaning in a low voice. Christian straddled the woman as she stirred, pinning her arms and looking upon her dirty face with its sunken eye sockets and gaps between her teeth.

'Who the hell are you?' Christian demanded, 'and how many more of you sods are there?'

The woman gnashed. Her head jerked from side to side as if trying to twist itself from her torso. The motion gradually subsided as she realised her efforts were in vain. Christian felt her muscles relax as she eyed him with something between fear and hostile curiosity.

'You's a Peeler's man?' the woman croaked.

Christian grimaced. He disliked the moniker but nodded. 'Aye. I'm a constable. Now, how many others of you are there? Tell me true and I'll see you're well treated between now and the gallows.'

'Came by yerself? You can get me away?' the woman spoke in quick, desperate breaths.

'Answer my questions, vixen,' Christian snapped.

The crone closed her eyes and seemed to sink into the earth with a long sigh of resignation. 'Me name's Pat Treagle. I been stuck here. Now you're stucked too.'

Christian frowned. It took him a few seconds to place the familiar sounding name: Patricia Treagle was a miller's wife – she had been abducted during a robbery on the road from Tavistock some six months earlier. Her husband had been among the men that had turned back at the Devil's Cauldron – he'd given up his wife for dead months beforehand and begun courting anew. The miller was a man of middle age, but it was impossible to guess the age of the malnourished thing pinned to the floor.

'Forgive me,' Christian said, removing his weight from the woman and taking hold of her arms to help her to her feet, feeling only bone and sinew beneath her grimy clothes, which he realised were likely the garments she had been captured in. 'I will remove you from this foul place. I've marked the way back.'

Mrs Treagle groaned. Her eyes flashed and her fingers became like claws again, raking his cheek as she screamed. 'Peeler! Peeler's man 'ere!'

Christian caught her wrists and wrestled the maddened woman to the ground. He placed his hand over her mouth, drawing it back with an oath when she sank her few remaining front teeth into his palm.

A crack of twigs and rustle of leaves announced approaching enemies. Christian Pushed Mrs Treagle to the ground and glanced about desperately for the pistol. He put his fingers on the smooth polished wood handle as he saw boots pounding the ground in his peripheral vision. His fingers fumbled in the hurry to grasp the weapon and instead pushed the firearm an inch or two further away, creating enough time for the nearest assailant to kick the weapon out of reach. The rushing feet came to a halt with the unmistakable click of the hammer of a flintlock pistol being primed.

Christian let his arm fall limp as he looked up at the three men blocking the only exit from the alcove. The nearest, a rotund man with long greasy hair and a sweat-stained white shirt, stared at Christian down the barrel of a pistol aimed at the constable's chest. The two other men were similarly dishevelled: unshaven, with torn and dirty clothes. One of the men was even shoeless with feet blackened from the peat.

'I'll send you to hell, Peeler!' the armed man snarled.

The shoeless man swiped the weapon aside. 'Fool! If he's in, he's same as us!'

'Same? He's a peeler, setting to hang us I don't doubt!'

'Not for us to choose,' the shoeless man said, regarding the constable with suspicious curiosity. 'we'll take him to the boss.'

Two of the men advanced, roughly taking Christian by the arms and pulling him to his feet. The constable offered no resistance other than by way of expressions of distaste.

The rogues led him through the labyrinth with Mrs Treagle skipping behind, jabbering and screeching until one of the captors released Christain's arm and turned to the woman, raising his hand like he would strike her, and warning to go back to her camp if she knew what was good for her.

It was impossible to keep track of the paths they took; the men moved quickly, without even glancing at the many signs and markers. The maze was certainly unnatural: carved out, Christian presumed, by the rouges over a period of many months. They passed other little camps in alcoves – all similarly decorated with coins, trinkets of gold, and jewellery, yet otherwise completely destitute, with discarded pots, clothes, and the leftovers of meals. Curious faces peered out at them: most were men, dishevelled and fearful. The few women Christian saw bore haunted or vacant expressions, suggesting the sufferance of such torments as to have ripped the very sanity from them. They may have once been pretty but had come to resemble the starving shells of people Christian recalled lying dead in the snow on the retreat to Corunna back in the Peninsula. He had little doubt that each of the women had been captured during robberies and forced into being comfort women for the thieves and murderers.

Eventually, they came into a wider clearing where roasted meat on a spit hung over a smouldering fire. Chests, barrels and furniture lay scattered around, making Christian wonder at the effort the villains had gone through to drag such booty down into this place, or if they had another more easily accessible entrance. Again, treasures decorated the branches while coins were spewed across the floor with disdain alongside rotting food morsels. Several men occupied this space – all much better dressed than those he had seen already, with clean shirts, robes of fine colours, and even silks. A bearded man smoked a pipe as he reclined in a chair with a knee-high boot resting nonchalantly on one of the chests. Christian recognised him straight away from descriptions in reports: Josiah Gupney, the leader of the Gupney gang.

Josiah's hair was long and greasy like that of his followers, but there the similarities ended. He looked to be in his thirties, clean shaven, and much better fed than his men, as evidenced by the pot-shaped bulge that hung over a wide belt. He wore an old bicorn hat tilted at a precarious angle as if mocking those higher-born people whose dress he sought to mimic. He blinked in apparent surprise on sighting the constable, pausing with the mouthpiece of his pipe just short of his lips which spread into a yellow-toothed smile, then almost immediately morphed into a snarl of cruel pleasure.

'Oh, my. What has the Master brought us?' Josiah said in a sing-song voice to which most of his gathered henchmen forced a chuckle.

Christian looked around at the other men, wondering if he had misidentified the ringleader, but when Josiah stood, those seated around him stood too, gathering behind him and adopting similarly wide stances as their leader.

Josiah pointed the pipe at Christian. 'Tell me, Peeler. How'd ye find a way down here?'

Christian stared at the gang leader, saying nothing until one of the men holding his arms squeezed and the other pressed a what felt like a knifepoint into the small of his back.

'Followed your vagabonds in. The rest of my men have gone back to gather reinforcements. There'll be yeomen slashing through this mess of a forest by tomorrow morn.'

Josiah tipped back his head and blasted out long barking laughs. His followers chuckled along.

'My dear Peeler. Nobody can get in lest the master alloweth it. And once you in, you only gets out by way of parole.'

Christian shook his head, more to clear his mind of the nonsense the man was talking than to indicate his lack of understanding.

'Let him be.' Josiah waved his pipe.

The henchmen released their grip on Christian's arms and the point was retracted from his back.

Christian rubbed his arms, aching from the rough grip of the rogues. He glowered at the ringleader, resolving to remain defiant even in the face of this small mercy.

'Go on then, Peeler.' Josiah grinned, gesturing with the clay pipe. 'Be on your good way. Go to your yeomen if you can. None shall impede your progress. Or lack thereof.'

All of the thieves laughed and regarded the constable with sneering superiority.

Christian backed away, suspecting a trick or trap. Josiah waved him away with his pipe. Needing no further encouragement, Christian turned and ran. Sprinting through the narrow passageways, turning off each time the route branched, hoping to evade the pursuers he expected would soon give chase. Only once his chest was heaving from the effort and his lungs aching for air did he stop to rest and formulate a plan.

It was clear that without marking his progress, escape could take days. He dug into his pocket for a small three-inch knife with a dull blade that he kept on his person as a general tool. He used it to mark his chosen route at each turn by carving a small *X* on the twisting trunks above the existing marks, wondering as he did so how many others had done the same before him while trying to flee this labyrinthine oubliette.

The constable wandered at a steady pace, deciding to save his energy in case he should need to fight or flee. He marked many trunks – twice finding himself coming back upon marks he had already made. Darkness came on suddenly, like a black cloud descending unseen until the last moment. With no light source, the night was impenetrable. Christian sat with his back to a trunk and rested his chin on his knees. The night air was cold despite his thick blue coat. He hugged his arms around his legs and exhaustion soon brought sleep.

Christian awoke with a start, blinking into the shadowy dusk, wondering where he was in the confusion of the waking moment. He took out his pocket watch and found the time to be a little after seven – he presumed in the morning. His throat was parched and so he licked fresh dew from leaves, leaving a sour taste on his tongue and failing to sufficiently quench the thirst. He could only hope that his men had been quick about reporting his pursuit, and that the yeomanry would be sent for, but the difficulty of crossing the Devil's Cauldron and navigating the routes beyond meant that any relief might take days, and if the yeomanry were not sufficiently provisioned, they might even give up the cause as lost long before the constable could be reached.

Christian moved on, soon passing a campsite that looked like one he glimpsed the previous day. Observing three forms submerged in rags and furs, he snuck into their camp, looking about for some scrap to eat. He picked up a tin flask; the weight indicated it was empty and let it drop. The only foodstuffs he could find were the bones and gristle of beasts consumed perhaps many days ago. Christian grimaced at the remains of rodent bones among those of rabbit and even badger.

'Do our fare not please thee, Peeler?' a head said from the furs, raising only a few inches before resting back down and watching the constable with cool grey eyes. 'Go on. I won't stop you should it please you to suck on the bones of stoat and rat, such as I've had to sup on this past year.'

'Pity thee, should I?' Christian said, suddenly angry. 'You chose this life. Reap the reward.'

The man sat up and swept tangled hair from his face. 'Chose? I chose nought. A bloody stonemason I were until snatched on my way home and brought here. Forced into this existence between life and death.'

'Fear not, Stonemason. After I'm out, I shall return for you, and bring such a quantity of rope to hoist all of you out of here by your necks.'

'Bring enough for yourself then!' the ruffian shouted as Christian left him.

Each path appeared little different to the one before or after, yet seldom did Christian find one of his own markings on the wood. He encountered one of the highwaymen at a turn in the path. The Constable held his knife out and adopted a defensive posture.

The thief glanced at the small knife with half-shut eyes and walked on without otherwise acknowledging the constable's presence.

Christian wandered for hours. Sometimes falling into desperation and running, even calling out for help. His stomach groaned and his heels were rubbed raw against the leather of boots not yet properly broken in. He spent a second night tucked up against a tree, praying for salvation until he lost consciousness.

The third day brought not sight or sound of a soul, yet the markings on the trees were still infrequent, indicating a huge size to the labyrinth. Christian despaired at how rare his markings were and how dispersed they seemed to be: as if his marks were disappearing, or the lanes were somehow changing. Or perhaps, he considered, he was losing his mind.

On the morning of the fourth day, Christian found another empty campsite. It may have been the one he passed days before, he wasn't sure: all those he had seen were in a similar mess. He found some bones with greasy morsels still attached. He didn't pause before stuffing them into his mouth to suck the fetid juices, crunching the smaller bones before swallowing them.

Christian sank to his knees as he came to the wide clearing where Josiah sat in his same arrogant pose, tankard in one hand, pipe in the other, humming a ditty along with a companion who sat on the floor beside him.

Josiah raised his tankard in salute. 'Welcome back, Peeler. Knew you'd decide to stay. Glad you found your way back here. Not everyone do.'

Christian opened his mouth to speak but could form no words. His throat was raw, his clothes heavily soiled, and fingertips bloody from where he tried to claw his way through the knotted forest with his bare hands. The small knife was long lost to him. He'd stopped counting the days after a week, and now he was only glad to have found his way back to the presumed centre of the maze where a small fire burned and a rabbit carcass glistened and dripped enticingly above a crackling fire.

Josiah picked up the branch that speared the skinned rabbit and walked to Christian, holding the offering before him, jerking it away when Christian's grasping hands reached out for it.

'In good time.' Josiah put a fatherly hand on Christian's head. 'A peeled rabbit for a peeler! I shan't deny you, but the master needs your parole firstly. Think of this foul toil what you've endured as a sort of initiation.'

Christian groaned and might have cried if it were in his ability to do so. Instead, he gaped at the food, drooling and the smell of dripping animal fat. His attention was so fixated on the meat that he didn't at first notice the strange sculpture which two henchmen were attending to. It was an ugly creation, an assortment of sticks and bleached bones which had been arranged into the semblance of a man seated in a crude high-backed chair roughly fashioned from twisted branches. The torso of the effigy was dressed in dead leaves, and the decaying head of a goat with its tongue hanging out one side of its mouth was perched upon the body; the two horns of the rotting beast were straight and long and looked like they had been sharpened. Claw-like twigs in place of a hands held a staff topped by a small human skull.

The gathered robbers knelt in the presence of the putrid totem, except for Josiah who bowed before the statue and then turned back to his captive policeman.

'The master ensures that such beasts as can sustain us fall into this realm between realms. Enough to keep us alive, but seldom enough to thrive. I were first here and pledged my soul for the promise of riches and the protection of the master while in his realm.' Josiah sighed and shook his head as if recalling some sad memory. 'Alas, we must return here every night or our souls are lost, and what good are riches here except to decorate our cells? I tricked or captured such peoples to bring here and keep me company in this hell.'

Christian groaned, deciding he would say whatever he these madmen wanted so that they would feed him. He would make good his escape when he was stronger.

Josiah laid a hand on Christian's head and regarded him with what looked like a sympathetic smile. 'I know well as you're thinking, but he'll never let you leave, little hare, caught in the Devil's snare.'

The statue jerked as if someone had nudged it. Josiah and his henchmen put their foreheads to the ground. Someone made a whimpering sound. Sticks and old bones cracked as the totem shifted. The head turned stiffly upon its body of decayed nature. The dead goat's eyes, once dark and lifeless, now blazed.

Christian felt a warmth in his crotch as his bladder loosened. The statue of the Devil creaked as it stood, glaring down on the policeman with eyes that seemed to look into his very soul.

'He'll never let you escape,' Josiah hissed, his head turned sideways in the dirt to regard Christian with one eye. 'Swear your allegiance and he will let you exist as we do. Give your parole – tis your only hope.'

The Evening Standard, September 12th.

The search for the body of Constable Christian Hare has failed to establish any trace of the late officer's remains some three weeks after townsfolk of Lydford saw the Constable fall into the tumultuous waters of Devil's Cauldron while in pursuit of criminals. Meanwhile, attacks on merchants and travellers in the locality continue and the parish puts it trust in the newly arrived Constable Rufkin, who all hope and trust will rise to the task of bringing the so-called Gupney gang to justice.

The Legend of Vixana

'Where you a heading, stranger?' The red-haired man asking the question was leaning on the bar in a familiar, slovenly slouch and raised his near full tankard in salute to show meant no offence by the question or the labelling as an outsider.

'Tavvy. Visit me old ma,' Oliver said, aware that his voice was high and scratchy in comparison to the more manly baritone of the local man. 'I come from Widecombe way, but I grew up in Tavvy. Visiting me old ma as I do every three month or so.'

Oliver gulped down some of his stout and wiped the foam from his mouth with the back of his hand, smacking his lips, then thumping the glass down on the bar. A little of the brown liquid sloshed over the side of glass and down over his fingers, making them sticky. He ignored being nudged by a thin man to his left who was heatedly talking to his companions in a rasping voice and seemed oblivious at his proximity to Oliver – or that it was the third time his elbow had dug into Oliver's rib. The pub was full of miners and stone cutters at the end of a hard day's work. They all wore tall dirty boots and heavy Woolen trousers covered in granite dust. Their bowler hats were discoloured around the rim from the smoke of pipes which hung from the corner of every man's mouth. Had they been in a line-up of criminals, Oliver thought they might only be differentiated by height and the style of moustache. All that is, except for Oliver and the flame-haired local who studied him with an amused half smile.

The man's style of dress was not dissimilar to the others, but he bore no trace of masonry work. His shirtsleeves were rolled up but his white shirt, although slightly stained from spilt drink, showed no signs of sweat or grime from rough labour. He wore a cap with the peak high rather than a bowler, with bushy tufts of curling red hair exploding from under his cap. The fiery muttonchops down to his chin, playful glint in his gaze, and a nonchalant pose gave him the appearance of a leprechaun from a child's tale.

The redhead slid along the bar, nearer to Oliver until their elbows touched. Oliver might have drawn back a few inches if not for the agitated drinker on his other side who was now resting his back against Oliver's arm.

'William,' the big ginger man said, offering a thick fleshy hand supported by a freckled and hairy forearm. 'But call me Billy.'

Oliver took the offered hand; the movement caused the thin fellow to remove his weight from Oliver's arm. He felt the man's breath as he turned his head in Oliver's direction and tutted with irritation.

Billy's hand enveloped Oliver's smaller one, shaking with confident and dominating firmness.

Oliver mumbled his name, then seeing Billy tilt his head and wince questioningly, said it again, too loud and high pitched. Oliver's hand was released several lingering seconds after it felt polite to do so; he instinctively wiped it on his trouser leg, regretting the involuntary motion when he noted that Billy registered the action with another of his half-smiles before drowning the expression in a mouthful of beer. Oliver reached for his own drink, taking it around the circumference of the glass instead of the handle, making his palm sticky again.

Oliver took several gulps of drink, watching his new companion over the rim of his glass and regretting his decision to walk into the pub at that time: he'd visited the inn several times before as it was a convenient hours' walk into Tavistock from the pub, and all downhill, but he'd never stopped by so late in the day and hadn't expected the pub to be so packed.

'Pay day,' Billy said, smirking as if he'd heard Oliver's thoughts. 'Not usually this busy, but pay-day they all has a few before going home for weekend.'

'What's your work?' Oliver said, leaning against the bar. Billy's smile widened a fraction and Oliver realised with some embarrassment that he was emulating Billy's posture. He straightened and bumped the man behind him whose curse was accompanied by the pitter-patter of a slosh of beer splashing the floorboards.

'Hey!' the man said, shoving Oliver's shoulder. 'You split my beer.'

Oliver turned, stiff and wide-eyed. He was faced by three men with dusty coats and serious moustaches. Other patrons of the bar turned their attention to the sudden confrontation.

Billy's rough hand clapped on Oliver's shoulder, levering him out of the way and taking his place.

'Hey now,' Billy said, his voice having dropped a several octaves. 'You lost but a drop and you've been jostling my friend without a thought since you walked in here. You shan't get a free pint out of that dribble o' spillage.'

The offended man bristled, squaring his shoulders and jutting his chin forward. Although his baggy work clothes made him look thin, his grim countenance and bent nose marked him out as a probable brawler. 'You taking the side of that stranger?'

'I am too, because we was talking and you interrupted us. Best you take your guffaw further down the bar unless-'

Oliver jumped at the sound of the innkeeper's palm slamming the bar. The burly barkeep frowned at the arguing patrons over the rim of tiny spectacles. 'I'll not have any fighting – as you both know. If you must fight, have at it outside: but you ain't coming back in if you do. Neither of you.'

The disgruntled drinker snorted into his moustache and turned back to his friends. The low rumble of chatter returned as men picked up their paused conversations.

Billy turned around, reaching past Oliver to take up his pint before leaning back on the bar. He rolled his eyes and nodded his head toward the thin man and his companions. 'Some folk'll try anything for a free beer.'

The offended fellow turned, glowering at Billy's back before returning once again to his companions.

'Well, it's been nice meeting you,' Oliver said, tipping the remaining half-pint down his gullet.

'Hold your horses,' Billy laughed. 'Don't let the stone brigade scare you off.'

'No, I must be going really. It'll be dark before I get to my ma's.'

Billy shrugged. 'Fair enough. If it do get dark on you, just stick to the road and you can't go wrong.' He muttered some half-heard words of discontent at being abandoned, although his eyes were already searching the tables and benches for fresh company to intrude upon.

'Oh, I don't take the road,' Oliver said, straightening to leave. 'I go by the lanes. Know the area well: remember, I grew up here about.'

'Lanes?' Billy frowned, suddenly interested.

'Yup. Down past Yellowmead Farm, o'er the river and through the lanes between the farms.'

Billy put a light hand on Oliver's arm and shook his head. 'Oh, shouldn't be doing that. Haven't you heard the legend of Vixana?'

Oliver shrugged. 'Witch or something wasn't she? I recall something of it.'

'Oh, my boy.' Billy's arm encircled Oliver's shoulders, pulling him back to the bar while with his free arm Billy motioned for the innkeeper to refill Oliver's glass.

'I must go, really,' Oliver said, but the hand on his shoulder held him fast.

Billy's breath was hot and stank of ale as he leaned close to Oliver, who noticed for the first time that the big ginger man's eyes were bloodshot and watery, whether from the tobacco smoke that hung in a thick cloud at just over head height, or from consumption of beer, he did not know.

'This one's on me. Let me tell you the tale of Vixana. Then you can decide which route to take to your dear ma's.' Billy downed his drink and held the empty glass out for the innkeeper who had just finished pouring Oliver's beer.

Billy released Oliver's shoulder to dig around in his pocket, quickly retrieving a sixpence which he tossed onto the bar where it spun with a tinny ring.

Oliver glanced to the door and considered escape, suddenly suspecting his new friend was setting him up for a confidence trick or scheme of dubious nature, but he envisaged taking but one or two steps before Billy's meaty fingers would snatch his collar. He stared at his refilled glass, the foam still frothing atop it, and mumbled his thanks.

'Everyone this side o' the moor knows the tale of Vixana and knows not to venture near her haunt alone – especially not near dusk.' Billy paused to take a long swig. 'Vixana was a witch, yer right there. She would climb up on Vixen tor and look for lone travellers crossing the moor. Close by Vixen Tor lies the line of crosses marking the old path across the moors to Tavistock Abbey which many would follow on way to church or market: course, you knows that. Anyways, she'd look out for travellers come that way, and would use her magic to call down a deep thick fog, thick as any you'd ever seen, so that no man could tell his way even if he were familiar with the terrain.'

'Aye,' Oliver nodded, parts of the story coming back to him from his childhood.

Billy gestured like a mummer as he spoke, enthralled in his own tale. 'And then, lost in the fog they would fall afoul of the mire where they would become stuck and sink to their doom to slowly decay alongside the bones of others who'd fallen prey over the generations.'

'But that's not the end of the tale, is it?' Oliver said, taking a small sip. 'Didn't one traveller get the best of her? I'm sure he did.'

'Aye. Aye.' Billy drummed his fingers on the bar. 'Did so, he did. He wore a magic ring of invisibility, and so Vixana – whose gaze could penetrate the fog – couldn't see him. She peered over the edge of the tor, and the traveller: he snuck up behind her, he did – real quiet like, and pushed her head over heels into the bog below where she met her own demise.' Billy threw his head back and laughed.

'Well, I'll consider the route made safe then.' Oliver said in a tone which denoted his imminent departure.

'If only it be so, lad.' Billy snatched Oliver's sleeve before it could be withdrawn out of reach. 'For, on a night like this when there be fog, Vixana can be heard up on the tor, cackling and screeching. Her spirit looking for souls to join her in hell.'

Oliver smiled weakly. 'You don't believe that, surely. Big fella like yourself.'

'Let's see,' Billy said, setting his glass down on the bar. He laid both his hands on Oliver's shoulders and steered him toward the door, marching him out into the cool evening air.

Nearby King's Tor was lost in a haze of grey, as was the mighty Great Mis Tor. The depths of the wooded valleys along the River Walkham were cast in gloom, yet gaslights from the streets of Tavistock radiated a distant dim glow through the veil of fog.

'Vixana is out tonight it seems,' Billy whispered into Oliver's ear, 'working her magic.' He chuckled and then straightened, releasing Oliver and calling out a greeting to two men in brown tweed and feathered caps who sauntered down the track toward the pub. 'Ah! I been waiting for you two for an hour! Good job I've had Oliver here to keep me company.'

Billy released his captive with a clap on the back before walking to his friends, waving a friendly hand in Oliver's direction when he joined with them. 'I've got to attend my work with these follows now. You just take heed of my warning and stick to the road into Tavvy: you'll get there safe n' sound.'

The two new men greeted Billy in thick Irish accents. Oliver thought they looked like gypsies. A black and white mongrel dashed between their legs, barking and nipping the air until one of the Irish men kicked a clot of earth at it and snapped 'Back to wagon with yer!'

Oliver waved and watched the men head back down the track. They didn't rejoin the road, but cut across the grass, chatting loud and amiably among themselves, Oliver apparently immediately forgotten. With a sudden alarm, Oliver dug his hand into his pocket, sighing relief when feeling the paper banknotes which he intended to give to his mother. He shook his head and laughed at his own suspicion, feeling foolish that he'd mistaken the overbearing drinker for a pickpocket. He wondered vaguely what the men did for work, his earlier question going unanswered after the interruption from the belligerent drinker.

Deciding to finish his drink before departing, Oliver ducked back under the low door and went to the bar. He reached between two men and picked up his drink, noting that Billy's had been left near full. He downed the last of his beer, nodded to the innkeeper, and went back out into the evening gloom.

Oliver didn't even consider following Billy's impudent advice, imagining it was intended more to tease than to warn. Besides, he'd travelled this route dozens of times, including after dark on occasion when he had been slowed by the weather. He set off downhill, passing Yellowmead farm and scores of partially cut stones, many still bearing the marks of the wedges which had been used to split the granites, and others with smooth surfaces and straight edges. He passed within sight of the darkening silhouette of an old medieval cross and soon after reached the river at a small ford. Finding the water level slightly higher than usual, he splashed through the ankle-deep crossing, cleaning some of the dust and dirt from his boots. Then the mist clinging to the heights cleared enough to reveal sight of Vixen Tor.

The sheer rockface; jagged, grey and threatening, towered over the trees lining the hill below it. The valley was already descending into dark; Oliver scolded himself for feeling apprehension brought on by his drinking companion's childish tale. He pushed on, climbing up past the tor and toward the trackways which brought him near to Feather Tor. He glimpsed a dim light from a nearby farmhouse which was soon lost as the fog thickened again.

Oliver stopped, looking for Vixen Tor to get his bearings. The tor had been engulfed in misty grey, but he felt confident that it stood to his right. The ground around his feet was soggy; his feet sank an inch as brown liquid seeped spilled over his boots. It was fine, Oliver assured himself, he knew the way and he would know if he was venturing into the mire before it became a danger.

A shriek from somewhere up high pierced through the thick grey air. Oliver gasped, feeling his pulse quicken. The sound had come from the direction of Vixen Tor. Silence followed the short, sharp screech. He listened, hearing only his thudding heart and feeling the fog's moisture form a wet layer on his face.

'Hello?' he called out weakly.

The scream again – this time further away and higher.

Oliver groaned and released a long breath of relief: it was a hawk or some other bird of prey, transported by mere imagination into the ghost of an ancient witch. He laughed, glad that nobody was around to witness his humiliation. Still shaking his head, he continued on, spying the light from the farmhouse which he knew lay near to the track to Feather Tor.

Wet ground sucked at his steps until he got to the droveway which ran down between the hedged boundary walls of two farms. The bleating of sheep comforted him: a pastoral reminder of nature's company among a shadowy landscape made suspiciously supernatural as visibility diminishes. Oliver's boots crunched gravel shavings. He whistled a tune to keep himself company, feeling more confident now that he knew he was not far from his destination: past a few more farms and he'd be on the outskirts of Tavistock.

The whistle died on his lips after a few notes. Oliver tilted his head, thinking he'd heard voices. A lamb called for its mother – otherwise, all was silent. 'Stop imagining things, Olly,' he scolded himself.

'There! I told you I heard something!' a voice hissed.

Oliver stopped. He squinted in the direction of the voice, seeing nothing, imagining ghouls just off the track amongst the clitter, waiting in ambush for an unwary traveller to pull into the mist and drag down to hell. He shuddered, silently berating himself as a coward, then walked on, not quite finding the courage to call out to into the gloom.

'There!' a voice said, louder.

Oliver stopped again. He recognised the voice. 'Billy? Is that you with your mates?'

A muttered curse answered him.

Oliver strode on, emboldened at the familiar voice. He laughed aloud: had Billy and his friends been afraid at the spirit in the mist just as he had been? 'Don't worry. It's not Vixana! Jus me: Olly.'

Shapes emerged from the fog as he advanced: two silhouettes, then a third, surrounded by sheep. Further behind the men Oliver could make out the outline of wagon and heard the snorting the draft horse attached to it. He discerned the nearest shape as belonging to Billy, resting his weight on a thick walking stick.

'You're farmers then?' Oliver said, drawing near enough to see Billy's face. 'I should've thought so. Why you out gathering your flock up this time o'night?'

He stopped dead. Halted by Billy's sour expression. The two gypsy men moved from behind Billy; one circled around to Oliver's left, the other headed right as if to outflank him. Billy lifted his stick, which Oliver realised with a creeping horror, was in fact a club.

'You… you're sheep thieves.' Oliver stammered.

Billy sighed and slapped the club into his open palm. He advanced slowly. The shadowy men to the left and right closed in.

'I told you to stick to the road,' Billy said, sighing as he lifted the club.

The Whaler

It was the proudest moment of my life, standing outside the newly refurbished pub I had purchased the previous summer. The Whaler Inn sits on the old road between Tavistock and Okehampton, so the mayor of Tavistock – the nearest of the two towns – had turned up to cut the ribbon in front of a small crowd which included local press reporters and photographers. It was the Third of May, Nineteen Fifty-One. What started off as a wonderful, happy, sunny morning would by the day's end mark the beginning of weeks of terror.

At eleven o'clock, I poured my first pint: for the mayor, of course. There's a photo in the *Western Morning News* of myself leaning on the brass pump while the mayor and a local councillor raised a glass along with a small crowd of local men. The pub had previously been a coaching inn but had laid derelict for decades. Old tales of headless coachmen and highwaymen waylaying travellers, along with newer stories of disembodied hairy hands pursuing drivers had attracted visitors to the area, and the correspondent from the Western Morning News asked me pointedly why I had gone with a nautical theme for the new inn rather than capitalising on local history and legends.

'Well…' I said, gathering my thoughts as to where to begin. 'When I first bought the coaching house, it was falling apart – much worse repair than I bargained for. The floorboards needed replacing and I remembered reading – in your very newspaper I believe it was – about the wreckage of an old whaling ship being sold for scrap. So, after buying a wrecked inn, why not buy a wrecked ship to go with it?'

The reporter and all the moustached, flat cap wearing, countryfolk in our company laughed; their shirtsleeves were all rolled up as was their style, and pipes adorned their mouths instead of the cigarettes preferred by city folk.

'But, Mister Grayson,' the correspondent said, licking the tip of his pencil, 'what made you decide to adopt the character of the whaling ship rather than just break it apart for the planks?'

'Laziness,' I said, with a wide grin as I pulled another pint of stout for one of the local men whom I hoped might become regulars. 'Seriously: I wanted the place to be unique and memorable. I found myself scouring chandler stores and bartering with captains for the old lamps which hang from my ceilings and all the other brick-a-brack I've decorated the walls with.'

The men turned to admire the décor, as if only now noticing it, with smiles of amused approval. The far wall was covered in a fishing net, from which hung harpoons, replicas of various fish, and other nautical adornments. Tables were set into alcoves designed to feel like tiny smugglers caves with candles lighting the cubbyholes, while part of the dining room had the character of a ships' cabin, with lanterns hanging low over the tables. Photographs and paintings of various vessels decorated walls along with steel rimmed portholes. My bar top was originally a table on which ship's crew ate. Creaking floorboards and low ceilings gave the impression of the lower decks of a tall ship. The strangest feature of all was that of a human skull – missing its jawbone – which had been found in a chest in the doctor's cabin. The harbourmaster who sold me the wreck told me the skull was likely something the ship's surgeon retained as a reference piece in case of performing head surgery. Regardless, the strange curio was displayed on a shelf above the bar where drinkers could gaze up at it and, I supposed, coin some nickname it. Naturally, the skull attracted the attention of the press, and it was brought down and passed around to impromptu amateur performances of Hamlet and a couple of photographs with the skull held like it was some manner of trophy.

Once the dignitaries had their photographs and obligatory pint, they left. The local press and then the workmen departed in dribs and drabs until soon just three customers remained; two of them wanted to open a tab, which by their soiled clothes, red noses and rheumy eyes I doubted they could repay. The third man, an aging local farmer by the name of Jebediah, sat at the bar with his sheepdog by his boots.

'Don't you be worryin' about curses or the suchlike?' Jebediah said, scrutinizing the peculiar surroundings with a wince of distrust. He scratched the grey whiskers on his cheek at the same moment the sheepdog scratched his own cheek with his back leg. If dogs and their owners look alike, that certainly was true for Jebediah and his grey dog with its patchy fur and gammy legs.

I laughed, thinking Jebediah was jesting, but he curled his lower lip, harrumphed, and muttered something into his pint of mild.

'What kind of curse?' I said, leaning on the bar and trying to look attentive.

Jebediah's wrinkled face screwed up into knots; he shook his head, incredulous as my lack of understanding. 'What kind, ye say? You made a tavern out o' a wreck. It's bad luck at the least, but if she were a cursed ship, whatever blackness soaked into those planks is flowing through these walls and floors.' Jebediah gave the room a panoramic glare and then took a long draught of his drink before wiping wet lips with his sleeve.

'If the Inn's cursed, why drink here?' I said, immediately regretting giving my first potential regular reason to prefer frequenting *The Dart Inn* a mile down the road.

'Drinking ain't the same as owning the place,' Jebediah fixed me with a stern gaze, challenging me to dispute his superstitions. 'Anyways, Gerty will alert me to lurking evils. They got a sense for such things, they has, dogs.' He reached down tickle Gerty's ear.

'Well, Gerty looks quite content so hopefully we're safe from curses and evils.' I smiled, satisfied that I had closed the peculiar topic without upsetting my patron. I was jolted from my smugness by a cascade of mild from the pump at my elbow. Beer poured freely from the tap, sloshing over the slop tray in a torrent and onto the floor.

I spent the next couple of minutes disabling the pump while Jebediah helpfully caught the free-flowing beer in glasses – of which I felt obliged to let him have two on the house.

'So, ain't cursed, says you?' Jebediah said over the rim of his glass.

I found myself wondering if the old coot was likely to put off other regulars, reasoning that if there was a curse it was likely to be Jebediah and his mangy pet.

A few customers wandered in throughout the day, but the inn was empty by half seven. I closed up at around eight o'clock. I didn't let the lacklustre start put me down: telling myself it was a Monday and that on Friday the quarrymen and commuting workers would be thirsty from a weeks' work. I stacked chairs on the tables as I had seen done at other establishments and was about to put the lamps out when I saw, by the corner of my eye, one of the lights wink out – and then the adjacent one went dark, and then the next, casting the far corner of the bar into gloom. I shivered and then immediately felt silly: I'd put the same amount of oil in each of the lamps and so they had just happened to go out at the same time. I thought about what Jebediah had said about the curse and chuckled.

'Thanks,' I said to the darkness. 'You saved me the work of putting out the lamps.' I had no sooner spoken than a dozen other lights went out in the same instant. I shuddered – and this time I didn't feel silly for it. I called out 'hello', feeling cowardly for the nervous sensation prickling my spine. I waited for the best part of a minute, hearing only the ticking of a grandfather clock. I released my breath and walked to the lit lantern that was nearest to those which had gone out, intending to extinguish it before I could be alarmed by any more lamps running out of oil.

I reached for the latch on the lamp and paused as I saw movement: a hand loomed out of the darkness on the opposite side of the lamp. I jumped back with a cry of alarm just as the light blinked out. I scrambled backward into a table, sending chairs clattering to the floor. I was about to take to flight when my senses returned, realising what I had likely seen was the reflection of my own hand in the glass. I put a hand to my heart and laughed nervously.

I set the chairs back on the table and went about seeing to the other lanterns with more trepidation than such a menial task warrants. I had decided to leave one lamp on in the window to serve as invitation to knock for any late travellers on the road who might require accommodation.

As I was about the shut the door to the bar area, I noticed a figure standing beside one of the alcoves: only a partial profile was visible in the dim light from the solitary remaining lamp, but I could make out some form of workmen's cap and knee-high boots, but little else.

'Hello,' I called out, nerves tickling my voice.

There was no answer. I dared hope it was some trick of the low light, or that it was a customer who had woken from sleep in a corner without my noticing, but I had not long ago walked through the very spot where the man now stood, unmoving.

I hailed the shadowy figure again without response. I strode into the hall where I picked up a lamp from a low table and marched back into the bar: there was no sign of the man. I searched the entire ground floor, checking all the alcoves and under the tables, finding nought. I retired to bed, putting the whole incident down to tiredness and nerves.

For the first time since moving into the countryside I felt truly isolated. The night-time view from my bedroom window was that of deep oily blackness. Pulling the curtains closed only brought a sense of confinement. I lay on the bed, staring at patterns of dancing candlelight on the ceiling which gave me the impression of motion much like that of a ship on a rolling sea. I blew out the light, but the sensation remained with me, making me feel ill. When sleep came, I dreamt of plunging waves, greasy wet ropes, and commands shouted over howling winds. The dream remained with me for some moments after waking at dawn with a taste of seawater in my mouth.

My cook arrived on the second day: a middle-aged man who had travelled up from Plymouth by train. I met him at the station in Okehampton and had him settled into the inn before opening time. The day was disappointingly quiet – just as well since the cook had to go out to buy ingredients. I spent much of the day dusting and tinkering; I attempted to fix the pump on the mild, but it seemed to be working fine. By mid-afternoon the disturbed sleep from the night before had caught up with me and I found myself yawning. Worse was that I kept seeing things in my peripheral vision: glimpses of someone loitering nearby, watching or waiting, but when I looked directly at them there was nobody there. I concluded that a sight test was in order and tried to shake off the constant sensation of being observed. That night I slept fitfully again, waking several times, dreaming always about the sea. The dreams were remarkably vivid; I could feel the oily wet ropes in my clutches as I braced against a torrent that surged over the deck. I could even smell the stench of fish guts from the cargo hold.

'Not been getting much custom,' Jebediah said accusingly that evening.

'It'll pick up,' I said, deciding that I'd kick his dog the next time Jebediah went to the outhouse to relive himself.

'Got bags under your eyes. Looks like you ain't slept a wink. Thinking of selling up already?' Jebediah stared at me with a blank expression, either not registering my red-faced indignation or not caring about it.

An empty glass smashed on the floor at the end of the bar. My two other patrons paused conversation from their alcove. There was nobody within two yards of the glass.

'Must be the headless coachmen letting you know he wants another pint,' said one of the men in the alcove with a chuckle.

'Ain't no headless horseman,' Jebediah said, not bothering to turn to the men. His eyes remained fixed on me as he took a sip of ale and smacked his lips.

'Just a jest, old timer,' said one of the men.

Jebediah sniffed. 'Plenty of things to make yer skin crawl around these parts but horsemen – headless or nay – ain't one of them.'

'Tell that to the skull up there,' the patron said. His companion laughed.

I cleaned up the broken glass, aware of Jebediah's unblinking gaze upon me. I felt irritated, as if the grouchy old chap was bringing me bad luck. Jebediah was the last to leave that night, wincing as he climbed off his stool. Gerty rose, staying ever close to his master's side. Jebediah raised a hand in farewell as he reached the door, whereupon Gerty froze.

The dog's hair rose on his back. Gerty stared into a corner where a lamp had gone out, snarling and shaking with the tail curled between his back legs.

Jebediah and I followed the dog's gaze, but there was nothing to be seen other than an empty alcove shrouded in shadow.

'C'mon, Gerty,' Jebediah said, nudging the dog with a mud-encrusted boot.

Gerty remained petrified, unable to move beyond the shaking that wracked his withered frame. Jebediah reached down to grab the dog by the collar: only then did Gerty react – snapping at his owner's hand. Jebediah's surprisingly quick reflex stopped the dog from taking a fingertip. The old coot made to give the dog a backhander, but the animal crumpled into a whimpering mess with a puddle of urine spreading out from under him.

'Maybe it's time to get a new dog,' I said without malice.

Jebediah shot me a blazing glare and scooped the dog up from the floor, carrying it with both arms to the door. He stopped at the threshold and half turned toward me. 'Told you the blasted place is cursed.'

I bolted the door behind Jebediah and turned to the puddle I'd have to mop up, catching a glance of a figure in a long coat and a cap in the corner where the hatstand was, but when I focused on the spot I saw only the empty stand. I shook my head and went about my labour.

I must admit a sense of trepidation as I set about putting out the lanterns, but all remained lit until I extinguished them. This allowed me some good measure of comfort and the belief that I had probably let my imagination get the better of me over the last two days. Yet, once again as I slept, I dreamt of the sea. I dreamed of arguing with a bearded man with a thunderous expression and dreadfully scarred cheek, but when I woke the detail of the dispute – if indeed there had been any – was lost to me.

Things continued much the same way over the following five or six days: glimpses of a shadowy man, a picture or piece of decoration falling from its proper place without draft or vibration to have caused it, and nightly dreams of the whaling ship which left me feeling exhausted through the day, as if I had spent the night toiling at sea in the ethereal realm. Nobody else mentioned the shadowy man, so I became convinced that I was seeing things. I travelled into Tavistock to have my eyes examined and, finding them to be in good working order, went to a doctor who prescribed me sleeping pills to dispel the dreams.

The night I took the first sleeping pill was the worst: I slept straight through until after ten o'clock in the morning, awaking to bedsheets soaked with sweat and the most vivid recollection of the dream yet. The pills had kept me trapped in the ethereal, and the strange recurring dream had become a nightmare I couldn't awake from.

In this dream realm, I was one of the whaler's crew. While before I had experienced rough seas and felt myself thrown about deck, this time the ship had become trapped in ice. Several crewmen carried a lifeboat across the snow to the water where they planned to row to a whaling station to seek help, but I knew they would never return. I dreamed that we were trapped there for weeks – months perhaps – the nerves of the crew growing ever more frayed as idleness set in and rations ran out. The bearded man I had quarrelled with blamed me for the misfortune. He was always there in my peripheral vision, glaring at me and telling anyone who'd listen that I was bad luck for the ship.

I was late opening the pub, but there was only the cook waiting to be let in. My thoughts remained on the ship and the strange man who stalked me. I took the skull down from its shelf and studied it, looking for any trace of scarring on the cheekbone but finding none. I couldn't help but shake the feeling that the threatening bearded man represented the shadowy figure I kept glimpsing.

As there were few customers – none of which were eating – I asked the cook to watch the bar while I took my old car out for a drive up to Appledore; intent on questioning the harbourmaster about the strange wreck I had bought. I cursed myself on the way for not asking prudent questions at the time of purchase, seeing the ship as mere salvageable planks and beams.

The harbourmaster was every bit the sea-faring type: nautical hat and close-cropped beard with a pipe hanging from salt-dried lips. 'The whaler?' he said after I asked what he knew about the vessel's past.

I resisted an urge to snap that it was the only ship I'd purchased from him, but I suspect impatience was apparent in my tone when I replied 'yes, the whaler.'

The harbourmaster shrugged. 'The Orca. Wrecked off Baggy point two-mile north o' here.'

'How many hands were lost?' I asked.

'None,' the Master said, frowning. 'They got blown against the rocks. The hull cracked and the masts snapped, but it didn't sink. There was time to rescue not only the crew but the entire cargo of whale oil.'

'So, why was it sold in pieces?' I asked.

The harbourmaster chuckled like I had asked a childish question and gestured with his pipe as he spoke. 'The Orca was towed into harbour as salvage, but the hull started to split apart, and the ship got stuck on the sandbanks for another few days where it was an obstruction to shipping. By the time she were pulled out o' the sea she were falling to bits: she never properly recovered from stress to her hull from being trapped in the ice over winter.'

'She was stuck in ice?' I asked, unable to mask my shock.

'Aye,' the captain eyed me with suspicious curiosity. 'It were a common enough danger in arctic parts. Why the sudden interest?'

I insisted to the harbourmaster that my interest was purely in relation to telling the ship's tale to curious patrons. He suggested that I write to the vessel's owner enquiring of the full history, and he kindly gave me the firm's London address.

'And you're quite certain there was no loss of life?' I asked from the doorway of his office.

The harbourmaster nodded. 'I were a tug captain back then and helped salvage the cargo. Twenty years back but I remember it well. Not a soul died on that wreck, I promise you.'

'So, what about the skull?'

The harbourmaster laughed. 'Ah, that. It was in the surgeon's chest. He probably bought it landside. Crew are buried at sea or brought home; we don't keep their skulls, Mister Grayson. We're mariners, not pirates.'

I left the harbourmaster with more questions than answers. The knowledge that the ship had been trapped in ice forced me to consider that my dreams reflected reality. Anticipation of where the story would lead kept me awake that night, while the incessant creaking of timber, which I had until then dismissed as the mere noises of the night, now became in my imagination the manifestation of a haunted ship.

Later that morning, a crash of shattering china brought me running into the kitchen where I found the cook trembling and staring into an empty space with his mouth agape and the shards of a large bowl scattered around his feet. The poor chap was unresponsive to questions even as I shook him. I sat him down and boiled the kettle for some tea. Before I had even time to fill the teapot, the cook had recovered enough to stand, remove his apron, and throw it to the floor.

'That's it!' he cried, still shaking. 'I'm done with this place.'

He refused to relate what had shocked him so, but at the door I caught his sleeve and looked him right in the eye. 'You've seen something haven't you? Something you can't explain.'

He licked his lips nervously and nodded. 'Thought I were half crazed at first. I don't know who that man is, but he's not of this world.' With that he was off, refusing the offer a lift to the station.

I went to the bar and found myself staring up at the skull. From its prominent position it felt like it was watching the comings and goings with a cruel malevolence I hadn't previously recognised. I took it down and put it under the bar with a beer towel over it and went about my work.

'Got rid of the blasted skull, did ye?' Jebediah said that evening as he took to his usual stool.

'I've just taken it down until I can decide where to put it. It's scaring customers away.'

Jebediah looked around the otherwise empty inn and shrugged. 'Throw it away. Or bury it. Either way it looks like there's only me left to frighten off and I've seen enough peculiar things out on the moors; that a bit of bone ain't gonna send me running into the night.'

Jebediah's words of advice remained with me as I turned in for the night. I dreamed of struggling with assailants as my boots slid on a wet deck. I awoke the small hours, still with the sensation of hands pinning me down. I thrashed in the darkness and cried out, scrambling from the bed and slumping against a wall as I caught my breath and my heart rate returned to normal.

As my eyes adjusted to the dark, I noticed the bedroom door was ajar: I always close it. I reached out for the brass handle and gasped at the sight of a pale face staring back through the crack in the door. It wasn't the bearded face that stalked my dreams, but a smooth round face with white skin and dark eyes. I recoiled and cried out in alarm. The face vanished. I snatched the door handle and yanked the door open, finding nothing on the landing and all the other doors closed. I returned to my room, turned on my bedside light, and went back to bed. Perhaps thanks to exhaustion due to lack of sleep the night before, I was easily able to return to slumber. I slept a dreamless sleep but awoke in the morning to find the bedroom door ajar.

I didn't open the inn that morning. Instead, I put the skull in a bag and took it to the priest at St.Mary's church, a quarter mile down the road. I found the priest in his house next to the church and sat with the bagged skull on my lap as his housekeeper brought us tea. I allowed myself to enjoy twenty minutes of idle chat in the reprieve of a peaceful residence under the presumed protection of the almighty. The priest eyed the bag with interest, perhaps hoping it was a donation. Disappointment mixed with shock and mild disgust registered on his face when I revealed my grim offering. I asked for skull to receive a Christian burial with a simple marker. The priest was initially not amenable to interring remains of which the origins were dubious; I insisted and, after promising to attend service regularly, he relented and said he would perform a short service the following week where the head would be buried in a corner of the churchyard.

The relief I felt was complete. I couldn't repress a wide grin as I thanked the perplexed priest and bid him good day, whistling my way back to The Whaler. The tune died on my lips when I found every glass from the bar smashed in a large pile on the floor. Nothing else had been disturbed, but the small mountain of shards reached knee height. Deflated, I walked outside and sat on the doorstep with my head in my hands. That was where Jebediah found me an hour later.

He didn't ask what was wrong – just watched and waited for me to get up, dust off my trousers, and walk inside with him following close behind.

'There,' I said, gesturing to the pile of glass. 'That's your curse.'

Jebediah held onto Gerty's collar; not that he had to worry about the dog stepping on any splinters as the mutt remained as ever at Jebediah's side. 'Reckoned there was something about the place,' Jebediah said as matter-of-factly as he might have told me it was like to rain that afternoon. 'Reckoned too that a couple times I saw some fella in the shadows where there ought not to have been a fella.'

'Why didn't you say something?' I snapped.

Jebediah shrugged. 'Ain't nobody wants to listen to an old timer's tales of ghosts. The skull still behind the bar?'

I shook my head. 'No, so it can't be the skull that's doing this. You know, I thought about burning this damnable place down just before you got here.'

Jebediah sniffed and shook his head. 'Wouldn't do you no good. Whatever it is it's latched onto you I reckons. What did you do with the head?'

I told him how I'd given it to the priest for burial, Jebediah shook his head again and sighed. 'Get it back. Find out what it wants. It sure ain't burial or you wouldn't have a pile o' glass on yer floor.'

'So, it *is* the skull's work?' I said, hopeful that the old coot had the answers.

'Who can say? Seems like as not.' Jebediah turned about and headed for the door.

'Where are you going?' I called after him.

'The Dart for a pint. They got glasses there.'

I thought about putting the place up for sale, but I couldn't in good conscience pass the nightmare over to another. Besides, if Jebediah was right, I'd still be haunted by the shadowy man and I couldn't bare the thought of the locals scoffing that I'd failed to make a go of my oddball pub.

I could sense something watching me as I cleaned up the broken glass. I looked up to the empty shelf, thinking that removing the skull had been a mistake: I had angered the spirit.

'What do you want?' I shouted at the space where the skull had been.

A lamp blinked out. Then another.

'Just bugger off!' I snarled, stomping out of the bar and toward the stairs. 'And stay out of my dreams, damn you: I've had enough of it!'

My request was not honoured. My dreams were on the ship, as always, yet it didn't rock with the motion of waves. I was below deck in the cargo hold among barrels of whale oil. It was freezing cold and my breath came in moist clouds of vapour. I knew without going topside that the ship was stuck in ice. Muffled voices came from the deck above where the crew's quarters were. I couldn't make out much of what was said, but I felt in fear of them.

My stomach ached. My throat was dry. It felt like days since I'd eaten; somehow, I knew we'd been on the ice for weeks. Boots thudded on the steps, descending into the hold. I looked for a weapon, finding nothing, I snatched up a gas lamp and held it over the nearest barrel.

'Come for me and we'll all burn,' I said. It was the first time I'd heard my voice in the dream: I had a thick northern accent.

Five or six men faced me. At their head was the scarred man. His smile was cruel. He gestured for his companions to get me. They surged forward with teeth bared and hands grasping, yanking the lamp from my grip before I could react. Other hands pressed me down to the floor, pinning me. The scarred man's face filled my vision; his breath hot against my cheek and stinking of tooth rot. He held a knife in the small space between our faces, turning the blade so I could see how sharp it was.

I woke with a jump as a sharp pain jabbed into my ribcage. I tore at my pyjamas looking for a wound and found nothing. The pain faded, as did the sensation of fingers gripping my limbs. Then I saw the figure in the shadow – in the darkest corner of the room – motionless, watching me. I felt like he might have advanced on me had I not seen him, but there he remained in the black. My vision adjusted to the dim light of the first rays of dawn, allowing me to make out the long blue overcoat, cap, and tall boots the man wore.

'You murdering bastard,' I breathed.

The figure moved. I blinked, then it was gone.

I closed the inn – no longer feeling safe to remain there. I left a note on the door stating that the inn was closed until further notice due to unseen circumstances, and thought, wryly, that nobody could ever have foreseen the circumstances I found myself in. I gave thought to staying in a guest house, but didn't want to be recognised by locals who might question why I had abandoned my pub so soon. I decided to take the train to London and visit the ship management company. First, I called from a telephone box and spoke to the company secretary, who informed that they held a copy of the ships log in storage, and I was welcome to study it at my leisure so long as the log remained in their offices. I was delighted: my first stroke of luck since opening the pub.

I arrived early at the company's offices, following a rough night's sleep in an overpriced Kensington guest house where it was proven that distance from The Whaler did not provide sanctuary from nightly incursions by the vessel's long deceased crew. The company had several logbooks covering the period from the vessel's commissioning in eighteen-ninety, until the date it was wrecked in April nineteen-thirty-one. It didn't take long to establish that all the information I needed was in the final book.

The Orca had become trapped in ice October nineteen-thirty and had remained stuck until the following March when the ice melted. The Orca then went to a port in Greenland where they replenished supplies which had completely run out, and then back to North Devon, arriving just a month after being freed from the ice. It seemed Jebediah was right about it being a cursed ship. The final log entry recorded the ship's wrecking in a gale after the sails had torn. The log confirmed that all hands were rescued; included were a list of names – eleven in total. I flipped back to last entry before The Orca left Devon, which included lists of stores as well as a roster of the officers and crew for the final voyage. Eighteen crewmen were listed. I skimmed through mundane entries and the meticulous detailing of the reduction in ship stores during the icy incarceration and found the entry I was looking for: the day the missing men set out to find the whaling station. There were six names listed. I cross referenced my three lists to come up with a missing name: Gordon Bell.

Gordon was listed as being twenty years old when he joined the ship and wasn't on any of the previous crew lists, nor was his name mentioned anywhere else in the log: I had found the man who I became in the dreams. Now all I had to do was find his killer.

It wasn't difficult to narrow down the suspects among the crew. The log gave me the ages of all the crew and I knew my man was around forty years old. Among the eleven surviving crew members there were three who were around that age: the master, this ship's doctor, and an able seaman by the name of Arthur Browning. I was further guided by log entries stating that Browning was disciplined for assaulting one of the crew in the first week of the voyage. Fortunately, the list also stated the town or city of residence for each crewman next to their name and age. Browning was from Watchet: a small coastal town in Somerset. I retreated to the guest house to contemplate how best to confront Browning – if indeed he still lived.

That night I woke to find the bed shaking; the posts rattled and I was unable to move. A black fog formed above me, swirling like billowing smoke until it took on the form of a man with hollow eyes. There was no detail in the face, just a charcoal mist, like the shade of a man.

'Please, I am doing all I can. What else do you want?' I demanded.

The posts of the bed trembled in response. A neighbouring guest thumped our adjoining wall. The mist dissipated. I slept a dreamless sleep for the rest of the night but awoke exhausted. I went to the train station to book a ticket to Bridgwater: the nearest stop to Watchet. As I queued, I saw the dark figure in my peripheral vision standing by a newspaper stand. I jolted; shocked to find the apparition appearing to me outdoors in broad daylight. It was gone in a moment and nobody else seemed to notice it. I sensed that it was trying to communicate something to me: I thought about the face I had seen in the smoky apparition above the bed, realising that it had resembled the skull.

'Next!' The teller prompted, stirring me from my reverie.

'One ticket to Exeter,' I said, 'and then on to Okehampton.'

I knocked at the priory door and was admitted by the housekeeper. The priest was surprised to see me and when I asked for the return of the skull he was only too glad to hand it over. He said nothing but I could tell by his apparent relief that he had suffered some ethereal visitation.

When I arrived at The Whaler I didn't even go inside; instead going straight to my car and then on to Watchet with the skull on the passenger seat. I was left in peace for the duration of the journey: I don't suppose it would have done the deceased seaman's presumed desire for justice any good if I was to have an accident along the way.

My thoughts during the drive were concerned with what I would do if I found Mr Browning. I couldn't very well go to the police without evidence. It seemed unlikely that the man would confess. I could only rely on the skull having designs on a course of action and to be guided accordingly – and hope that the spirit would then leave me alone. I felt that we had an unspoken bargain to that effect.

Arriving in Watchet, I went straight to the harbourmaster and asked if he knew Mr Browning and if the man still resided in the area. The harbourmaster asked if I was a debt collector or police officer and directed me to a local inn where he assured me Browning was a regular.

The inn was small and dirty. The sort of place where customers aren't fussy if their glass is dirty and the owner doesn't mind what the customers get up to provided it doesn't hinder trade. The tables were old beer barrels – something I might have thought of for The Whaler – and the once white walls were stained with nicotine. The few customers eyed me with a suspicious scrutiny I expect was reserved for outsiders, but Browning wasn't among their company. I took a seat in the corner and kept the skull in a leather holdall at my feet as I nursed an ale that had the consistency of gravy. I didn't have to wait long.

Arthur Browning limped into the tavern, wincing with each waddling step. His beard and mop of hair, so black in the dream, were now completely grey. His face was wrinkled and broad shoulders hunched. He walked with the aid of a cane which stabbed the floor as the old man ambled toward the bar, taking a seat alongside one of the locals.

I decided to observe the fellow and take his measure before engaging. Browning threw back one whisky after another. I listened to bragged tales of old seafaring days and complaints of how young sailors now have it easy without such deprivations as the old salts had to endure. After a time, Browning's companion ran out of coin, belched loudly, and lurched off his stool toward the door. Browning downed a whisky and reached for his stick, apparently about to leave.

I gave thought to confronting Browning there but decided it best to follow him home. I kept my distance but need not have taken such care as my quarry was too intent on maintaining his balance as he struggled to walk on a gammy leg, cursing at anyone who came within a few feet of his path. His residence was down an alleyway of wet stinking pebbles. The cottage door was rotting and one of the windows was boarded up. I cleared my throat to announce myself as Browning turned the key in his door.

'What the hells you want?' Browning said as he half turned toward me, presenting his profile with a scowl.

'I'd like to talk to you inside, if you please.'

'Bugger off.'

'It's about The Orca.'

Browning paused with one foot inside his abode and turned toward me. His expression of slack-jawed surprise quickly turned to malice. 'Got nothing to say.'

The door began to close.

I rushed and stuck my foot in the doorway. 'I must insist,' I said. 'Otherwise, I shall have to take my findings to the press. Or the police.'

Large grey caterpillar eyebrows pressed down on Browning's narrowed eyes as he tried to gauge what I knew. I could feel his mind working as his eyes flicked over me – likely wondering if he could overpower me. With a splutter and a snarl, Browning opened the door.

Browning's home was as detestable as he no doubt deserved: a clutter of empty bottles and chipped furniture. He lived alone. The one sofa chair in his living room was frayed and the few belongings were coated in thick nicotine-yellowed dust. He had electricity, but there was no bulb in the lamp and the heavy curtains were drawn, casting much of the small room in darkness.

Browning took the seat, grunting and lighting a cigarette. He watched me with one eye wide and the other narrowed as he blew a long plume of smoke.

'What do you know about Gordon Bell?' I said, deciding to get straight to the point.

Browning's eye twitched. His hand shook as he took a drag from the cigarette and stubbed out the inch of remaining tobacco before lighting a new cigarette.

His apparent surprise at the mention of Gordon Bell's name made me wonder what other dark things lay in this foul man's path.

'Tell me what you did with him, you blackguard.' I said, finding courage in the dishevelled man's shock.

'How do you know about him?' Browning said, struggling to keep his lower lip from quaking. 'Pearson tell you?'

I remembered the name Pearson from the crew list. I shook my head. 'No. Gordon told me. Showed me actually.'

Browning gulped and forced a laugh. 'You're fishing. You don't know naught.'

I put the holdall on the floor and unzipped it, removing the skull. I held it out toward Browning, who fidgeted in his seat like he wanted to escape but was held transfixed by the jawless skull.

'You killed him, didn't you? Why was that? Cheat at cards, did he? Threaten your position on the ship? What was it? What made you drive a butcher's knife into the boy?'

Browning stared agape at the skull. The colour drained from his face, making his own drawn features appear skeletal. The cigarette dropped from jaundiced fingers onto the scratched wooden floor. 'Twasn't murder. Twas the law of the sea. Fairly done.'

I shook my head, confused. 'Law of the sea? To murder a young lad? For what?'

'We were starving!' Browning roared, the fierceness I witnessed in my dreams returned momentarily in his snarl. 'Weeks we were trapped in the ice after the stores run out. We had to eat something.'

'What?' I said, suddenly understanding but refusing to accept the truth without confirmation.

'We drew lots. The boy drew short. Twas the law of the sea. I did the deed, you're right, and I had no love for the lad, but everyone ate of his flesh – not just me. Everyone. He fed eleven of us for four days. We got clear of the ice before needing to draw lots again. Sailed for the whaling station a hundred miles down coast where we restocked before heading back to England.'

I nodded slowly. 'That's why he wants you. You killed and ate him. But it's more than that: you did the lots didn't you? Made sure he drew short.'

Browning didn't answer but looked down at his scuffed boots. When he looked up again his eyes went wide at the sight of something behind me. He sucked in his breath and a dark wet patch formed at his groin.

The hairs on my neck prickled. I turned and saw George Bell, standing in his blue sailor's coat and cap. His pale face was expressionless and cold. There was only blackness where his eyes would have been but he looked otherwise as he might have in life.

I set the skull down in Browning's lap and leant forward to whisper in his ear. 'I suspect you've had your last good night's sleep. Oh, and don't think to get rid of the skull: it won't do any good, believe me.'

Browning snatched my sleeve as I made to move past him. I tore myself free of his grasp and walked to the door to the sound of Browning's whimpering.

I stayed the night in Watchet and drove home at dawn. The day seemed somehow brighter than any I had experienced since opening The Whaler. I had not long returned when Jebediah came in and took his usual stool.

'Had yourself a bit of a holiday, have you?' Jebediah grunted. 'Thought you'd packed it in. That was the talk anyway. I just heard from the postmaster that your car was back outside, so I thought I'd come down and see for myself.'

I laughed. 'Nobody came here while I was open, but I leave for a day or two and everyone knows I'm gone.'

'It's cos of your haunted skull,' Jebediah said as if it were obvious. 'It's the talk of hereabouts. What you gone done with it anyway? The Vicar said you took it back.'

I blinked, unsure how to answer, then the door opened and two young men came in, smiling and laughing.

'Where's the ghost then?' One of them said.

'Is it true the ghost sends glasses crashing off the bar?' said the other.

I frowned at Jebediah. 'What have you been telling people?'

Jebediah shrugged. 'Only told folk what I saw.'

Before long there was a small crowd in the pub. People from Okehampton, Tavistock, Plymouth and even day trippers from Exeter and beyond stopped by, hoping to catch a glimpse of the restless spirit. The journalists were back too, albeit briefly, taking photographs and listening to increasingly far-fetched stories from locals. Tales abounded that I was the keeper of the skull of a headless horseman who rode past The Whaler nightly, seeking his missing head.

The three rooms of the inn were soon rarely vacant and the bar was busy enough that I was able to hire a member of staff to help out. It took some scrounging about, but I eventually found an old skull in a bric-a-brac shop which I positioned above the bar and insisted it was the same skull found in the surgeon's trunk.

It was a few weeks after I returned from Watchet that I read a brief article about Arthur Browning, who had died of a heart attack and was remembered in the local press as one of the crew rescued from The Orca. I hoped that George could rest in peace and felt no malice for the many shocks he had given me.

That very same night I awoke sweating. The room swayed as it had often done when I emerged from a dream of The Orca. I had dreamt of George being held down as Browning wielded the knife, but the dream didn't focus on the killer, but rather a balding, yellow-toothed man who pinned one of George's arms.

A figure in the corner became apparent as my eyes adjusted to the dark. It was George Bell. He stood there, watching me as he had watched Arthur Browning wetting himself in his armchair. I shouted at the spectre and threw a pillow which passed through to strike the wall behind. A rustle of paper on my bedside table distracted me. I reached for the lamp and turned it on, holding the paper up to the light.

It was the newspaper, opened onto the page about Browning. I didn't understand at first, then my eyes settled on the part of the article where the journalist had listed the eight other crewmen who were known to still be alive. There was even a photograph of two of them. The first one was a balding man, much older than he appeared in the dream, but there was no mistaking him: Pearson.

'My god,' I sighed, feeling a tightening in my chest as I realised what George's ghost wanted of me. 'They all ate of your body. You want me to go after them all! Will you not let me rest?'

The hollow eyes stared at me. George Bell remained motionless, resolute.

Part II: Tales of the Present

The Grey

Simon sucked in damp moorland air as he struggled to regain his breath from the climb. Panting, he turned to look back the way he'd come; the carpark had become a mere smudge in the distance through a light haze of misty rain. Wind ruffled his greying hair and threatened to dislodge him from the rocky highpoint of the tor. He leaned on his hiking stick, waiting for exhausted lungs and racing pulse to recuperate, unclipped the water bottle from his belt and took a long draught.

A quick check of the smartphone's navigation app indicated that less than two miles had been walked: it had felt like more. Simon wiped the lenses of his glasses and tried to ignore the protesting ache from disgruntled hips – preferring to believe such pains were more to the weather rather than age related struggles agitated by uphill walks.

The onward route required an abrupt turn west toward a cairn. Simon pivoted, blinking through veils of vapour as he looked for his next waypoint, and turned into a swift thrust of wind. He wobbled. A boot slipped on wet granite. The sudden shift in weight sent the other foot sliding from under him. Flailing for balance, the hiking stick went spinning out of his grasp and off the granite outcrop. Simon followed, grasping at air.

Looking up at grey sky, Simon patted himself down, satisfied that nothing hurt: not even the usual aches. Propping himself up on his elbows he looked up at the outcrop he'd fallen from. The tumble had been about ten feet onto damp grass – somehow managing to miss landing on any of the many stones that covered the ground. He was lucky, if clumsy. He touched his face, realising the absence of glasses resting on the bridge of his nose.

A thick fog now encompassed the tor in place of the misty rain. Simon wondered at how the fog had descended so quickly and wondered if he might have been knocked out for a minute following the fall. Visibility was reduced to about a dozen metres, everything beyond which was a swallowed in swirl of grey. Simon searched on hands and knees, finding his glasses in a clump of wet Molina grass. One of the lenses was cracked. He tutted and put them into a pocket; he could just about see well enough to struggle on without them.

Simon stood and took a few careful steps. Legs and lungs felt ok. The walking stick was nowhere to be seen. He decided he could walk back without it as the carpark was downhill. Simon sighed and looked about the miserable hilltop, suppressing a sob: the moor was telling him he was too old to deal with the tough terrain. Until a few years ago he could walk ten miles before tiring. Five years before that he could walk twenty. Now he was defeated in under two.

'Alright,' Simon said into the wind, 'I'll take the hint. You can keep the stick. Maybe someone who can make use of it will find it.' He took a last look around at the granite boulders and tangles of sodden grass fading into a sea of grey, then began the walk down off the moors for the last time. He had only made a few steps when he noticed the silhouette of a figure walking up toward the tor.

'Hello!' Simon called, waving a greeting. The echo of his voice seemed to carry forever through the moist greyness.

The figure made no acknowledgement but marched directly toward the summit with a purposeful stride. The fog seemed to swirl more thickly around this dark shadow of a man. The arms remained rigid – not even swinging with the motion of walking. The fog grew even denser the nearer the figure came.

'Hello,' Simon called in again, his tone weaker and cracked.

There was something threatening about the man's bearing and gait, marching with a machinelike intensity. He wasn't walking toward the tor: he was heading directly for Simon.

A shiver of fear shook Simon. Where was that damn walking stick? He looked about for it – anything he could hold onto for security. He dashed a few steps, finding only rocks and slippery grass. He turned one way then another, searching. The striding silhouette was mere metres away: it was not even a man but a black man-shaped opaque mass. A shadow or void given life.

Simon retreated, moving as quickly as wobbling legs permitted but finding himself penned in by rocky outcrops. He clambered over the nearest. The shadow followed with long, noiseless strides.

'What do you want?' Simon snatched up a hand a handful of small stones and threw them at the figure. They passed through. Still the faceless shadow advanced undaunted.

Simon fled. Heedless of snags on the ground, oblivious to direction or purpose other than to put distance between himself and pursuer. A flash of colour caught his attention through the fog: a hiker! Resting on the grass below a plateau of granite.

'Help!' Simon pleaded, scurrying toward the walker. The man lay on his back. Hiking stick at his side. Simon halted, gaping down at the sight of his own pale, lifeless face. The twisted body lay below the very rocks he had fallen from. Dead eyes stared up into the grey. He became aware of his shadow behind him. Simon shut his eyes.

Beast

A panorama of granite flecked hills and valleys engulfed in shrub stretched to the horizon. There was not a soul to be seen – not a human one anyway. Sheep were mere specks of white on distant slopes; other darker oddities might have been ponies or cows. The only movement on the landscape was from the shadows of slow-moving clouds and the gentle breeze brushing over long grass; the same caressing wind caused the ends of Mel's hair to tickle her cheeks.

Mel pulled her beanie down over her ears and tucked a few errant strands under the rim. 'We're so far from the car. I can't even see a road,' she said, unable to keep a tinge of worry from her voice.

Rufus hopped down from a nearby granite bolder and approached with an easy smile and put his arm around Mel's shoulders. His ginger curls bobbed as he laughed. His breath smelt of the coffee they'd just finished drinking. 'Don't worry. I've been out this way a couple times; I know exactly where we are.'

'Would you say that even if we were lost?' Mel said, forcing a chuckle.

Rufus kissed her on the cheek and withdrew his arm. 'I guess I would, but we're not.'

Mel scanned the horizon again. Fern trees in tightly packed rows stood guardian upon a steep hill which they had passed over an hour before. A few glints of reflected sunlight in the far distance might have been indications of civilisation but the only firm sign that humanity still existed were the fading contrails between gaps in the clouds. The afternoon breeze was colder up on the exposed hilltop, bringing out goosebumps on Mel's bare arms. She took her pack off and dug out her microfleece.

The sound of water rushing from somewhere in the valley below suggested some unseen stream, while birds chirped and whistled from their ground nests among long yellow grass and the remains of dried-up brown ferns from last summer.

'Told you it was a great view from here, didn't I?' Rufus said, his wide grin baring seemingly oversized horse-like teeth on his thin freckled face.

'Yeah,' Mel said without conviction as she put her arms back through the straps of her pack. She thought back to when her PE teacher, Mr Trevaskis, had tried to press gang her into the annual Ten Tors event. That had been when she was sixteen – six years ago. She whimsically thought that Mr Trevaskis probably led the Ten Tors trainees the same way Rufus led her: with a chuckle at complaints and a sigh of impatience at requests for a break.

'Oh, come on,' Rufus laughed. 'You can't lounge at home all the time. You enjoyed Snowdonia: this is better.'

Mel narrowed her eyes at him, but Rufus had already turned away and began to trudge downhill into the valley. He had spoken lightly enough, but it was the first time he'd mentioned Snowdonia without bringing up what had happened. Mel wondered if he was moving on. 'I don't stay at home all the time.'

'If you say so, lazy bones,' Rufus said in a sing-song tone.

Rufus walked with a swagger that Mel found pretentious. His ginger locks bouncing as he moved, confident, carefree; he was enjoying himself a bit too much. Mel wondered if this was what he was like when he went out hiking alone or if he was just savouring her lack of enthusiasm for the great outdoors. She hurried after him, picking her way between rocks and the larger piles of animal dung, trying to catch up before Rufus could get too far ahead and then stop, as he often had, with his head inclined and hands on his hips as if she were slowing him down.

'How much further?' Mel called out, hoping he would stop to answer.

'Not far,' Rufus said over his shoulder.

'How could it be not far? We're miles from anywhere. I could've used GPS if you'd let us bring phones. We're definitely not lost, right?'

Rufus chuckled. 'Trust me: I know what I'm doing. We're coming up to a fun bit – you'll see. Phones are a distraction. Besides, there's not much signal out here.'

The valley floor below them opened into a swathe of bright green, dotted with reeds and barely a stone in sight, contrasting with the surrounding sun-bleached hills. A large pond in the centre of the emerald basin reflected the cloudy sky.

'You're heading right toward that pool of water,' Mel called out.

'Yeah, I seen it. Don't worry – we'll be skirting around it.'

The ground become softer near the base of the hill; rocks and dung gave way to large tufts of long grass, hiding hazardous dips while soggy peat sucked at their boots. Mel cursed as she struggled through this new terrain, waggling outstretched arms to aid her balance. The grass was too long and thick for her to see where she placed her feet. Twice she almost fell.

'You okay?' Rufus said, standing on the far side of this rough patch with his hands on his hips.

'Yes! Couldn't we have gone around this bit?'

'Want me to come back and help?'

'I don't need any help.' Mel's foot sank to the ankle, throwing her off-balance. She fell cursing into a thicket and rolled onto her back, possibly crushing the remains of lunch in the backpack.

A frightened bird burst from nearby undergrowth, eliciting a startled gasp from Mel. A rustle of reeds and a superior chuckle announced Rufus's approaching aid.

Mel struggled to get to her feet before he could rescue her. She brushed nature's detritus from her fleece and trousers, casting a warning glare at her grinning boyfriend.

'Sorry, Babe,' he grinned. 'I should've stayed near. The ground is a bit tricky here. We're at the fun bit now though.'

Rufus led the way through the tall grass, pointing out any difficult steps, and soon enough they emerged onto the spongy plain at the foot of the hill. The view across the valley was clear; yellow flowers grew among sparkling emerald knots of grass, and tufts of what looked like wool topped an expanse of reeds like a field of cotton.

'What's fun about this place?' Mel said.

'Watch,' Rufus said. He took off his pack and set it down by his feet then walked on twenty or so paces before stopping and seeming to test the ground with his foot. He proceeded bit further and repeated the action, then turned back to Mel. 'Watch this!' Rufus made a little jump, like a bunny hop, and upon landing the spongy emerald ground around him wobbled. Laughing, he bounced up and down.

'What the hell?' Mel said, laughing.

'Come on. Give it a try!' Rufus waved her over.

Mel rushed toward him. The ground underfoot was soft and she could feel it reverberate with each step like she was walking on the skin of a drum. She bounced. The ground wobbled. She did it again, laughing. 'This is so weird. What causes this?'

'It's even bouncier further out toward the pond,' Rufus said, pointing.

Mel moved in the indicated direction, bounding from one foot to the other like she was walking on the moon. She realised the ground wasn't grass-covered at all, but it was a glistening green moss that blanketed much of the valley floor.

'It's like a bouncy castle, isn't it?' Rufus shouted, sounding almost like an excited child. 'How high can you jump?'

Mel leapt, tucking her knees up to her chest and untucking them on the way down. She laughed. Then the ground swallowed her.

It happened in an instant. Her feet pierced the mossy surface and she plummeted through, sinking up to her chest. She flailed, looking for something to grab onto. Stinking water splashed her face and went up her nostrils. Moisture, cold and thick, soaked through her clothes.

The ground sucked at her. The pack strapped to her back dragged her down like it was an anvil. Mel scrambled with one hand to try to find the clasps to undo her pack while slapping at the filthy bog with her other hand in an attempt to stay afloat.

'Help! Help me! Rufus!' She screamed. Splashes of bog water went into her mouth.

Rufus approached with light steps, taking care to tread carefully, testing the ground with his toes before putting his weight down. He stopped about ten metres short.

'I'm sinking!' Mel stretched a hand dripping with brown sludge toward Rufus.

'Stop moving!' Rufus snapped. 'You'll sink faster. Just try to float.'

Mel flailed and gasped in panic. More brown water went into her mouth; she swallowed some and began to choke.

'Mel, calm down! You'll sink. Listen to me. Look at me, Mel.' Rufus leaned forward, hands on his knees. His expression calm but stern.

Mel locked eyes with him. She spread her arms out four buoyancy and tried to tread water with her legs. The bog came up to her collar bone: she was still sinking.

'Get me out!' She trembled.

'Calm down. I can't come there or we'll both be stuck. That's no good to either of us.'

Mel sobbed. She leant forward and tried to swim but the movement just made her sink another few centimetres.

'The backpack is weighing you down,' Rufus said. 'I want you to try to unclip it. Hold onto it for support.'

'I tried already.'

'Try again.'

Submerging her arm felt dangerous – like the lack of ballast would sink her. She treaded ferociously in the thick, stinking soup to compensate while she fumbled for the buckles. Both calves already ached from the effort of kicking through the paste-like substance. Fingers found a clasp and unclipped it. Taking off the pack was more delicate, requiring the use of both arms. Legs kicked frantically. She sank an inch lower.

'Are you kicking?' Rufus demanded.

'I'm sinking!'

'Stop kicking. Try to raise your legs and lay flat. Otherwise just stay still. Moving makes it worse.'

It required a struggle against survival instinct keep her legs still, but once she stopped struggling the sinking seemed to subside. Carefully, Mel tugged at the strap on her left arm and unloosed the pack. Then the right arm. She dragged the bag around toward her front.

'Careful. Careful,' Rufus said, gesturing for calm.

Finally, the pack was at her chest. Only the very top of the bag was above the swap. Mel rested her weight on it, but the backpack instantly began to sink so she just held onto it.

'Do something,' Mel said, her voice wavering.

'I will. I just wanted to make sure that you're not going to drown before I do.'

'Get me out.'

'I'm going to.' Rufus looked around. Hands on his hips. He chewed his lower lip and hummed.

'Do something!'

'I am! I'm looking for a branch or something I can use to pull you out.'

'Rufus. You need to get me out of here fast. It's cold and I'm in this up to my neck.' The bog water, cold against Mel's skin, had already begun to make her shiver.

Rufus held up his palm. 'You're right. I'm going to go get a long stick. I'll head back to the forest. There's bound to be something that way.'

'What? No. It's too far.'

Rufus turned and began to walk away.

'Rufus, wait! It's two hours away. I need to get out now.'

He turned. Hands on hips again. He shrugged in exasperation. 'What else can I do? I can't come there or we're both stuck. Maybe I'll see someone on the way who can send for help. Anyway, I'll hurry so it'll only be an hour to the forest. I might even find something beforehand. This is the best plan.'

'No, Rufus. What if you can't find your way back?'

'I told you: I know this area. I'll be as fast as I can. You just stay there.' He smirked, realising the irony. 'Sorry.'

'Rufus!'

He turned and broke into a jog. Heading back the way they had come.

'Don't leave me! Rufus!'

He waved in answer – not even looking back.

The retreating form of her boyfriend quickly became obscured by the many clumps of reeds which surrounded the bog. Moments later the soft padding of his footfalls dissipated to nothing. Mel was alone.

Reeds rustled in the wind, giving the impression of an unseen presence gliding through the terrain. The landscape dimmed as a large cloud passed in front of the sun, bringing with it a stronger gust of chilled air.

'Rufus!' Mel yelled. 'Come back.'

The wind answered with a cold rush of air, blowing up tiny fragments of detritus into Mel's face.

'Rufus!' Mel screamed.

Silence.

Mel realised the wind was blowing in the opposite direction to that which Rufus had set off, carrying her voice away from him.

'Hurry back,' Mel whispered. Shivering. She broke a hand up through the surface of the mire. Brown sludge coated the entirety of her arm. She reached out, feeling around the surface of the bog, hoping to find a spot of solid ground or something that could be used to pull herself free. There was nothing.

A speck of rain slapped Mel's cheek. She began to sob. The forlorn blubbering sounded lonely and pathetic to her own ears. The release of tears made the shivering all the more uncontrollable. Mel bit her lip, willing the crying and shaking to desist, holding her breath until both tears and quaking gradually subsided.

The spattering of rain stopped. Sunlight broke through the clouds.

'Thank you,' Mel said, looking up at the clouds before blinking the remaining traces of wetness from her eyes.

A rasping sound like a saw through hard would carried through the weeds. The source was obscured from view, but it sounded close.

'Hello?' Mel called out.

The noise stopped for a few seconds before picking up again.

'Is anyone there?' Mel shouted, wondering if an acoustic trick of the valley had carried the sound from far away. There were no trees nearby: it made no sense to saw wood in this desolate place.

The sound stopped, leaving only the breath of wind through grass and intermittent chirping of birds.

Mel wondered if she imagined the strange noise, or if it was perhaps an effect of hypothermia. She wiggled her toes and fingers to make sure they still had circulation. Even her socks were sodden with the thick goo, but there was still sensation in all the extremities.

'Come on, Rufus. Hurry back.' Mel scanned the horizon for any sign of her boyfriend, or anyone else. Nearby reeds and foliage obscured much from her low field of view, but what could be seen of the hillsides were bare of life. *He wouldn't leave me here – would he?* she wondered. There had been many disputes and misunderstandings of late, but they were past it. *It was his idea to jump on the swamp – could he have set me up on purpose?* She shook her head: even if it had been part of a cruel trick, he'd have surely planned how to help her get out. It had been perhaps twenty minutes since the moss floor gave way – too long to maintain an immature prank.

'Rufus!' Mel screamed. She screamed again and again.

The sky darkened from a light blue to an oily dark blue. The clouds had grown moody and increased in mass. The temperature dropped at least a couple of degrees and rays from the sun, now lower in the sky, only brushed across the landscape in occasional waves when gaps in cloud cover allowed.

Mel gave up calling out for help. Her throat was sore and her tongue was coated with the taste of sour bog water. The nauseating thought that she might have to drink the stinking brown soup for sustenance if help didn't arrive soon had begun to feel like a real possibility. It had been at least two hours since Rufus had left – more likely three.

It had become difficult to move the toes. Wrinkled fingertips were cold to the bone. The quagmire felt like it was thickening; each movement was countered by a squelch that threatened submersion.

A nearby sound of soft footfalls and swish of reeds announced someone approaching.

'Rufus? Rufus!'

The steps ceased. The sawing sound resumed. Nearer, yet out of sight.

'Hello?' Mel said, in a lower, faltering, tone.

There was no answer. The sawing desisted. Reeds rustled and then silence.

Mel closed her eyes, causing tears to spill over the eyelids and down her cheeks. Her nose ran and lip trembled. She made a small noise of despair then swallowed the sore lump in her throat and clamped her teeth together, setting her lips firm. 'Be Strong,' she whispered. 'Be strong, Mel.'

'Mel!' The voice came from the left. Rufus.

'Here! Here! Oh, thank God! Rufus, I'm here!' Mel lifted an arm, flecking her face with globs of decaying vegetation as she waved.

Rufus huffed as he jogged down the hillside, easily navigating his way through the tall blonde grass. He stopped at the edge of the bright green ground near where he had left his pack. He waved with a jovial grin.

Mel's return smile was so wide it hurt her cheeks. Tears filled her eyes again. She swallowed more dirty water as she sobbed and laughed with relief.

'You look a right state, dear,' Rufus laughed. 'Proper hog monster.'

He stood with hands on his hips, in that way he always did, yet this time it didn't infuriate Mel. She adored him for it. She would give him a big yucky hug when he pulled her out – she

119

imagined him playfully protesting at the state of her, but she would cling onto him and make him all yucky too. Everything would be fine after all.

'Rufus, I'm so glad to see you. Get me out of here.'

'You forgot to say *I'm a celebrity*.'

'What?'

'Before you say *get me out of here*. Doesn't matter. How've you been coping in my absence?'

'Great. Just get me out.'

'Ah, problemo.' Rufus raised a finger. His smile dropped.

Mel felt a sudden cold permeate her entire body. Her mouth fell open. Only now she realised he had returned apparently empty handed. 'Rufus... did you find anyone? Or a branch... some rope? Rufus, get me out. Now.'

'Rope?' The hands went back onto his hips. 'You really aren't an outdoors person, are you? Do you think there are coils of rope stationed around for emergencies or a ready supply of hemp which I've spent the last few hours twining into something to pull you out with?'

'Rufus, get me out of the goddamn swamp!'

Rufus sighed. He shook his head and ran a hand through his red curls. 'Problemo, dear: I couldn't get any help.'

'What?' Mel's lip trembled uncontrollably. Her vision blurred. 'Rufus... I'm going to die here.'

'Not if I can help it.' He allowed the flash of a grin.

'Rufus, stop screwing about!' Mel splashed, trying to swim, feeling the bog attempt to swallow her with each limb movement. She stopped almost as soon as she began the futile struggle.

'The only problem is...' Rufus sat on his pack and scratched his cheek, wincing as if hesitating to announce bad news.'

'What?' Mel wanted to throttle an answer out of her posturing boyfriend. Scarcely believing that even now he had to keep up the arrogant posturing that had driven them apart in the first place.

'Well... the thing stopping me from getting you out is that... I kinda like you fine where you are.'

'Rufus, this isn't a game. I'm freezing. I can't feel my toes.'

'Well, rest assured they're still there. Pretty sure the mire isn't piranha infested. Be quite funny if it was though.' He made a show of casting his gaze around the mire with his hand to his brow, shielding his eyes and feigning a search for signs of carnivorous fish.

Mel felt a hollow sickness in the bottom of her stomach – he was toying with her because of what had happened in Wales. She wondered how long he would keep it up before getting her out. The sky was growing darker by the minute. Even if he let her out now, they'd be walking back in the dark. 'You knew I was going to fall through that moss, didn't you? How long have you been planning this?'

Rufus slapped his forehead, grinned, and shook his head. 'You really are stupid. Did you not consider that it seemed odd that I'd brought you to an isolated spot which I told you I knew well, and then had you jump up and down on a featherbed bog?

'Walkers know to give this bit a wide berth. Eight metres deep they reckon. I had a close call here about six weeks ago and started thinking about how to use it. I've been out here a few times since. Never once seen another person. Of course, I didn't know for sure how well it would work – but it worked brilliantly, didn't it?'

Mel remembered him coming home with brown matter stuck to his clothes up to his waist. She complained about the stench and Rufus said he'd had to wade through a mucky stream: he'd been plotting all that time. That had been a fortnight after Wales and a couple of weeks before he told her she was forgiven.

'You bastard,' Mel sneered.

Rufus either didn't hear or ignored the insult. He had moved off his pack and was pulling something out of it, humming as he did so.

'What are you doing?'

'Hmmm?' He didn't turn around. Instead, he pulled out a roll of bright green material which he began to unpack. 'I'm putting up a tent. It's getting dark.'

'You can't leave me in here!' Mel's voice came out hoarse.

'Oh, I won't leave you all on your own. What if someone finds you before you freeze to death or drown? I'll be in real trouble.'

The shock of his harsh words stunned like a physical blow. Mel's mouth hung open in disbelief, doubting that even someone as jealous as Rufus would actually murder her, but knowing that plotting for weeks to leave her trapped in a mire overnight was a sure death sentence. She knew from the few times she'd been camping before that even in the summer the nights were freezing cold, and on the windswept highlands of Dartmoor in late February, it was sure to be even colder.

Mel quietly watched Rufus set up his tent, hoping that he would grow bored of tormenting and lend assistance.

Rufus hummed as he went about his task, not sparing a glance at his captive until the little dome tent was put up, the sleeping bag put inside, and his small pillow inflated. He hung a little plastic lantern at the entrance to his tent and turned on the light, standing back to admire his handiwork.

'There. Up in less than ten minutes! I only brought a light snack – sorry there's not enough for two. I suppose all your food has turned to mush inside your pack by now.' He sat cross legged outside the tent and opened a packet of crisp, seeming to make an effort to create as much noise as possible by crunching the packet and munching the crisp with his mouth open. He held the open packet toward Mel. 'Want one? If you can get here, I'll let you eat the lot. No? Too lazy to make the effort? Thought so.'

'It's really cold, Rufus.'

'Yes. It is a bit nippy. I'll get inside the tent shortly. I'll leave the lamp on for you.'

'Why are you doing this?'

He screwed up the empty packet and frowned. 'You know damn well why.'

'Because I chatted to a guy in a pub? You're pathetic.'

Rufus scrambled to his feet. He made as if to move toward her, fists clenched, but thought better of stepping onto the moss.

'It wasn't *just* chatting. I can't believe you're falling back on that story.'

'Did you feign being over it this all that time just so you could get back at me now?'

Rufus shrugged. 'Wasn't easy. Pretending I'd forgiven you for being such a massive slag. To tell the truth, there were moments where almost I forgot about it. A couple of times I even thought about not doing this, and that I'd tell you my plan one day, years from now, and we'd laugh about it. But I knew you'd betray me again someday. Once a cheater...'

Mel shook her head. 'Unbelievable. You gaslighting creep! You really are the most pathetic person I've ever met. Arrogant ginger tosser.' Mel spat the words and watched him clench and unclench his fists, pacing around the edge of the swamp. If only she could agitate him, maybe he'd come for her and in the ensuing struggle perhaps she could somehow get out. It didn't seem like much of a plan, but it was the only one she had.

Rufus pointed an accusing finger. 'I knew it. You always looked down on me. Within twenty minutes of me going up to the room while we were on a holiday *I* paid for, you were snogging a stranger in the bar.'

'I don't know what's more pathetic, Rufus. The fact that you can't let it go, or the fact that you spied on me after feigning going to bed with a headache just so you could test me.'

'I always suspected what you are. I just needed proof.' He paced, combing his fingers through his hair as he often did when stressed. He huffed and kicked at the ground. 'I should've left you in Wales and drove back on my own. Left you with lover boy.'

'He kissed me, Rufus. I pulled back. Of course, you chose not to notice that.'

'Liar.'

'I'm not going to argue about this again. In fact, I was going to finish with you after today. I had been trying to summon the nerve to do it for weeks. The only thing stopping me was that I knew you'd react badly, but I'll give you credit: I never imagined you were this much of a psycho.'

Rufus stopped pacing and stared at her. His cheeks flushed red. He sniffled and wiped what may have been a tear from his eye. '*You* were going to finish with *me*?'

'Are you surprised?' Mel went to gesture with her hand and found the movement sluggish. She realised she no longer felt cold, but wet and sticky. Hypothermia had begun to set in.

Rufus went to his pack, dug his hand in and pulled something out. He marched the few steps back to the edge of the mire and held out a knot of blue rope in his fist. 'Well, I've got a surprise for you. I planned all along to pull you out after you'd had a good scare and we'd established a few ground rules, but now you can get yourself out.'

Rufus tossed the bundle of rope, which plopped onto the moss several metres from Mel. He turned on his heel and stomped to the tent where he yanked the zip down and ducked inside. His hand shot out and retrieved the tiny lantern. The zip was refastened from the inside.

Only now Mel realised that the sky was almost dark. The moon and the brightest of the stars had already appeared. The lantern in the tent went out. Mel muttered a curse, realising she had followed the wrong strategy: appeasement might have gotten her out already, instead she had antagonised him into murdering her.

'Rufus, I'm sorry! I was kidding – I mean, I spoke angrily because... well, you did leave me in a swamp. Of course I wasn't going to finish with you. If I was going to do that, I'd have done it in Wales, right?'

'Shut up!' Rufus screeched from the tent. It sounded like he'd been crying.

Mel rolled her eyes and cursed again. There was no way he'd see reason if he was in one of his self-obsessed moods. She wondered, not for the first time, how she'd managed to let a beast like that attach himself to her. He was charming at times, often funny, but deeply troubled from years of being bullied at school and work. Mel had never loved him, maybe she felt sorry for him and amused by his conspiracy theories and oddball beliefs. Perhaps, she thought, he'd realised the truth of it and that was why he was always so jealous and controlling for most of the nine months they'd been together.

Mel stared at the tent. Waiting for movement or a sign that Rufus was going to come out and rescue her. She decided to remain quiet, hoping that he would wonder why she wasn't shouting for help, prompting him to come out to check. If the strategy didn't work in five or ten minutes, she would start calling out again.

Mel's breath came in puffs of vapour. Her teeth rattled so she clamped them shut. Her body felt strangely numb. It wasn't quite dusk, and she was already waning. Mel knew she would not survive the night.

The rasping sound returned. Mel looked about but saw nothing. The light in the tent flicked on, confirming that she hadn't imagined the sound.

The tent unzipped. Rufus stuck his head out. 'What's that racket?'

The sound stopped.

Rufus opened the zip the rest of the way and stepped out of the tent. He went on tiptoes, scanning the surrounding landscape. He looked worried, refraining from calling out to some unknown presence that might take a dim view of him luring a young woman to her death.

'Help!' Mel screamed.

'Shut up!' Rufus hissed.

'Help! He's trying to kill me!'

Rufus gestured wildly for her to stop. He stomped his foot as Mel continued to scream for assistance.

'Shut up, you stupid cow! You don't know what that is out there.'

Mel stopped, registering the look of genuine fear on his face. Was it fear of discovery or fear for his life?

'What is it?' Mel said, her voice becoming increasingly hoarse.

Rufus sputtered. 'Ghost. Aliens. Psychos. I don't know, but it's not natural.'

Mel laughed at him despite her predicament, then sucked in as much air as possible and screamed as loudly as she could.

Her scream was answered by a low growl.

Rufus pulled a small torch from his back pocket, flicked on the light, and fanned the beam over the long grass.

'Rufus, what's there?'

'Sush!' he snapped.

'Rufus, get me out of here. Quickly.'

'Ok. Hang on.' The mocking superior tone had gone. Rufus put the torch back in his pocket and laid out flat on the ground at the edge of the mire, distributing his weight as best he could he moved along on his belly, gradually shortening the gap between them. He stopped occasionally, splaying himself out when the ground wobbled too much, then continued.

In a few minutes that seemed to stretch on forever, Rufus reached the coiled rope. He picked up the bundle and unwound a length of it. Keeping hold of the loose end, he threw the coiled end toward Mel. 'Tie that off around you if you can. Hold onto it if you can't. I'll go back to the edge and pull you out.' Rufus shuffled back toward the edge of the swap, moving like a worm.

Mel stretched a hand toward the rope. The coil was a good metre outside of her reach. 'I can't get to it. Can you throw it again?'

Rufus cursed. He went to the edge of the mire before pulling on his end of the rope and dragging the bundle back toward him.

'What was that growl, Rufus? Was it the same thing that made the sawing sound?'

'I think so.' He didn't make eye contact, keeping his attention on the rope. 'I think that sawing sound was it panting. Or roaring.'

'Oh, God. What was it?'

Rufus didn't answer. The coiled rope was within reach. He stretched out an arm and plucked it up. Remaining prone he lifted the rope, poised to throw. 'Ready? Catch it in the air if you can.'

Mel nodded.

A rush of motion erupted from the reeds. A black shape slammed into Rufus, pinning him facedown. Golden feline eyes glared from over his shoulder.

Rufus cried out. The sound cut short as the creature clamped its mouth around the back of Rufus's neck, shaking him, its black nose wrinkled in fury.

Mel screamed and flailed heedless of the pull of the mire.

Rufus was limp and unmoving.

The huge black cat flicked its long tail and again shook its victim by the neck, causing Rufus's arms to flop uselessly. The beast released its grip once satisfied that life had been extinguished and began noisily sniffing Rufus's ear before pawing the body, turning it over onto its back and ripping at the shirt with its paws. With a last glare at Mel, the creature sat down and tore at Rufus's torso, ripping flesh with a muzzle already dripping with blood.

Mel averted her gaze from the horrid sight and squeezed her eyes shut, trying to stifle sobs of despair which escaped as high-pitched squeals. She shook uncontrollably and felt a heavy sickness in her stomach at the wet tearing sounds the beast made as it ate its fill.

There was no way to know how long she waited, expecting at every moment that the creature's hot breath would imminently be on her cheek, stinking of blood and raw meat. Mel cautiously opened her eyes when she realised that there hadn't been any sound from the beast for a while.

Darkness enveloped the entire landscape, obscuring both beast and deceased boyfriend. Moonlight illuminated only the horizons and the silhouette of the most prominent of jagged bushes – any one of which could conceal the creature.

Mel listened carefully, hearing only the wind. She strained to see where Rufus had fallen. As her eyes adjusted to the dark, she could make out the outline of his corpse, laying face-up. There was no sign of the cat. A rustle among the reeds brought a cry of shock to her lips, but nothing charged from the undergrowth, leaving her unsure if it had been the wind, a rabbit, or the creature, which she felt sure must be a black Jaguar.

127

A desperate desire to live was urging Mel to scream for help. It took all her self-control to refrain from calling out: there was no help to be had. Any sound could summon the beast. The chattering of teeth couldn't be controlled, nor could occasional whimpers when some gust of wind emulated the rushing of the feline monster through the undergrowth.

'I'm sorry, Rufus,' Mel whispered. Looking at the prone shape. She wasn't sure why she apologised – the whole predicament was his fault – but he had tried to save her when he could have fled. She gagged when realising her best hope for survival was that the Jaguar had eaten its fill already.

Mel retched twice, trying not to vomit. The third time she couldn't help but be sick with such violence that it hurt her stomach. Warm stinking matter stained her lip and chin, quickly cooling and solidifying in the cold night air.

'Please, God. Save me,' Mel gasped through rattling teeth, then letting out a cry upon hearing the return of the beast's sawing grunts. It was further away, sounding like it echoed through a chamber of some kind, but stopped after a few short rasps. Mel let out a long breath and waited, helpless, for whatever would happen next.

Mel awoke with a start at some horrible noise, the resounding of which rang in her ears. She jolted, momentarily forgetting where she was or why she couldn't move. She blinked as eyesight adjusted to a dim light, making her wonder how long she had slept, and how sleep had even been possible. The resonance of the sound in her ears faded, leaving her unsure if she had dreamed it. Her eyes fell on Rufus's ravaged remains.

The exposed skin was white. His eyes, now black hollows, stared at her. His lower jaw was missing and it looked like the tongue was gone too. Ribs protruded through ravaged skin and tatters of cloth. The stomach cavity was completely torn open.

A sudden movement behind the remains brought a yelp to Mel's lips.

Black ears flicked. Golden eyes fixed on her. Small, pointed white teeth grinned with evil intent. The creature made a yapping noise and returned to tearing at its meal.

A growl and a swish of black charged from nearby undergrowth. The smaller creature which had been feasting on the body now yelped and ran for its life. It wasn't fast enough. The jaguar caught the fox just a few feet from Rufus. Its mouth clamped around the fox's neck as it had with Rufus, shaking the smaller beast which almost instantly hung limp. The jaguar dropped the body and turned its golden eyes on the mucky head in the swamp.

Mel screamed.

The jaguar lowered its profile – ready to pounce. It snarled, showing huge gleaming canines. Keeping low, the leopard rushed across the ground toward its prey.

Mel shrieked as loud as she could. She flailed, swallowing bog water.

The creature paused. A paw pierced the surface of the bog, sinking an entire foreleg. The jaguar recoiled, growling at the ground. The long black tail flicked back and forth as the creature moved a few paces left, testing the ground again. The paw submerged through the moss again. The jaguar hissed, baring its teeth, then turned and slinked away, flopping down next to Rufus's remains where it rested its chin on the corpse's chest.

Mel struggled to regulate her breathing and hoped to slow the thundering of her heart, the pulsating of which reverberated through her entire body. She could feel the beast watching her as it relaxed by its kill. Mel kept her eyes down, knowing that eye contact with a feline was construed as a challenge. Although the creature had shied away from entering the mire, Mel felt it was likely that the ground could hold the beast's weight if it chose the right route.

There was nothing to be done but remain in silence, waiting and hoping. Mel was beyond tears. Her dry throat burned. Every muscle that still had sensation ached. She no longer trembled; after hours of despair, imminent death was certain – the only factor was whether the end would come from jaws and claws or from hypothermia and dehydration.

The morning sun peeked over the hilltops, its brilliance made Mel wince and turn her face as if trying to force her gaze back toward the grizzly scene. Instead, she closed her eyes. Despite the dazzling glare, the sun brought little warmth.

Mel let her head loll to one side, hoping the beast would forget her, or lose interest, or that death from cold might come before the jaguar. She remained motionless for what seemed at least an hour before the jaguar stirred.

It stood and moved to the edge of the bog, pacing, making that gruff sawing sound and flicking it's white-tipped tail in apparent agitation. The creature was staring at a fixed point somewhere in the distance. Ears pricked up alert. Whiskers twitched. The hair on the beast's shoulders stood erect.

Mel followed the line of the jaguar's gaze, initially seeing nothing, then spotting movement on the hill she had descended the previous day. A white shape bobbed along the hilltop. Mel's hopes deflated: a sheep.

The cat intently watched the movement, lowering its profile as if stalking.

Mel squinted at the white blob, wondering what so interested the jaguar, or if it just attacked anything to come in sight.

The white shape moved fast for a sheep. Sun glare made it hard to focus clearly on the figure at least a hundred metres away and partially obscured by elevation and vegetation. A glint of sunlight reflected off the figure. Mel gasped: it was a person. The light was from a watch face, phone screen, or an item of jewellery.

The jaguar stayed low by the reeds. It watched the movement intently, tail arched like a cobra ready to strike, yet content to remain concealed.

'Help!' Mel shouted. The cry was half lost in her hoarse throat.

The white figure continued. It was a man in a white t-shirt, jogging.

Mel coughed and tried to clear her throat. 'Help! Help!' Her voice cracked, the higher tones trailing off into a whisper. She raised an aching arm in a sluggish wave.

The jaguar hissed its fury before loping off through the long reeds and out of sight.

Mel called out again, her voice came a little louder. She hoped the jogger wasn't wearing earbuds. She shouted again and again as he the man continued, nearing the crest of the hill which would take him out of sight. And then he stopped.

He looked about, shielding his eyes against the sun's glare with a palm.

Mel screamed, waving both arms, sinking down into the murky mass up to her chin and kicking for buoyancy with numb legs that responded sluggishly to her desperate desire.

The man put his hands on his hips in much the way Rufus did, then began to descend the valley. He wound through the undergrowth with ease, padding along in a leisurely jog, stopping on a small granite outcrop to survey the valley again.

Mel waved frantically, shouting and sputtering as more filthy water splashed into her mouth.

The man's head pivoted as he scanned the mire. Finally, he looked directly at Mel and covered his brow to get a better look before breaking into a jog again.

'Oh, thank God!' Mel gasped, blinking away tears of relief. 'Over here! Thank you.'

The man slowed his pace as he neared the mire and removed his black sunglasses to get a better look at the mire's captive. His thin legs and black shorts were flecked with mud. He stopped at the edge of the bog, eyes already trying to track a path toward Mel. 'Wow, girl, you're pretty well stuck. Ain't been here all night, have you?'

'Yes. Please help; there's some rope there if you can get to it somehow.' With a jolt of shock Mel remembered the jaguar, momentarily forgotten in the relief of imminent rescue. 'Watch out – there's a jaguar. It killed my boyfriend.'

'What?' The man looked around with his face contorted in puzzlement. Sighting the tent he took a step toward it, then abruptly halted on noticing Rufus's remains. The man cursed. He crouched, looking about sharply as if expecting attack at any instant. 'Where is it?' he hissed.

'It went off that way through the reeds. It's probably not far. Have you got a phone?'

The man unfasted a phone which was strapped to his arm and shook his head after a moment contemplating the screen. 'I'd have to go back up the hill to try for a signal.'

'Don't leave me.'

The man looked at Mel for several seconds and then to the hilltop. He released a heavy sigh and stood. 'My name's Mikey.'

'Mel.'

'Hi Mel. I'm gonna to try for that rope, but if I can't get to it, or I can't pull you out, then I'm gonna have to run up that hill and call for help, okay?'

'Okay,' Mel said weakly, knowing she would protest if this saviour tried to leave her for a moment.

Mikey knelt at the edge of the mire and touched the mossy surface. 'I've run through bogs before, but always gave this one a wide berth – especially this time of year. Even so, I've never heard of anyone get stuck as badly as you have.'

Mel was too exhausted to formulate a conversational response. She willed Mikey to hurry but could see he was calculating how to get to the rope and so remained silent.

'You sure it's a jaguar?' Mikey said, looking at the coil of blue rope.

'It's a big black cat with blacker spots. I don't care what else it is if not a jaguar. I just want out.'

Mikey nodded and put his sunglasses back on, flashing a grin of perfectly white teeth. His confidence betrayed by trembling hands. 'I'm gonna try and crawl to the rope then throw it to you, okay? You loop it under your arms. Got it?'

Mel nodded.

'If this works, you'll be out in ten minutes.'

Mel kept watch on the reeds in the direction the cat had gone.

Mikey followed her line of sight and then turned back with a weak smile. 'I know you're scared, but big cats like that are afraid of people. It's probably starving, that's why it attacked. My arrival probably scared it off. Most likely it's half a mile away already.'

Mel nodded, unconvinced.

Mikey took a small backpack off his back and took out a water bottle, taking a long draught before setting it down along with his phone and sunglasses. Then, slowly, carefully, he laid out prone as if about to do press-ups and began to crawl commando-style over the mire.

The ground wobbled, but not as drastically as it had when Mel jumped on it. She figured the athletic Mikey didn't weigh any more than she did, and with care the swamp should hold his weight. The pulse throbbed through Mel's body. Sweat stung her eyes. Breath quickened.

Mikey remained focused on the rope, advancing at a steady and purposeful pace, pausing occasionally when a hand of foot broke the surface of the swamp. When the ground rippled too much, he paused and waited a few seconds for it to abate before continuing. Within a few minutes he passed Rufus's remains and, keeping his eyes averted from the body, reached the end of the rope. He gathered in the line until he could pick up the bundle, then threw it to Mel.

The rope bounced off Mel's waiting palm and landed just a few feet away. She stretched, fingertips touching the bundle, releasing a strangled sound of frustration and despair that salvation would again prove to be just out of reach. Mel gritted her teeth and reached out until it felt like her arm might dislocate from the socket, managing to use her middle finger to pull the rope a few centimetres closer – enough that she could grab it. With a shuddering sob of relief, she pulled the rope to her chest, clutching with both hands.

'Quickly, tie it off around you,' Mikey said.

Mel nodded. Fingers fumbled; the digits sluggish, numb and reluctant. It proved difficult to put the rope around herself as motion threatened further submersion. She rested her weight on the now fully submerged backpack and, leaning forward as best she could, dug her hands down into the mire and passed the rope from hand to hand behind herself, pulling the lose end around to her front and looping it, forming an awkward and loose knot: the best she could manage.

Mikey nodded, gave a thumbs up and looked around, licking his lips. 'I'm gonna start heading back. Let the rope go slack. I'll pull you out when I can stand.'

Mel watched Mikey's retreat with anxiety and the expectation that the beast would burst from the undergrowth to maul her saviour.

Within a few minutes, Mikey was standing and wiping his bog-stained hands on filthy shorts. He gathered in the rope until it was taught and then pulled, bracing himself like a tug-of-war contestant at a country fair.

Mel gripped the rope with both hands, feeling it dig into her back. She could do nothing to help extract herself, managing only to hold onto the lifeline.

Mikey huffed and gritted his teeth.

The mire gave up a few inches hold on its captive with a wet gulp.

'Yes! It's working!' Mel gasped.

Mikey heaved on the rope. The bog gave way to his strength but rather than pull her out of the swamp, Mikey's effort was dragging her through it.

Sweat already glistened on the runner's forehead and cheeks. His breath came in gasps as he dragged Mel slowly nearer. In a couple of minutes toil he had pulled her little more than a metre. He paused to wipe perspiration from his brow. 'It's gonna take a little longer than I thought. Hopefully, you'll feel firmer ground under your feet soon and you can wade out.'

'I can barely move my legs. My boyfriend said the bog is really deep. What if it's deep all the way to the edge?'

Mikey puffed and braced to pull again. 'It's about fifteen metres to the edge. I'll pull you all the way if I must, but it might take a little while. Just keep an eye out for that big old pussy cat. Ready?'

Mel nodded, feeling secure under Mikey's guardianship; his mask of fearlessness wasn't convincing, but that he stayed to save a stranger when he was clearly afraid made him seem all braver. The rope pulled tight against Mel's back and under the armpits. Gripping the line with both hands, Mel tried to pull herself along it. The rope constricted her airways, but there was movement. A few inches of progress.

Mikey puffed with exertion, pausing for a moment before straining again.

Another few inches of movement.

The bog sucked against her, unwilling to release its bounty.

Mel gritted her teeth. Wet hands slid on the rough rope which scratched her palms.

'You got an anchor beneath your knees there?' Mikey said through gritted teeth. Then with a gurgle of surrender, the bog seemed to relinquish its hold and Mel was pulled at least a couple of feet.

'We got it. Stop struggling. Just lay flat,' Mikey gasped in a pause between pulls.

Mel tried to kick as if swimming despite Mikey's warning, but found the legs sluggish and reluctant to respond.

Within a couple of minutes, half the distance was covered. Mikey let the rope go slack as he paused for breath, resting with his hands on his knees. 'Just give me thirty seconds then we'll get you the rest of the way.'

'Shall I try to touch the bottom?'

'No. The bog might get a good hold on you again.' Mikey examined his hands, the palms of which bore scarlet rope burns.

'Can you still pull?' Mel said.

Mikey nodded, gathering the blue cord in his hands and taking a stance ready to resume his effort. 'Ready?'

Mel nodded, gripping the rope tight as she could.

The jaguar bounded from the reeds, covering the clear ground in as little time as it took for Mel to notice the blur of black in her peripheral vision. Mikey had only begun to turn when the beast pounced, sending him sprawling to the ground with the big cat upon him.

Mikey lifted his head, but the predator's weight was on his back. Huge black paws pinned his shoulders. Mikey looked at Mel the same moment the beast's jaws clamped around the back of his skull. Mikey's sunglasses hung from one ear. His expression went from open mouthed shock to a grimace of pain. With a loud crunch Mikey's face sagged. His eyelids half closed. Blood poured down his cheeks.

Another crunch.

The beast released him. The lifeless head thudded to the ground. The monster hissed through reddened fangs. Golden eyes glared hungrily.

Mel locked eyes with the creature, watching it prowl the edge of the mire, staying low as it tested the ground again. 'Damn you!' Mel screamed. 'Damn you! You didn't need to do that!'

The beast's tail twitched with anticipation as it moved further down the mire, finding ground that held its weight. It crept along parallel to Mel, nose near the ground, slinking nearer.

'Oh God, oh God,' Mel breathed, seeing that the beast would soon be upon her. She slapped at the mire around her and found the ground to be mushy – it definitely wouldn't hold her weight, but she realised it might easily hold the cat's.

Mel pulled on the rope, finding that it was still taught – Mikey had braced it around his waist – if she was strong enough it might be possible to pull herself free. Mel heaved on the rope and tried to kick. She gained a few inches of ground, but the jaguar was sure to reach her first.

Dropping the rope, Mel tried to swim, flailing desperately in the muck, failing to propel herself far. Legs tingled and ached as desperation forced them into action. Her right hand sank until it met resistance – the mire again sucking against the effort of withdrawing it. In a final desperate effort, Mel sank her legs and touched something solid – maybe rock or even hard ground underneath her. She stood, rising to waist depth in the bog. Any relief at release washed away by the proximity of the beast. Mel dared a glance to her left, finding yellow eyes staring at her from a dozen metres away.

The cat snarled.

Mel waded through the mire, stumbling. She tore at the moss-covered surface with her hands, hoping to find more solid ground to pull herself out by. She fell forward, flopping onto the stagnant mess but didn't sink. She scrambled, crawling on her stomach. Still the legs were sluggish in operation and reluctant to obey. Her hand found a rock that was fixed to secure ground and used it as an anchor to pull herself along. Her other hand found some reeds which tore out of the ground in her grasp, then grabbed another handful which she was able to pull herself toward. Then she realised she had cleared the mire.

With a cry of relief mixed with desperation, Mel tried to stand. Her entire body was caked in brown. Her legs wobbled, but she stood. She tried to run but fell after a few steps.

There was no hope of outrunning the predator. Mel looked about for a weapon: a big rock, or a sharp stick, but saw nothing. A rocky outcrop near the bottom of the hill provided hope of some fist-sized stones that could be thrown at the beast – perhaps even scare it off.

She dared to look behind. The beast was in the mire, not far from where Mel had been a minute before, testing the ground with its paw. It snarled in apparent frustration and turned back the way it came, rushing with frightening speed.

Mel lurched toward the rocks, noticing a small opening between two large granite boulders, daring to imagine that it might be possible to wedge herself between them and remain unnoticed by the beast. Even as she climbed over the lower rocks the hope felt forlorn, but it was the only hope there was.

Mel dragged her legs over a ledge into the recess, finding it deeper than expected. It formed a small cave that only went back a few metres but, absorbed in panic, the sight of shelter was too much of a temptation. She clambered deeper, breaking fingernails against granite in her haste and crawling through a mess of detritus on the cave floor.

The reeds outside swished as the jaguar bounded after her; all effort at stealth abandoned. Claws scratched at the granite as it closed in with unbridled haste.

Mel scrambled to the back of the recess, startling when something soft and warm under her hand made a yapping cry.

Blue-grey eyes looked up at her. Grey whiskers twitched and the little black creature showed tiny needle-like white teeth.

Mel gasped, recoiling. It was only then she noticed the half-eaten sheep carcass she had hastened over. A second set of tiny eyes watched from beside the sheep's deflated chest and protruding rib bones.

Daylight was blocked out by the black shape of the mother filling the entrance. The golden orbs glared with fury as the beast snarled, furious at the trespass into its lair.

Mel snatched up the nearest cub by the scruff of its neck. The tiny thing pawed the air as she held it as a protective talisman toward the mother.

The big jaguar paused, hissing hatred.

Mel grabbed the other cub, holding both at arm's length.

The mother lowered her profile as if ready to pounce but didn't move. She locked eyes with Mel and waited motionless with ears pricked up like a sandstone sphynx.

'I'm sorry we came into your territory,' Mel said, her voice cracked and broken. 'I didn't know. I just want to leave.'

The big cat lowered her torso to the ground, but her head remained upright, alert. The eyes ignored the dangling cubs and remained fixed on the intruder.

Mel shivered, unsure if it was from the cold, fear, or hypothermia. Her outstretched arms already ached. She wondered how long until help might arrive: surely someone knew Mikey's route. Someone would miss him. How long could it be before rescuers came looking? Five hours? Six?

The jaguar sat sentinel at the alcove entrance, seemingly satisfied to wait until the enemy tired. She kept a stern stare fixed on the human, silently threatening what would come.

Mel dared not break the gaze, sensing it was a challenge of her resolve. She swallowed a sob. Her arms burned; she wanted to put one of the cubs in her lap to rest her aching limb, but any overt movement might prompt the beast into action. All she could do was to wait.

Passage

Father Brendan waved farewell to the last of the congregation as they filed out of the churchyard amid a swirl of brown and golden leaves. The priest shivered and blew into his cupped hands as he retreated inside the church, pushing the heavy studded-oak door shut with a thud that echoed through St Petroc's.

'Heard it again,' a voice close behind announced in a nasal, accusing tone.

The church should have been empty. Father Brendan spun about, slamming his back into the door. A startled cry wilted on his lips as he recognised Mrs Pascoe, the cleaner. He coughed to try to mask his involuntary outburst, but the cleaner's withering stare over the rim of her pointed spectacles evidenced the futility of the effort and made his cheeks burn.

'What is it, Mrs Pascoe?' Father Brendan said, unable to keep a sharp edge from his voice.

The cleaner pursed her thin lips and winced. She shook her head, making her purple-dyed curls dance like medusa's coils. 'The sound from the basement!' Mrs Pascoe put her meaty paws on her hips and let out an exasperated, if exaggerated, sigh.

Father Brendan navigated around the rotund form of the elderly cleaner and headed toward the altar to tidy away the sacred vessels. He waved a dismissive hand over his shoulder. 'Dear Mrs Pascoe, there is no basement – as I keep telling you.'

'There is too – you just ain't been here long enough to know of it. Father Norsworthy knew, and Father Brian before him. Heard the ghosts too.'

Father Brendan groaned. He pulled his green and white vestment over his head and rolled it up, keeping his back to Mrs Pascoe. 'No church has a basement, nor any ghosts for that matter. What you hear are moorland winds blowing through the belltower, or the squeal of mice through rusty pipes, not the shaking of chains and wails of the dispossessed.'

'Never said naught about no chains. Anyway, this time it wasn't sobs and cries. Was whispers and shuffles.'

Father Brendan slammed a chalice on the altar with a little more force than intended. The ringing from the brass base rebounded off granite walls along the length of the nave. He spun about to face Mrs Pascoe. 'You see?' He pointed at the rafters. 'This mere cup echoes like a bell, does it not? The vaulted ceiling amplifies and throws sounds. Please, Mrs Pascoe, I beg you: forget this talk of spirts. Does The Bible not tell us in Hebrews 9:27 – *Man is destined to die once, and after that to face judgement.* Does that not tell us that spirits do not linger, but ascend to face the Lord?'

'Matthew 27:52 – *The tombs were opened, and many bodies of saints raised, coming out of their tombs they went into the holy city and appeared to many.*' Mrs Pascoe allowed herself a smile and nod of superiority on the presumption that her words ensured victory.

Father Brendan permitted the upstart cleaner a moment of self-satisfied smugness as he fixed his quarry with a rigid stare. 'Mrs Pascoe, you have deliberately misquoted The Bible to support your argument. I have served in churches as old as this for near on forty years and have yet to see or hear anything that can't be explained. I won't have you putting off the congregation and upsetting the choir over talk of the supernatural. If you persist, I shall have to ask diocese to reconsider your contract.'

Mrs Pascoe's eyes momentarily bulged before returning to their natural state of narrowed suspicion. She twisted the apron in her talons as her frame visibly shook with silent rage.

'Furthermore,' Father Brendon pressed home the assault while his quarry was checked. 'I will not listen to another conspiracy theory regarding the fate of my predecessor. I don't believe for an instant that Father Norsworthy was abducted, murdered, snatched by aliens or piskies from the high moors. I am certain that in time, once he has settled his crisis of faith, he will return to us by God's grace.'

The duellists stared at each other for a long and unflinching moment until Mrs Pascoe swallowed and brushed down the front of her apron before quickly wiping away a glistening drop from one eye. 'I shall go and hoover the parochial house then – if you've no objection to that.'

'Of course,' Father Brendan said, in as gentle a tone as could be managed. His shoulders slumped; deflated in victory at the visage of the diminutive sixty-year-old waddling off to clean his home while sniffling to suppress tears. He turned and looked up at the form of Christ on the crucifix and crossed himself. 'Apologies, Father,' he muttered once the church door had thud shut behind the cleaner. 'She is sent to test me. I should do better.'

It took but a minute to collect the communion cups, oils, and paten dish from the altar and onto a tray to be taken for cleaning. Usually, a choir boy would stay to help but he had sent them all home after the service because the wind had picked up and worse still was forecast. Even from within the sanctuary of the thick-walled church, the trees lining churchyard could be heard groaning their protests at rough treatment by gusts that bellowed through the valley from the high moorland.

Father Brendan walked to the door, intending to repair to the parochial house for a late-morning cup of coffee and steel himself for an apology to Mrs Pascoe. The sound of his footsteps reverberated through the high-ceilinged chamber. He paused with his hand on the black iron door ring and swept an inspecting gaze around the nave: over empty pews, the lonely font, and the cold grey lectern.

A screech of stone rasping against stone gave Father Brendan pause as he was about to turn the door ring. He cocked his head, listening. A distinct creaking was followed by what sounded like a whisper. The words were not loud enough to be distinguished over the rush of wind which brought with it a sudden drumming of rain on the roof. The disembodied voice continued only a few seconds before falling silent. Father

Brendan shook his head, deciding that Mrs Pascoe's musings had infiltrated his imagination. He turned the iron ring and was about to pull the door open when he once more heard the scrape of stone.

'Hello?' Father Brendan called out. He waited, but no further sound came. He marched back down the length of the church toward the chancel, peering into the north and south transepts as he passed. A brief check around the altar revealed no trace hiding children or destitute refugees from the elements.

The sound came again, followed by a hollow clunk which sounded like a slab being slid into place. The noise had come from the southern transept. Father Brendan dashed the short distance, finding only that one of the few lit votive candles had blown out. A thin wisp of smoke rose to the rafters from the extinguished wick: something had blown it out, but nothing else was out of place. Father Brendan marched along the pews with footsteps pounding the stone floor to show he meant business. After the last empty bench, he found himself back at the door. He turned, casting a careful gaze about the interior.

'If there's anyone here, I'm going to lock you in. I don't normally close-up during daytime, but if someone's hiding, I must suspect you have devious intent. Come out now, or you'll spend the night.'

A wait of a few seconds yielded no response. Father Brendan opened the door and braced against the thrust of wind that blasted him, sending withered fragments of nature's autumnal detritus fluttering across the threshold and over flagstones. He stepped out, locked the door, and marched down earthen track toward the one-bedroom cottage that served as the parochial house avoiding the puddles which had accumulated during the short downpour.

The sky was a gloomy grey even though it was not yet midday. Yellow, orange, and brown leaves swirled around the cottage and crunched underfoot. Once inside the parochial house, the vacuum cleaner could be heard from upstairs, humming its tune like an irritated bee, and so Father Brendan retreated into the parlour where he found a cup of tea, lukewarm to the touch, on the table beside his armchair. He carried the tea out to the kitchen, tossing the cup's contents down the sink before spooning in some instant coffee and boiling the kettle.

'Tea instead of coffee. Every time,' he muttered, shaking his head.

The buzz of vacuuming trailed off into a dying whirr and then to silence; the sound of the plug being tugged from the socket announced the cessation of cleaning. Floorboards creaked as the vacuum was carried downstairs accompanied by the grunts and laboured breathing of the cleaner.

Father Brendan flicked the kettle off – not wanting the housekeeper to detect that he was replacing the drink she had made. he steeled himself for the humility of his imminent apology which he had no doubt would later be weaponized against him.

Mrs Pascoe padded past the kitchen door, glancing sideways at the priest and moving on without acknowledgement.

'Mrs Pascoe!'

She sighed and stepped back so that her side profile was framed by the doorway.

'Mrs Pascoe… I wanted to apologise for my hasty words. Of course I shan't write to the diocese. You do a proper job here.'

The purple curls bobbed as she nodded, but she did not look at him and remained with her lips pursed and the vacuum held like a soldier with a rifle at *order-arms* on the parade ground.

Father Brendan rubbed his chin, knowing what could be said to abate the cleaner's resentment, but reluctant to explore that path. With a heavy sigh he gave in. 'Mrs Pascoe… where exactly did you hear these strange sounds?'

'I can do without your pretence of interest, thank you,' she snapped, still not meeting his gaze. She seemed about to march on when she frowned and stiffly pivoted her head a few degrees toward the priest. 'Unless… you heard something?'

Father Brendan nodded reluctantly. 'Maybe something.'

The vacuum clattered to the floor as a squealing Mrs Pascoe advanced on the priest with chubby fingers outstretched and trembling with excitement.

Father Brendan backed up a step. The edge of the kitchen worktop pressed into his lower back. He went to raise his hands defensively but, realising his overreaction, instead fidgeted with his collar.

The cleaner clapped her hands on Father Brendan arms. Tiny dark eyes stared through thick-rimmed glasses. The cleaner's face loomed dangerously close, with breath reeking of parma violets. 'I knew it!' She squeezed the priest's shoulders as her eyes widened eagerly. 'Tell me what you heard.'

Father Brendan related his experience as quickly as he could, hoping the conclusion would bring distance between himself and his domestic assistant.

'Stone scraping on stone?' Mrs Pascoe released her grip and stepped back as her gaze wandered, apparently musing what the priest's news could mean. 'Perhaps the sarcophagus?'

'Oh, Mrs Pascoe!' Father Brendan snapped. 'I wish I said nothing of it now. There's no need to add zombies to your list of theories about what is going on in St Petrocs!'

Mrs Pascoe's slowly raised a finger as if to beg silence for the revelation of some great discovery that she could barely compose herself enough to declare. 'A secret passage!' she blurted, patting her chest as if almost overcome with emotion at the realisation.

'Lord have mercy,' Father Brendan spluttered and covered his eyes with his palm. He slid the hand down his face, revealing the sight of the cleaner glaring over the rim of her glasses.

'Why, Father Brendan! It is clear to me now that Father Norsworthy is somehow hidden or trapped under that church. It is up to us to save him!' Mrs Pascoe shook her fist with determination, making her fleshy arm wobble.

Father Brendan sighed and leant back against the kitchen counter. 'Father Norsworthy has been missing for months. If he was trapped in a sarcophagus, or anywhere else, he would have died of starvation or suffocation.'

'We owe it to him to find out – and I mean to!' declared the housekeeper. She turned on her heel, marched out of the kitchen, pausing at the coat rack in the hall long enough to retrieve her jacket, and went out into the November gale. The door slammed behind her – either by her action or that of the wind.

After a moment's hesitation, Father Brendan hurried after her. The cleaner's purposeful waddle had brought her to the church door before he was even halfway there. She turned upon finding the door locked and made an exasperated gesture.

Father Brendan came to her side and unlocked the door. 'I shall help you search for ten minutes, and not a moment more. I don't want the place reduced to mounds of smashed masonry in your quest to discover our missing cleric.'

Mrs Pascoe barged into the church, making her way directly to the stone sarcophagus of a Tudor priest who was interred on the southern transept. The cleaner ran her hands over the stonework, peering here and there and muttering to herself. 'Shan't you help?' she snapped over her shoulder before returning to her labour.

Father Brendan suppressed a remark and made a show of looking about as he pondered how his effort at mollifying the cleaner had only made matters worse. He walked between the transept and the lectern staring at the post-medieval carvings in the ceiling which depicted faces, Tudor roses, gargoyles, and the coats of arms of Devon men centuries dead.

'What was that?' Mrs Pascoe turned from the sarcophagus. Her eyes scanned the floor near Father Brendan.

'What was what? I heard nothing.'

'When you stepped there, something sounded hollow. Retrace your steps.'

Father Brendan sank his hands into his trouser pockets, deciding that dumb compliance was the best way of ending the charade quickly. He walked back toward the transept.

'No! Not like that. Step heavier so's I can hear if it's hollow.'

Father Brendan bit his lip and about-turned, stamping across the flagstones until a startled cry from Mrs Pascoe stopped him.

'There! Did you hear it?'

'It's a loose pathing stone, Mrs Pascoe. The church is five-hundred years old.'

Undeterred, Mrs Pascoe went to her knees, feeling around the edges of the suspicious stone, murmuring and humming sounds of satisfaction. 'Fetch a crowbar,' she snapped without looking up.

'Of course,' Father Brendan said. 'I keep a few beside the altar for just this sort of happenstance.'

The remark elicited a momentary glare from over the top of the housekeeper's glasses before her attention was redirected to the flagstone where she tried to find purchase with her fingertips.

'Don't do that – you'll hurt yourself,' Father Brendan hissed. 'There are tools in my shed. I'll fetch something. Don't fiddle with that while I'm gone. The flagstones are medieval: I don't want them damaged.'

Father Brendan soon returned with a spade, a trowel, and a torch. The cleaner scurried aside and made a flurried gesture for him to hurry. The edge of the spade fit snugly between the flagstones and he was able to lever up the stone with a small puff of dust and a musky smell like that of aged books.

Mrs Pascoe dropped to her knees and grabbed the stone. Father Brendan put the shovel down and helped her lift the slab aside. They both reached for the torch on the floor at the same time but the cleaner swatted away the priest's hand before flicking the light, directing the beam into the dark space that had opened under the church floor.

'Stairs!' Mrs Pascoe declared.

'We shall have to remove this other stone,' Father Brendan said, already taking hold of the slab adjacent to the square hole on the floor. He lifted and pushed the stone aside and looked down into the blackness, where torchlight picked out seven or eight uneven steps leading into what looked like an underground chamber. As he opened his mouth to speak, the cleaner already had her foot on the first step.

'Mrs Pascoe! Please show some restraint: the structure might not be safe. We should– '

The cleaner descended into the darkness without so much as a backward glance.

Father Brendan set off after his supposed helper with flushed cheeks and a fresh intent to have her removed from employment. He kept one hand on the wall as he went down into a narrow passageway. Torchlight illuminated the rounded silhouette of Mrs Pascoe some ten metres ahead. A plea for hesitation received no greater attention than his previous effort and so he rushed to keep up.

The ground was unpathed but largely level, while cobwebs were thick enough on the walls to give the impression of a kind of cocooned chamber. The passageway was little wider than a person and Father Brendan's sleeves were soon trailing lengths of grey strands picked up from the walls. Mrs Pascoe's torch lit the tunnel for some distance ahead, but provided only flickers of illumination behind her, forcing Father Brendan to keep close.

'Footprints.' She directed the light to the floor as Father Brendan caught up.

Sure enough, the vague impression of modern shoes had left their mark in the dust: not one pair, but many. At least three different treads as well as barefoot prints were apparent leading both ways along the corridor.

'It would seem the tunnel is far from forgotten,' Father Brendan whispered.

'Father Norsworthy!' Mrs Pascoe bellowed. Her voice blasted down the tunnel and a moment later rebounded back to them from the darkness.

Father Brendan winced and steeled himself for some unknown threat to charge from the black. 'Mrs Pascoe,' he hissed. 'We should show restraint. Whoever is using this tunnel clearly believes we are ignorant to it. Have you thought for one moment that villains may have done away with Father Norsworthy?' He looked back down the way they had come and licked his lips, failing to suppress an involuntary shudder. 'We should go back and alert the proper authorities. This could be a county drug lines operation or… anything.' His mind quickly raced through which of the young villagers might be involved in such a plot. A few baseball cap-wearing spotty faces came to mind.

Mrs Pascoe grunted and marched on, leaving the way back in empty darkness.

'Wait!' Father Brendan seethed and bumbled after her, cursing as he almost tripped on a dislodged stone.

The passageway soon opened out into a chamber. Rounded pillars flanked cobweb-shrouded alcoves in which stone effigies of monks stood with head bowed over heavy granite coffins.

'A crypt!' Father Brendan declared.

A heavy, musty smell hung in the air. Torchlight illuminated dust particles which floated like slow-motion rain. The floor was covered in slate tiles, many of which were cracked: all were caked in dust. Scores of shoeprints crisscrossed the ground. Two more gloomy tunnels led out of the chamber – one seemed to continue for a long way, while the other opened into another chamber.

'This must have been built by Benedictines from the abbey,' Father Brendan said. 'If this joins up with the abbey, the tunnel is a mile long.'

'Told you the rumours were true,' Mrs Pascoe snapped as she moved toward the next chamber.

'Almost every medieval church has a myth about a secret tunnel. Who could have believed that any of them were true?' Father Brendan tried to keep his voice low – even so, it echoed through the tomb. He cast a cautious glance off into the dark tunnel they had yet to explore.

'I believed it,' Mrs Pascoe grunted. 'So did Father Norsworthy and Father Brian before him.'

Father Brendan followed the cleaner into the next chamber. Together their eyes traced the beam of torchlight as it illuminated mortuary alcoves like those they had already seen. Then the torch caught on something that reflected a glint of light back at them. Father Brendan gasped and involuntarily grabbed Mrs Pascoe's arm, only to then release it with some embarrassment. The reflection was from a small assortment of chalices on an altar much like the one in St. Petroc's. Together, they advanced on the altar: it was clear that the vessels were not mere brass but gold and boasting jewels. A gold dish was full of large round coins which Father Brendan immediately recognised as Crusader coins from the 14th century. He reached a quivering hand to the dish, his mouth dry with the anticipation of the riches.

A hand swatted his away with a tut. Mrs Pascoe turned the torchlight into his face, forcing him to shield his eyes.

'You blind me,' Father Pascoe hissed.

'No less than you deserve. That coin ain't yours – keep your thieving hands off.'

'Mrs Pascoe!' Father Brendan cried, too flustered to say more.

The beam from the torch circumnavigated the rest of the chamber until it settled on a twisted shape on the far side of the room. Father Brendan gasped when he recognised it for what it was: The slumped figure of a man in priest's clothes, suspended from the wrists by iron chains fixed to the wall.

'Father Norsworthy!' Father Brendan gasped. He cautiously moved toward the crumpled figure. A stench of excrement permeated the air and only grew stronger nearer the chained figure, whose knees hung a few inches above the floor – the chain cruelly not permitting enough leeway for its captive to even kneel. Father Brendan said the priest's name again and made to touch Norsworthy's white hair, but he curled his trembling fingers into a fist and let the hand drop to his side.

'He's dead, you know,' Mrs Pascoe said in a stern tone.

Father Brendan turned toward her and was startled to find her flanked by three black-robed figures with hoods hanging low over their faces.

'What is this?' Father Brendan cried out, scurrying back to the wall beside Norsworthy's corpse and only dimly aware of having moved through the dead priest's pool of bodily waste.

Mrs Pascoe kept the torch beam low so to not blind him. The monks fanned out to block any chance of fleeing past them. Their bare feet made no sound on the smooth, wet stone.

'This be your own doing,' Mrs Pascoe sneered. 'You might've been a guardian for the relics from the Holy Land which are spread throughout these crypts. Father Norsworthy had the same chance. Both of you failed and now…' her voice trailed off and the tone became sad, 'we must find yet another priest. If only the church could provide us with a worthy priest since Father Brian died.'

Father Brendan shook his head and pressed his back against the cold wall. 'I don't understand.'

'You stole the coin!' Mrs Pascoe snapped. 'We tested you – just as we tested Father Norsworthy. We put a couple of the old coins in the Sunday collection. You saw their value and kept them. You can't be trusted.'

'No,' Father Brendan said, remembering his glee at finding the gold coins, and after having them appraised, selling them for a tidy sum. 'What will you do? Kill me like you killed Father Norsworthy?'

'Tis a sin to kill. We just won't ever let you leave.' Mrs Pascoe growled. She advanced with slow and deliberate steps. The Benedictines moved in with her, their hands reaching out like the limbs of ghouls from their robes.

Hands grappled Father Brendan's flailing arms and grasped his shoulders. He heard a metallic rattle and click and saw Father Norsworthy's body finally collapse face-down onto the heaps of his own decaying filth. Father Brendan was dragged into the priest's place. He felt the clasp of rusty iron snap around his left wrist and then his right. Only then the rough hands released him. He screamed and struggled uselessly against the chains.

Mrs Pascoe put her face close to his, her expression scornful. 'You shall keep Father Norsworthy company. Hopefully the next priest will live up to Father Brian's legacy.'

Mrs Pascoe and the monks turned and filed out of the room, taking the light with them. Father Brendan called after them for mercy and pulled against the chains which bit into his wrists. The footsteps faded, leaving only silence punctuated by the echoes of Father Brendan's screams.

Crazywell Pool

There it was. After a two-hour calf-burning bicycle ride, including thirty sweaty minutes over rocky paths and lumpy grassy trails, Martha and Simone had finally reached Crazywell Pool.

'Is that it?' Martha said, letting her bike drop to the ground and wrinkling her freckled nose as she inspected the pool: about a hundred metres long, and maybe a third of that across, roughly diamond shaped with steep grassy banks on each side providing protection from the elements so that the summer breeze could only create gentle ripples on the surface, which was a cold grey in colour despite the splendour of the sun and the hazy heat of the afternoon. A dusty trail led down to the water on the far side of the pool, behind which hills in all shades of green stretched to the horizon.

'Yeah. That's it,' Simone said, taking off on her bike over the bumpy terrain toward the trail down to the water. She glanced over her shoulder after a short distance and came to a stop. 'Well? Coming?' she called out, continuing on without waiting for an answer.

Martha sighed and picked up her bicycle, checking that the handlebar hadn't landed in any of the poo which lay scattered over seemingly every square foot of ground. By the time she joined her friend at the water's edge, Simone had already kicked off her flip-flops, stripped off her blouse and skirt, and was testing the waters with her toes.

'Ouch!' Simone cried, jumping back from the water and shivering despite the warmth of the June day. 'Water's freezing! Maybe we shoulda worn wetsuits under our clothes instead of bikinis.'

Martha folded her arms and studied the water for signs of uncleanliness. The pool was very opaque beyond the first few feet. There was no apparent stream running into the water, so Martha reasoned there was little chance of anything polluting it. However, a dead animal having fallen in would putrefy the entire pond.

'Don't be such a sissy,' Simone scolded, having detected Martha's reluctance. 'It'll be fine once we're in. Let's do some yoga to warm up.'

'The bike ride already warmed me up.'

Simone moved into *downward facing dog*, before rushing through a yoga routine like it was a competitive sport. She didn't spare a glance at her friend until she came out *prayerful pose* at the conclusion of the exercise and opened her eyes to frown up at Marha. 'You're not even undressed yet.'

'I'm not sure we should go in,' Martha said.

'What?' Simone put her hands on her narrow hips. Her usually pretty face twisted into a scowl which bordered dangerously on rage. 'I knew you'd be like this. I haven't ridden all the way out here just to stare at water. I'm going in even if you don't.'

'It's very deep. Didn't you say this was a former quarry pit?'

Simone shrugged, tiptoeing into the water, wiggling outstretched arms for balance.

'There could be rusty old machinery on the bottom,' Martha called out.

'So what?' Simone snapped. 'People swim here all the time. Anyway, it's supposed to be bottomless so if there is any old machinery at wherever the bottom is, there's not much chance of getting tangled up in it.'

A dozen steps into the pool and Simone was chest-deep in water. She ducked her head under and came up a few seconds later, doing back stroke, gleefully flinging droplets of water into the air as her arms arced overhead. She laughed, making a show of enjoying herself much more than she probably was.

Martha sighed and decided to join in: it was too hot to stand and stare at someone enjoying the cooling waters – especially as

Simone would almost certainly be in a mood on the ride home if she didn't get her way.

Martha took off her t-shirt, jeans, and trainers. Her one-piece swimsuit was not very revealing but she still felt vulnerable undressing in the wilderness. She looked around to make sure nobody was watching, satisfying herself that not even the sheep were interested in the spectacle. She put a foot into the water and shrieked: it was very cold. Much colder than the warm day would leave one to believe. Martha wondered how deep the pool was for it to be so cold on such a sunny day.

'The best thing to do is to just jump right in and get it over with!' Simone said. She was standing on the slope of the bar bank. She dove in, gliding gracefully through the water's surface and swimming breaststroke out to the middle of the pool.

'I'm not jumping in,' Martha protested. 'We don't know how deep it is.'

'Bottomless!' Simone laughed, swimming back to the bank. She pulled herself out and sat with her arms tucked around her knees. 'Anyway, don't be worried about how deep it is, be worried about the legend instead.'

'What legend?' Martha said, backing out of the water. The sun's warmth on her skin prickled, threatening sunburn, forcing a choice between freezing cold submersion and days of searing irritation. *Caught between the Devil and the deep blue sea*, Martha thought, wondering where she had heard the phrase.

'The pool calls out the name of the next person to die. If you hear your named called out from the depths, it means you're about to die.'

'That's stupid,' Martha said. 'Where do they get these stories?'

Simone shrugged. 'Nothing better to do before someone invented TV, I suppose. Now, dive in – I dare you. Get the shock of the cold over with quick.'

'I'm not going to jump in!' Martha protested, putting her toe back in the water. It was cold even in the shallows.

'Get in or I'm going home,' Simone said, her face serious again.

Martha sighed. She knew Simone wasn't going to give up until she had her way – and if she didn't get her way Simone would give her the cold shoulder for the next couple of weeks.

Martha backed up a few steps, took a deep breath, and ran at the pool. Feet splashed heavily into the water. Within three paces the water was up to her knees. Two more and it was up to her thighs, but she was moving too fast to feel the cold. The next step didn't land on solid earth, which had apparently tapered away at a steep incline, plunging Martha face-first into murky water. The shock of the freezing water was instantaneous. Her bones hurt – particularly those at the extremities. She kicked and splashed but her limbs felt heavy and the water resistance made movements sluggish. It felt like she was sinking. Every direction other than up was pure black. Her heart thundered in her chest and ears – then she broke the surface.

Martha gasped, gulping in air. She was a passable swimmer, but the pool's waters were too cold. She thrashed in shock and panic. Her head went under and a moment later broke the surface again.

'Martha!' Simone screamed from the bank.

Martha swallowed freezing water as she gulped for air. Her heart felt like it was being crushed and the sound of the rapidly increased pulse thumped in her ears. Martha gasped, swallowing more water. She could hear Simone calling her name over and over. The pool enveloped her. Icy water filled her nose, mouth and lungs. A shimmer of sunlight on the water's surface seemed just out of reach – Martha grasped for it, but something – perhaps her own weight – was dragging her down.

'Martha! Martha!' Simone screamed. The sound was muffled and far away. Light from above faded into blackness. Martha was left with the echo of her name being called out as she sank into the depths.

Heathfield House

I met the estate agent on the gravel driveway outside the nineteenth century mansion on the southern edge of Dartmoor. I was struck by the imposing architecture, boasting huge stained glass windows and jutting gothic pillars designed to replicate the history and grandeur of a medieval abbey turned, post reformation, into luxurious domestic abode, but this century-and-a-half old construct was a facade of hidden truths. It had never been an abbey, and nothing more than an old farmhouse previously stood where the majestic weather-beaten country pile now towered. The lie of the age and ecclesiastical shape of the building was betrayed by the engraving '1859' in foot-high italics over the huge double doors to the main house. I was, however, only particularly interested in the second-floor flat which I would be occupying for the foreseeable future.

The staircase was creaky and the high ceilings cobweb strewn. The carpet outside my apartment was threadbare, but inside the flat all was clean. Much of the furniture was old, but the rooms had been given a lick of paint in recent years and the bathroom and kitchen had been refitted at least inside the last decade.

'The utilities are included in the rent,' the agent told me with a flash of a smile before checking her watch as she leaned against the marble worktop in the spacious kitchen. I wondered if the timepiece existed on her wrist merely for the purpose of hurrying along appointments like mine: a casual, mildly nagging, reminder to the appointee that time is money in age where everyone uses their phone to check the time and watches are nothing more than statement pieces.

Aging boards under the linoleum creaked the young lady moved to the kitchen door, evidencing that the modernity ran only skin deep in these old rooms. She wore a smart black skirt and blazer with a scarlet scarf which contrasted with her hastily combed and untied hair. The only visible sign of make-up was a faint red smear on her disposable coffee mug. She looked like a washed-out air hostess who had ceased to give a crap. I glanced at her hands, noting a ring. A perceptible compression of her eyebrows told me that I didn't stand a chance even if she hadn't worn, or didn't care about, the gold band. I was, after all, a good ten years her senior; my three days of stubble and shirt which refused to remain tucked into my forty-inch belt surely labelled me as an undatable. I was at that awkward age where everyone should be married, whether it be their first or third marriage. I locked eyes with her – Sharon, I think she was called. She blinked. My eyes swiped left, disregarding her as I had so many times on dating apps with girls who looked too outgoing, or too reserved, or too pouty or self-obsessed.

'There's a lot of interest – as you can imagine,' Sharon, or whatever her name was, said while looking at the floor.

'Screw it. I'll take it.' I said, with a nonchalant shrug, as if I had money to splash around on whims. 'At least the neighbours won't be keeping me up.'

Sharon smiled weakly and glanced at her phone. 'I'll get the application emailed to you. It's a six-month term with a possible extension.'

'Yeah,' I said absently, digging my hands into my pockets.

'You've got to keep all the plants watered. The gardener comes around once a week to weed and whatnot. You've got to keep hallway and stairs clean, and you're not allowed in the main house except for the top floor outside this flat, which is just full of junk.'

'Yeah, I read the listing details online,' I said, unable to hide a tone of bitterness left over from her poorly concealed disgust in me. 'Say, what's the ghost situation here?'

Sharon smirked and made eye contact for second before her attention was drawn to the blank screen of her phone. 'Don't worry. The house isn't old enough for that.'

'Yeah,' I laughed, wondering how old it would need to be for *that*. 'Just wondering who I'm gonna call if it was.'

'Huh?' she said, phone to her ear as she walked to the door.

Three weeks later, I was in. Arriving on my own with all my worldly belongings fitting, depressingly, into my Volvo estate. I had no need of furniture as the flat came complete with its sun-faded furnishings from the eighties or nineties: just as well, as I had none to bring since all that I had owned was still being used by my ex-girlfriend in what had been *our* flat in Plympton. As I stepped out of the car, a gust of wind ruffled my hair and blew some brown detritus across the gravel driveway. It made me shiver and suddenly feel very isolated.

The grounds of the estate were huge, and the nearest neighbour was a five-minute walk down a tree-lined country lane. I could hear the call of a pigeon and some other unidentifiable bird, but none of the background city noises I was used to. The sun was swallowed up by a passing cloud so that the huge granite mansion glowered in the gloom – all warmth seemingly instantly drained out of the cold blotchy stones. The windows of the vacant mansion were covered with heavy drapes, promising darkness inside even during the daytime.

I shuddered and considered myself lucky that I wasn't required to go into the main building, which was certainly enshrined in cobweb, mouse droppings and probably mould. I unlocked the oak door which accessed the stairwell to my flat, which I assumed was originally servants' quarters. There were fifty-one steps up. Every floorboard creaked. The stairs still bore the outline of where carpet once covered the central two feet on each step. Long windows along the stairwell were too narrow to provide much light, yet dead flies and other insects collected on each windowsill.

They keys clattered overloud against the door. Once inside, the flat carried a musty smell that hadn't noticed on my previous visit and suspected it had been masked by air fresheners. I made a quick inspection of the rooms and pulled back all the curtains, letting a little light wash in. The old mahogany sideboards in the living room needed a good dusting, and the thirty-year-old television was definitely not HD ready. Finding most of the room in gloom, I flicked the light switch, startling when shadows lurched as dim yellow light threw another angle of illumination on the clutter of furniture. As the flat was in converted attic space, the high walls angled inward, creating a lot of dark space in the corners.

It took me all of an hour to move my stuff in. I pulled out moth-eaten and mildewed tweed clothes from the wardrobe and stuffed them in a bin liner. I wondered what happened to the previous occupant: obviously a man, probably middle-aged or older judging by his choice of wardrobe. Half remembered horror movie scenes flashed through my imagination, sparking musings of massacres which had led to the house laying abandoned for years. Of course, the estate agent had told me the owner worked abroad in Monte Carlo, and that the house had been on the market for two years without much interest due to the extensive renovations required. The owner needed someone to live-in just to help cover some of the expenses and give the house the impression of occupancy to deter squatters and urban explorers from breaking in. I hadn't thought to ask if there had been any crazed murders, but I supposed they'd have to tell me if there were. I recalled Sharon's dismissive reaction to my enquiry about ghosts and wondered if it might have been to deter any further questions.

Moving into a fully furnished apartment feels strange: In the light of day, with the flat aired out, I had welcomed the savings I would make on not having to purchase my own furnishings and having to lug them up the fifty-one steps. However, when it comes to contemplating sleeping in someone else's bed in a dark, old, groaning house with the moorland wind blowing against fragile windows like it was trying to get at me, it was quite another thing. To make the place more my own, I put my fresh sheets on the old bed, hoovered, dusted and stuffed old belongings into black bags until well after midnight. By the time I contemplated sleeping, the windows – which in daytime provided views across the wooded valley and up toward Penn

Beacon – now only displayed my reflection in a mirror of black: there was not one light source in the world outside, and one could only make out the silhouette of the horizon by pressing face and hands up to the window, or by turning off the lights which I wasn't ready to do yet: yes, I, a forty-year-old man, retired for the night with the bedside light on. I told myself it was so I could navigate around unfamiliar surroundings should I rise needing the bathroom during the small hours.

I awoke with a racing pulse due to some fading dream involving an obscure yet imminent danger. I blinked into the blackness, wondering where I was – as one does when waking to unfamiliar surroundings – and remembering, with no small amount of worry, that I had left the lamp on. I reached for it, clumsily knocking a deodorant can to the ground which clattered with a tinny ring against the wall and then the floor. I swore. My exploring fingers found the lamp. I fumbled for the switch, although my straining eyes were already making out the shapes of the wardrobe, armchair and other furniture. The furthest curtain looked much whiter than the nearer one and contrasted with the oily blackness around it so that it seemed almost aglow. My sight adjusted further and I realised with a slap of shock that what I was looking the shape of a figure in a long white gown, standing in front of the curtain.

Perhaps I cried out. I know I sat bolt upright with my eyelids prised wide as possible around my straining eyeballs. There was definitely something there: no, not something, someone. A white robe, perhaps like a woman's nightie from days of old: frilly with long white sleeves. If there was a person inside it, they were hidden by the folds of the curtain and the length of the dress. I squinted and blinked as my sight became accustomed to the gloom. I could make out long matted locks of hair. Then I noticed an eye: a singular black orb peering through a tangle of hair. I compressed the lamp switch: nothing happened.

Cold crept up my spine and arms, prickling my follicles and making me shiver. I held my breath and found the floor with a foot, taking care not to move too fast lest I might cause this strange apparition to descend upon me.

The dress rippled like a boat's limp sail stirring to life when catching a sudden gust.

I lurched from the bed and raced for the light switch by the door, crying out as my toe slammed against something solid and wooden. I fell, hearing the fluttering of the dress close behind me. I scrambled to my feet, slamming my hand against the wall in search of the switch, crying out in alarm when light exploded throughout the room.

I turned back toward the curtain, blinking again as my eyes searched for the ghostly woman. The drapes billowed, startling me once more. The window was ajar: I hadn't closed it when I aired the room out. I dared to turn the light off for a second and then on again to see if the apparition reappeared: it did not.

A laugh escaped me: a nerve-wrecked sound of relief. I shook my head, embarrassed with myself, but when crossing the room to secure the window my eyes checked the recesses for any sign of the peculiar apparition. The main light stayed on for the rest of the night.

Waking to a warm bed and the sound of light Jazz from my alarm radio, I stretched out satisfied and lazy. I put the events of the night before to the back of my mind, thinking it all a dream until I noticed the light was still on. It was easy to dismiss the incident as an overactive imagination from waking on the first night alone in a creepy old house. The whole character of the house was improved with the curtains pulled back and sunlight washing through the dusty old room. Creaky floorboards no longer sounded ominous, and draughty places could be explained due to their proximity to windows or sealed-up chimneys than to the presence of otherworldly beings.

I made myself some breakfast and went about my work, cleaning scores of dead flies from each of the windowsills on the old staircase and removing such cobwebs as were within reach of the feather duster: I wasn't about to risk a broken neck by standing on a ladder to reach the higher webs on the ceiling. I was sweeping outside when I had the impression of being watched from the house, shuddering with a sudden chill on my spine, but upon inspecting the windows, saw they were all still boarded or heavily curtained. The whisper of wind through the yew trees took on a sinister character which it had lacked moments before.

'Pull yourself together,' I said in self-admonishment, wondering if this was how I was going to be affected during the day, how should I hope to cope at night with all the strange noises of the house settling and the peculiar shadows? More than once throughout the day I felt as if an invisible presence observed me, causing me to spin about in fright as I made a cup of tea, and look over my shoulder squinting down the shadowy corridor as I went out to turn off the light in the hall outside the apartment.

Not only did I sleep with the light on, I left the curtains open too.

'If that doesn't do the trick, you're coming down tomorrow,' I told the curtains as I swept my legs under the bedcovers. Sleep overtook me quickly enough – but not for long.

I awoke with a fright. As with the previous night, a fading dream of danger and fear left only a vague impression: this time of struggling to breathe, gasping for air. I rubbed my chest and sucked in deep breaths, then I was hit with what I can only describe as an invisible wave of energy.

I jerked as if jolted by electricity and sat bolt upright with a ringing in my ears. The air itself felt suddenly still as if a void had occupied the room, blocking out all external sight and sound. The lightbulb dimmed: it didn't go out, but reduced in brilliance so that the corners of the room became dark portals from which some terror might emerge. I found it impossible to draw breath: I'm unsure now if that was by through fear or if some strange oppression had power over me. My pulse throbbed in my chest and my eyes widened, alert for danger, sensing that something was about to happen.

My fingernails bit into my palms as I waited, tense and alert, for whatever danger should reveal itself. My throat was dry, my body trembled despite my overwhelming desire to remain still, hoping that if I didn't move at all, perhaps whatever the strange presence was wouldn't notice me.

A dark crescent appeared on the white ceiling and quickly became circle, as if something had drawn the shape on the plaster, a perfect dark ring. Clear liquid trickled down as the ring thickened. Cold drops landed on the bedcovers and on my exposed foot. The touch of the drops lurched me out of whatever spell I was under. Breath escaped my aching lungs and I sucked in fresh air. The droplets were mere water: more of it trickled down. It smelt odd and I realised it was probably from some rusty pipe or old boiler in the attic. Relief flooded through me; the strangeness of the last few moments again discarded as an overactive imagination.

I moved the bed so that it was out from under the dripping and went to find a bucket to place under the wet circle. When I returned, the circle was gone. I felt the bedcovers and found them to be dry.

The best thing to do seemed to be to to get away from the house for a bit. In the morning, I took a walk to the nearby village: ten minutes by foot through narrow lanes. The village centre, such as it was, consisted only of a small shop, a memorial cross, and a pub which was not yet open. I could've done with a pint, but decided to stop into the shop, where I was greeted by a friendly young woman. I wasted no time in asking what she knew of Heathfield House.

'Oh, that's a lovely house isn't it?' she said, smiling broadly. 'Pity it's been left empty for so long. Could do with a lick of paint; I dread to think what the inside is like.'

'You don't know the half of it,' I said, unable to keep a tone of bitterness from my voice. 'What about the last fellow to live there? The caretaker before me.'

'Oh! There's been a few. Mostly they only stay a few weeks or even just days. Bit creepy on yer own innit?'

'Surely they've not all been scared off by creaky floorboards and dark shadows? How many have there been?'

The shopkeeper shrugged. 'Only been here two year myself. You're the third or fourth that I've known of. I don't know if they've been scared off: it's mostly students who house sit for the summer then quit, or people who wanted a country escape then miss the city life.' She blushed, chewing her lower lip – probably deducing that I was one such absconder from the city.

I paid for the newspaper and supplies, including a four-pack of ale, and bid the shopkeeper good day. She called out after me as my foot was about to touch the pavement outside the store.

'Been bothered by the ghost of the maid, has you now?'

'What?' I said, spinning about.

The shopkeeper's smile disappeared. She lowered her gaze and shrugged. 'Sorry. Just heard folks before talking about a ghost of a maid what haunts the place. Probably just locals trying to scare each other, innit?'

'Quite so,' I said, forcing a laugh. 'Takes all sorts, I suppose. Good day again!'

The shopkeeper's smile returned, and she gave a little wave as I turned away, but I couldn't help but think she'd be telling the next customer about the crazy grouchy fellow who was now occupying Heathfield House.

The shopkeeper's words haunted me on my return to the house. I felt that I should've asked more but was embarrassed to give such superstition any public validity. As I passed the front of the house I looked over all the windows, as had become my habit, but found nothing of note. The hallway was dark even during the day, and so I switched on the light to ascend the stairwell. Three steps from the top, I heard the front door slam. Hard. I jumped, nearly dropping my shopping bag. I leant over the rail and looked down: there was no light from outside. In fact, there was no light at all. The bulb just inside the doorway had gone out and the windowless ground floor was in near darkness.

'Hello?' I called out, squinting into the gloom as I waited for a reply. I wondered if what I'd heard was the lightbulb blowing rather than the door slamming: after all, I'd not heard the door open despite seemingly all the hinges in the house being in dire need of some oil. I deposited my bag at the top of the stairs and walked back down. My footfalls sounded overloud and resounded throughout the stairwell.

It grew darker still as I reached the first floor. The rungs of the banister cast long shadows which turned like spokes on wheel as the light changed. I looked up, noticing sunlight through the stairwell windows had dimmed considerably; I thought that perhaps a cloud had passed over. I returned my attention to descending the stairs. That was when I saw the face staring up at me through the wooden bars of the banister.

The oval face was unnaturally pale. Deathly white. The eyes were large and wide, as if in shock, but with a glazed expression like there was no soul behind them. Long black hair clung to the cheeks in wet clumps as the thing just peered at me through the bars.

I stood transfixed, unable to cry out or move. My brain refused to accept what I was seeing and struggled to make sense of it. I shuddered and felt a burning cold in my left ankle. Only then did I notice the white fingers clasping my leg just above the shoe. Such cold spread from those fingers! The chill quickly spread to my knee, causing my calf muscles to crap and my leg to buckle.

I fell hard on the stairs, sliding down two or three steps on my back. The deathly grasp had released me, but the face at foot of the railing was now level with my own. I looked into the eyes; cold, ice blue, with dilated pupils in which reflected my own screaming face. The mouth of creature dropped open, revealing a gaping blackness like a void inside an empty shell of a body.

Somehow, I manged to scramble away from the demon-like form. I lurched up the stairs like an animal on my hands and feet, flailing for purchase on the smooth wooden steps until I had the presence of mind to stand and run, taking two or three steps at a time. I looked down the gap in the stairwell and saw the oval white face staring up at me with mouth agape – not having moved from the spot where it had grabbed me.

I kicked my bag of shopping as I ran past, slamming through the fire door at the top of the stairwell. I dropped the keys and fumbled them several times before I managed to put the key into the lock, slamming my back against the door once inside, hearing the drumming of my heart pounding through my entire body before I collapsed to the ground in a shuddering pile. I remained on the floor for perhaps an hour before it felt safe to move. A heavy cloying wetness and dark stain down my leg evidenced an involuntary bladder release I had been unaware of until that moment.

I bathed, remaining in the tub until the scalding hot water turned tepid. The heat felt like protection from the empty coldness which the thing on the stairs had emanated; I imagined that the monster could not occupy a place of such warmth, yet my eyes darted from one corner of the room to the next in case the thing should suddenly appear. This state of high alert continued throughout much of the day. I was unable to even contemplate opening my laptop and doing any work. Only in the evening did my logical mind start to try to convince myself that I had imagined the whole affair, although the red mark left on my ankle belied any efforts of pretence that the apparition was a daydream or indication of some kind of psychological collapse. I still hadn't the appetite to eat by the time darkness descended, or even quite the courage to go back out onto the landing for my shopping.

Sleep was impossible. Throughout the night I sat in a wooden chair in the corner of the living room, clutching a torch in case the light should go out. Although still troubled by my encounter, thoughts of phoning the police were banished: there was nothing they would do, and they would think me crazy. I fancied that I might even be cautioned for wasting police time.

Floorboards groaned. Creaking sounds came from outside, in, and above the flat. I remembered the appearance of the dark circle above the bed. As my gaze went up to the ceiling, I heard what sounded like running across the attic. I held my breath. My grip on the torch grew so tight that it hurt. I studied the ceiling, waiting for the rushing of feet or the wet circle to reappear, only releasing my breath in shallow wisps when my lungs felt on the verge of rupturing.

A cold wave passed through me, making me shudder. I saw the figure standing in the opposite corner of the room. Staring at me.

Those same vacant eyes were fixed on me. I saw the figure in its entirety now. The off-colour white frilly underdress, soaking wet and clinging to a waif-like form. Unkempt black hair dripped. The jaw fell open revealing the black emptiness again.

A trembling arm lifted from the apparition's side, extending a bony index finger as the arm rose. The long digit pointed at me, forcing a strangled whine of despair from my throat. Then the hand continued up as the creature pointed to the ceiling.

The dark circle reappeared – just as it had before – drawing a circle about two and a half feet wide. Dark liquid dripped down from the circle, and when I looked back at the ghostly woman she was gone. A glance upwards showed that the circle had also vanished.

The apparition was trying to tell me something.

I went out into the hall and looked up at the small square hatch which led into the attic. At night and in such circumstances, it looked as foreboding as could be. That little white square of wood was all that separated me from whatever terror dwelt in the attic.

The ceilings were high in the old house, and I'd need a step ladder to get to the attic. There was no way in hell that I was going up there at night: not that it would be any lighter in day, but I opted to wait for dawn before exploring. I continued to stare at the hatch until the hallway was bathed in light from the kitchen window, then went out to fetch a cobweb strewn ladder from down the hall outside the flat. Despite my earlier misgivings about leaving the apartment, I felt that as I was following the apparent bidding of the apparition, and therefore safe from encountering it. For now, at least.

The top floor was open planned had become a store for old or broken furniture and things that were no longer needed. I had to move mouldy armchairs, a pushchair, and a dusty dollhouse to get to the ladder. The unwieldy thing clanged against the doorframe as I tried to manoeuvre it into my apartment. I wondered at how much space there was up there: there couldn't be more than a crawlspace above. I don't have much tolerance for heights, and about two-thirds of the way up the wonky ladder is about where I started to feel a bit giddy when looking down.

I stood atop the stepladder with shaking legs, steadying myself with one hand on the ceiling. I pushed up one edge of the hatch, which gave way with a squeak. I looked through the narrow gap I had made and saw only blackness, cursing myself for not having the foresight to pick up a torch. I let the trapdoor drop back into place and went back down the ladder, feeling better about descending than the ascent. I picked up a Maglite from the kitchen, having decided that the light from my camera phone would have been insufficient – and that I might have dropped the damned expensive contraption down the ladder if caught in a fright. I put the small torch between my teeth, and my hands on the sides of the ladder, and looked up at the hatchway. The torch fell from my teeth, clattering against the ladder rungs as my mouth hung open in shock: the hatchway was wide open.

A perfectly black square hung above me where the white painted wooden board had been just moments before. I glanced around in case the square of wood had fallen down somehow, knowing it had not as I'd heard nothing in the seconds I'd been away. I shuddered as I stared into the darkness, knowing that I must ascend into it if I were ever to have any peace. My legs trembled as I climbed with hands slick with sweat on rough wood. I imagined those eyes peering over the edge of the hatch at me and the dark hair cascading down like tendrils.

I took the torch from my mouth, gripping it as hard as possible, I made sure that the beam was turned on before my head was level with the entrance to the attic. Slowly, I rose to peer into the attic. Dust particles were illuminated in torchlight, looking like a blizzard. Cobwebs hung like sheets from support beams. The loft was about six feet high at the highest point, but the roof narrowed sharply so that it was only possible to crawl through much of it. I cast the light around in an arc, hoping to survey everything from the relative safety of the hatchway.

Torchlight illuminated a small dusty pile of leather-bound books, a couple of old chests, and a barrel. I kept the light on the barrel, figuring it was around the location where the wet circle had appeared on my ceiling. I felt some relief, deciding that a roof leak above the barrel might have caused water to collect on the top of the barrel and then overspill down the sides, creating the circle of wet I had witnessed. The only thing for it was to investigate the barrel myself.

I climbed into the loft with some reluctance and crawled over the dirty floor; glad I had not worn good clothes, as all manner of detritus was being collected upon my person as I shuffled interminably forward, sneezing on the dust I was disturbing. Upon reaching the barrel, I felt the top: it was dry. I tried to rock the barrel: it was heavy and sloshed loudly. One might think that finding a barrel of presumed liquor in the loft might bring feelings of joy, but I was sure that whatever was inside was long spoiled. I checked for any printing which might indicate the contents but found nothing. I picked up one of the leatherbound tomes nearby and, blowing the dust off the cover, I opened it to see that it was some kind of ledger. The hardened and crackling pages were difficult to read, but I deducted that it was some kind of commerce log. I was able to discern some dates, covering the years 1859 to 1861. The next book was a diary, although the elegant handwriting was hard to follow, I imagined it to be contemporary with the ledger.

A sloshing sound made me jump. I dropped the torch again, cursing as I reached for it. The sound had come from the barrel. I wondered if I had nudged it without noticing but was fairly certain I had not – then I realised that rather than an old ale barrel in which a tap would be hammered into the bottom, this barrel had a lid. I was able to easily lift one edge with relatively little effort. A strong smell of liquor filled my nostrils. I was not overly familiar with spirits, but the scent was off: spoiled, rotten even.

I shone the torchlight on the surface of the liquid, finding the barrel to be quite full. I dipped a finger and then licked it; the liquor was bitter and left an aftertaste almost like rotten fish. I put my hand to the lid, ready to push it back in place when I stopped, feeling a shudder run through me.

Something pale moved in the barrel. It came to the surface with a swarm of thick black tendrils around it: a face, cold and dead.

I screamed and bolted for the hatch. I made the bottom of the ladder in seconds, somehow managing to not fall and injure myself. Not satisfied with evacuating the loft, I left the flat and the house, running down the driveway until I was clear of the entire estate. Only then I felt safe enough to call the police.

I stayed in a bed and breakfast that night, remaining awake with the light on. The police were able to discern quite quickly that the body was a century and a half old, but it wasn't until the next day that a kindly middle-aged policewoman sat down with me at the little station in nearby Ivybridge where I was given a warm cup of cocoa.

'I'm sure it was quite a shock finding that in your loft,' she said with grimace.

'You could say that,' I said, sipping my drink; still quite unable to fully cleanse the taste of the barrel's contents from my palate.

'Turns out the body has been there since eighteen ninety-one,' the policewoman said. 'Died of natural causes, so you've no need to worry about a century n' alf old murderer stalking your house.'

'She was a maid?' I said.

'How'd you know that?' the policewoman straightened and frowned as she might have done if a suspect had blurted out something incriminating.

I shrugged. 'Guessed. How'd you know she died of natural causes?'

'The diary. Turns out it was kept by the original owner of the house. One of the servants died during a harsh winter and her body was put in a barrel of rum to preserve it for burial in the spring. An entry two months after her death complains that the only known relative still hadn't come to claim the body. Looks like she was then just... forgotten. But don't worry, we're looking at getting her buried down the road in St. Michael's church.'

I nodded, lost in thought, wondering if the apparition had been trying to lure me into discovering her remains so she could be laid to rest. I felt some comfort in that thought, but the memory of the body in the stinking vat was sure to keep me awake for many nights to come.

'So, will you be going back to the flat in Heathfield House after that scare?' The police officer's eyebrow arched enquiringly.

I downed the last of my cocoa, the hot liquid searing my tongue and throat. I slammed the steaming mug down on the cheap laminate table. 'Not a bloody chance.'

The Circle in the Woods

'Hi, Greer. I'm at the woods. Just about to set off.' Eve pinned the smartphone between ear and shoulder as she zipped up her rucksack.

'I thought you were gonna call me before you got there,' Greer said, the pout detectable in her tone despite the weak phone signal intermittently making her voice sound digitized.

Eve took the phone back in hand, checking the signal strength: two bars. She looked up at the tall Douglas Firs surrounding the carpark. Row upon row of long, straight trunks with green bristles towered over a carpet of moss-covered boulders and scatterings of fallen branches. The little carpark felt like a tiny grey island under threat of being swallowed by cascading waves of firs blanketing seemingly impossibly steep hillsides.

'Hon, I don't think I'm gonna get much signal out here. The trees are like fifty metres tall, and the hills are massive. I'll be sure to call when I'm back at the car.'

'That's why you were supposed to call before you got there. It's so crazy going out on your own. You couldn't have just waited until the weekend when Jasmine and Nassir come down for the end of term break, could you?'

'C'mon, gimme a break, Greer. I told you I can't risk someone else discovering it before me.' Eve pushed swung the door of her Nissan Micra shut, locked the car, and put the keys in her pocket.

'Ok, ok. Evie-anna Jones. I know you gotta go find your precious stones. Just make sure you're back here by eight cos I wanna have drinks before we go out. Oh, and one other thing…'

'Yeah?'

'If you find the Ark of the Covenant, don't open it or the Nazi ghosts will escape.'

'Yeah. Thanks for that, Greer. See you at eight.'

'By eight.'

Eve hung up the call. She slung the backpack over her shoulders and jostled it into a comfortable position. Satisfied that she was ready to go, she tucked her jaw-length blonde bob behind her ears and opened the GPS app on her phone. The screen shimmered with the reflection of unusually bright March sunlight. Eve moved under the shade of the nearest tree where the screen could be clearly seen. She had already plotted the route, but it hadn't looked so steep on the app. A red line on the virtual map followed twisting pathways through the Woodland Commission's forest, then off-track through a few hundred metres of woods into a clearing where the mysterious stone formations should be found. The app indicated that the walk would take one hour, leaving plenty of time for archaeological examination, measurements, photographs, and a light picnic before going back for the usual Thursday night festivities at the student union club.

An information board beside the path declared *Welcome to Ferntor Forest*. A basic map displayed woodland trails and the nearby reservoir alongside illustrations of local wildlife, and a few black and white photographs of archaeological remains in the vicinity dating from the Bronze Age through the Medieval period and into the Industrial Age. Eve glanced over the board, wrinkling her nose at the thought of going out partying in the evening. It wasn't that she disliked the student lifestyle, but next year was the final year of her master's degree and she didn't want to still be spending two evenings a week holding back her housemate's hair as she puked up her Vodka Red Bulls.

Eve started off on the dusty track into the woods. The temperature dropped a few degrees under the gloom of the colossal firs; Eve wondered whether wearing her khaki shorts was the best option, but at least she had a fleece and a raincoat in the pack – just in case: you could never be too cautious with moorland weather.

The track started out with a gradual incline which evolved into steeper and longer slopes as it wound around hillsides. Occasional glimpses through the trees where avenues of firs had been felled provided wonderful vistas of the reservoir and the granite-flecked moorland slopes above it. The reservoir was a wonderful deep blue, glistening in places. Birdsong was an almost constant companion; Eve recognised the chatter of Wrens, chirping of Robins, and the rapid tapping of a woodpecker somewhere in the distance.

The inclines and descents soon worked Eve into a mild sweat. She stopped at a junction of pathways and sat on a wide, fallen log. She took off her pack and pulled out the water bottle, taking several long gulps, then checked the navigation app which indicated that a one-and-a-half miles had been walked in just under an hour: slightly over halfway to the destination. Eve grimaced: she hadn't factored so many ascents into the route, and places where she had planned to cut through the trees had proved to be either too steep or the undergrowth too thick.

The sound of trickling water caught Eve's attention. She turned to her left and noticed a narrow stream flowing alongside the steep path. The climb looked long, curving around a hillside with the top of the path out of sight. She sighed and took another swig, momentarily thinking it would've been wiser to wait for her friends to come down from Bristol to provide company and encouragement. She put the bottle back in her pack and braced for the climb – determined to conquer it in one burst without stopping.

Eve strode at the slope, keeping up a quick pace, tugging on the straps of the backpack as if to pull herself up the hill. She leaned into the incline, looking down at the dirt track to avoid concentrating on how far was left to go, and to remain mindful of occasional jutting stones or bits of half-buried root that threatened to trip the unwary walker.

A maroon splotch on one of the rocks caught Eve's eye. She quickly spotted another and wondered briefly it was blood before dismissing it as merely indictive of copper deposits from the stream having soaked into the path and somehow staining some of the stones. A few steps more and she saw a scarlet droplet about the size of a penny coin on the dirt.

'Now, that *is* blood,' Eve muttered. Her searching eyes picked out more dots.

The droplets became increasingly clustered together and larger in size. Something had been injured quite badly. Eve wondered what the casualty was: a rabbit mauled by a fox, or perhaps a pony that had cut its mouth on something someone had carelessly discarded. She hadn't seen any ponies, but their droppings were more than evident.

Eve determined to find the source of the blood. She had kept the phone number for Devon Livestock Protection and the two main animal charities programmed into her phone ever since discovering an injured sheep at the roadside the previous summer. She pulled the phone from her pocket and pulled a face: no signal.

The path levelled out and split into left and right routes. Eve looked back down the way she had come, surprised to have already reached the summit of the climb; her mission in following the bloody trail had distracted from the effort of the ascent – even though her calves ached a little. The blood trail continued along the right-hand route – the same route Eve needed to follow. The drops were barely a pace apart and sometimes clustering where the creature had presumably paused. The blood looked fresh. She but her boot on a drop that had landed on a smooth stone and managed to smudge it with a light rub of her foot. She wondered how long it would take for droplets to dry: not long, she presumed.

The blood trail crossed the path and the foot-high verge bordering the woodland. The undergrowth beyond was as thick with green shrubs, granite chunks, and broken branches. The density of trees blocked much of the sunlight, and although it wasn't too dark to walk into, it was foreboding enough to discourage the effort.

Eve squinted into the forest. There was no sign of any injured animal, but any small creature would be able to move freely among the foliage and mossy boulders with little chance of being spotted from the path. She decided to give up the chase: the risk of twisting an ankle – or worse – while searching the cluttered undergrowth was quite high, while the chance of finding the poor creature seemed very low.

Eve sighed. Perhaps she was following the blood trail the wrong way: maybe it had bled profusely to begin with, and then the bleeding had stemmed as the animal went down the trail. Eve was definitely not going back down the hill to look for whatever it was. Other people walked these paths – the forestry workers for one. If the animal could be helped, hopefully someone would find it.

The navigation app showed there wasn't much path left to follow before an off-trail route would need to be found that led to the suspected stone circle. Eve realised that if the terrain was very difficult, she might not be able to get to the circle at all. It had all looked much simpler on a virtual map. She told herself that the terrain would be fine. The ground near the circle wasn't likely too overgrown or rocky: if it had been, it wouldn't have been possible to discern a circle from the satellite images. She shook off thoughts of the stone circle being just a geological coincidence and moved on.

The next bend in the track provided a new obstacle: yellow and black tape crossed the path; tied off around tries and backed up by a couple of traffic cones. A sign on the left side of the path showed an exclamation mark inside a bright yellow triangle, the words underneath declared 'Tree felling'. A larger sign on the right side of the path showed a logo of a man's head in a hard hat above four lines of text:

Woodland Commission

Danger

Path Closed

No Entry

'You gotta be effing kidding!' Eve protested.

She looked about for a diversion sign, but the only route was back the way she had come. The navigation app showed only a few minutes' walk before she'd need to turn off the path, then a few hundred metres through the trees to the destination. It was too close to give up.

Eve listened. There was no sound of chainsaws. No chopping of axes. Only birdsong and the breeze. There had been no evidence of anyone working throughout the forest, or even any human life at all. She waited by the yellow and black tape for another minute, listening just to be sure, before ducking under the ephemeral barrier and continuing her way.

Soon after the tape was an avenue that had been cut through a line of trees, connecting the path with one lower downhill. A stack of trunks beside the track were guarded by a pictorial sign warning against disturbing the log pile for danger of being squished by a cascade of toppling trunks. Eve perched the edge of the bottom log and checked the app again: it was time to leave the path.

It would be all uphill to the destination. The undergrowth looked less severe than much of what she'd passed and there didn't seem to be so much clitter among overgrown thickets where hidden crevasses might trap an ankle. She studied the way up, trying to pick out a route between the rows of trees, patches tree detritus, and bushy undergrowth she'd prefer to avoid.

'What do you think are you doing?'

Eve shot to her feet with a startled gasp and fumbled with her phone, dropping it.

A rugged-looking man in a checked shirt, jeans, and a hardhat had appeared at the other end of the log pile. He stood in a nonchalant posture and made no attempt to hide his judgemental smirk at her alarm.

Eve stooped to snatch up her phone and backed up a couple of steps. 'Sorry, I'm… uhm. I just got turned around in the forest and was trying to find my way back,' Eve said, tucking her hair back behind her ear.

The man sniffed and wiped his nose with the back of a gloved hand. 'I meant what do you think you're doing sitting on the wood? The sign is there for a reason.'

'Oh,' Eve gestured at the log pile which was stacked higher than she was tall. 'Sorry. It was just... I wasn't thinking. No damage done, right?' She flashed a nervous smile.

The man returned the smile. His yellowed teeth spoiled his otherwise roguish good looks. Eve reflected that with his brown tangled hair and unshaven, angular jaw, he wouldn't have looked out of place in a catalogue for outdoors clothes – at least if his clothes were new rather than the well-worn attire he sported.

'Did you not see the tape across the path?' The man nodded in the direction of the makeshift barrier which was out of sight around a bend or two in the path.

'Oh, no. I must have come a different way.'

'Oh aye?' The man grinned again. 'Funny. Thought I saw you coming that way.'

Eve narrowed her eyes accusingly and looked him up and down, seeing an opportunity to put the lumberjack on the defensive. 'Are you spying on me?'

The man grimaced. 'No. I was marking trees for felling when I heard you plodding along. We ain't cutting today, so I was gonna just let you go on by. When I saw you sit on the trunks, I thought I best warn you off.'

Eve bit her lip, embarrassed. 'Yeah, sorry. Guess I'm not good with signs.'

'Where you trying to get to? The car park? I can direct you.'

'Uh, no. It's ok. I can manage.'

The man lifted the brim of his hard hat and crossed his arms. 'I worked here my whole life: nobody knows these trails like I do.'

'All your life? You're like, what? Twenty-eight?'

'Thirty. My pa worked here and his before him and so on. I dropped out of school at twelve to work here for a tenner a week which I gave to my mam. Got pretty much every inch of this place stored up here.' He tapped his temple.

Eve glanced at her phone, then off into the woods where she planned to hike. She wondered if she could trust him with her secret destination. She closed her eyes and took a deep breath, deciding if she didn't confide in the guy, he wasn't likely to let her just stroll off the path into the wilderness.

The man waited with arms folded and head tilted.

'Ok, Mister. I'll tell you, but you gotta promise to keep it to yourself. Ok?'

'Tell me what?'

'I'm a landscape archaeology student and one of my hobbies is remote viewing. You know what that is?'

The man shrugged one shoulder. 'Is it watching TV? I don't own a television. Not one that's worked in fifteen years anyway.'

'No, no. It's to do with satellites. I noticed the satellite data for this area was updated in the last couple months and so I took a look. I found what appears to be a stone circle not far from here and it looks like it could be an undiscovered archaeological feature – right on the highest hilltop in these woods. Right up there.' Eve pointed.

The man followed the direction she indicated. He seemed to think for a moment then looked up at the sky, taking off his hat. 'Satellites? Can they see us now?'

'What?' Eve chuckled, stopping when the man gave her an annoyed look. 'Uh, no. It's just the images for this area before weren't clear. The deforested parts are much clearer in these new photos. I just don't know how such an obvious feature escaped detection before.'

'There's nothing up there. All the stone remnants are down the valley nearer the water.'

'Well, that's what I want to find out. I just want to go and peek. Maybe take a few measurements and photographs. That'd be ok, right?'

'You're not allowed off the pathways. The info board in the car park says that. You really aren't good with signs, are you?'

'Terrible,' Eve smiled. 'So, do you mind?'

'Well, yes. If you get hurt, I'll get in trouble for allowing you to go up there. Nobody but me ever goes up there.'

'Not even the other lumberjacks?'

The man guffawed. 'Lumberjacks? We're rangers and tree surgeons. Anyway, I worked this hilltop for years and never saw any stone circle. Got a cabin down the road so I never even venture off the hilltop except to cash my paycheque and shop for supplies.'

'Cheque? What is this, the Nineteen-Eighties?' Eve stopped herself from laughing when the guy's straight expression didn't crack at her jape.

'I don't use a bank – if you must know. My point is, if there was a stone circle up here, I'd have seen it cos I'm always up here. Now, if you want directions down to the car park, I'll help you out. Otherwise, I think you best be heading back the way you came, Miss.'

Eve winced and sucked her bottom lip. She wasn't about to head back without even taking a look, but there didn't seem to be any way the guy was going to let her go on.

'Ok, dude. You know what? You're probably right. I'm just going to head back down to the car. I've been out here long enough anyway.'

The Ranger nodded. 'Want me to lead you down?'

'I can find the way. Just keep going down, right?'

'Can't go far wrong. I'll check the car park later to make sure you've managed to get back ok.'

'Thanks!' Eve smiled as she turned away and waggled her fingers in the semblance of a wave. She walked a dozen paces and turned to see the man give a small salute. She continued on, sensing him watching, making sure she left. She wondered if it was so obvious that she had no intention of departing. She walked back to the tape and ducked under it and stole a glance behind: there was no sign of the ranger. She knew it was possible he was watching from behind a tree or might follow at a short distance, so she kept going, looking back every now and then.

Eve walked a hundred paces past the tape to where the road started to curve more steeply back downhill. She studied the undergrowth in the woods: it was the tangled and untrodden terrain she wanted to avoid, but there was little choice. She watched the path for any sign of the reclusive ranger for a minute or two before deciding that she wasn't being stalked, then climbed over a small embankment and into the woods.

The ground quickly became lumpy and uneven. Twigs other detritus masked much of the surface. In places it was hard to see if the fallen green and brown matter lay on solid ground or covered one of the many hollows between mossy rocks. It was only possible to take five or six steps in a straight line before having to pause to calculate the best path for the next few paces.

'This is ridiculous,' Eve muttered. The app indicated that was nearly four hundred metres to the objective. She sighed, feeling resolve deflating. The terrain sloped upwards at about a twenty-degree angle, and already her calves were burning. She gave thought to going back and waiting until next week when there would be back-up. 'No,' she whispered. 'I'm here now. It's not that far.'

The ascent was accompanied by a gradual submergence into shadowy gloom. The trees were planted more closely together and seemed taller than those further downhill. Occasional toppled trunks leaned precariously against their former neighbours and creaked with each breath of the wind – Eve made sure to give those a wide berth and wondered with some irritation why the ranger didn't do something about them if he knew the hilltop so well.

Birdcalls were varied and constant companions, as was the sound of snapping twigs. Eve squinted at a particularly loud snap, trying to peer through dense undergrowth of brown and green vegetation, but was unable to discern if the sound was caused by some woodland creature or if it was merely a large branch falling.

Eve persisted: huffing, cursing, and stumbling more than once, until the incline seemed to plateau out. The app showed that the supposed stone circle was less than sixty metres away but the density of tree trunks and undergrowth obscured line of sight.

'You better be there,' Eve grumbled as she trudged on, taking a wide detour around a two-metre-deep crevasse that was criss-crossed by branches. She kept her phone in hand, glancing at it to ensure she was heading closer to her destination. The foliage became sparser as she neared a clearing which she knew marked her objective. A small diversion around a heather covered mound brought Eve to the edge of what was clearly a wide, circular grove. Eve stopped and stared, unable to process the relevance of the sight in front of her, daring not to blink in case it disappeared.

In the middle of the clearing stood a circle of some thirty large stones: each between one and two metres tall. Every stone was marked with black swirls and patterns of Celtic design alongside jagged symbols painted in red which Eve didn't recognise. A large mound, nearly as tall as she was, lay in the centre of the circle. The clearance around the stones formed an almost perfect circle, indicating that the trees had either been planted or cut to create the circular grove. Eve stared at the circle for a few minutes before collecting her thoughts.

She brought up her phone and snapped an image, taking wide shots of the circle and zooming in on the nearest stones. She intended to take photos from every angle, then measure the stones and the distances between them, as well as the diameter of the entire circle. The real prize, she hoped, was the mound at the centre which Eve dared to hope contained a sealed burial. Her imagination ran ahead of her: what if this undiscovered circle contained remains to challenge even those found at Whitehorse Hill? Even if the site had been robbed centuries ago, the circle was undiscovered by contemporary standards and would ensure her a career in landscape archaeology.

Eve paid the painted symbols little attention, figuring them to have been applied by the ranger or one of his chums. Then her spirit deflated: If some idiot had daubed the stones in paint, it wasn't a new discovery. There was no way the strange designs could survive even a season in the elements without being touched up: there was no doubt the Woodland Commission guys were responsible. Why were they keeping it secret?

Eve quickly looked around the circle. Not one of the stones were recumbent: how likely was it they had stayed upright for three thousand years? All the erect Dartmoor circles had been righted in the Victorian era, and even some of them had fallen down again since. She groaned inwardly: what if the stone circle wasn't ancient at all? Perhaps the rangers made it for a laugh, or as an art project, or even some kind of wiccan ceremony.

'One way to find out,' Eve murmured. She knew that if an empty burial chamber lay at the centre, it would confirm the site was likely to be ancient. Eve stomped toward the five-foot high mound. As she neared the top, Eve could see that it dipped downward in the centre – an indication that the ground had collapsed or been dug out. She reached the summit and then stopped.

The middle of the knoll descended into a small pit, at the centre of which were four flat granite stones which formed a large rectangular burial cist some two metres long and a metre wide. Inside the rectangle lay a bulging, brown hessian sack which filled most of the burial chamber.

Eve wrinkled her nose. Why would someone leave that in there? What did it contain? Wiccan offerings? A dead animal? Or was it just a bag of leaves? A sudden rush of wind made her shiver. She rubbed her arms for warm. Then the sack moved.

The sack twisted, as if it were fidgeting. It was only then that Eve noticed the string bound around the sack in two places, dividing it into thirds.

Eve let out a startled cry.

The sack sat up and let out a muffled moan.

Eve turned and ran, sprinting for the tree line. The ground and trees seemed to wobble and contort like in a shaky-cam horror movie. She didn't stop until reaching the edge of the grove where she collapsed behind the nearest boulder that was large enough to conceal her and pressed her face against the green-flecked stone, holding onto the mossy boulder and screwing her eyes shut, trying to stifle a panicked sob.

It was a few minutes before Eve could move. She dared to peer over the boulder. Imagination conjuring an image of the sack-creature standing upright, twisting one way and then the other as it searched for her, and then charging headlong at her at an unimaginable speed when it sighted her sneaking a look from the hiding place.

There was, however, no sign of the sack-thing. The only disturbances in the glade were the shadows of a passing cloud slowly creeping over the grass and stones. Eve remained fixated on the central mound. Minutes seemed to pass without movement or sound. She forced herself to run the images of the frightful seconds through her mind: the moving sack, the bindings. She fleetingly wondered if she had imagined it – perhaps a result of having watched too many low-budget horror flicks, but it felt real. Whatever it was, it had been bound. Perhaps they needed help. Eve thought of running back down the hill to summon the ranger, but instantly changed her mind, deciding there was a fair chance the ranger was responsible: he had denied the existence of the stone circle and ordered Eve off the hill. She also considered that perhaps what she'd glimpsed was just a bag of leaves and the movement was nothing more than the work of the breeze.

Eve decided to go back and check. Whatever it was, it couldn't get out of the cist, so there wasn't any overt danger. Besides, if she ran for help and it turned out to be nothing, she would not only look stupid but could be in trouble for trespassing.

'Ok, you can do this,' Eve whispered, forcing herself from the hiding place. She trod carefully back into the clearing, taking an effort to create as little sound as possible. The tapping of a nearby woodpecker helped to camouflage footfalls.

Eve paused at the bottom of the mound, listening. There was no discernible sound from the cist. She held her breath and ascended. There was the rough, hessian sack. Eve thought she could see the rise and fall of breathing under the sack.

'Hello,' Eve said, barely above a whisper.

The top of the sack twisted, as if someone inside it had turned their head toward her. The sack didn't answer.

'Hello,' Eve said louder. 'Are you... stuck?'

The sack writhed and made muffled vocal sounds.

Eve looked about, fearful that some hidden danger might be waiting at the edge of the grove. She took a deep breath and knelt beside the cist, searching the sack for an opening. Finding it, she pulled it open. Two pale white feet wiggled desperately, but the rope prevented Eve from pulling the sack up far. She tugged at the bindings, but they were too tight to give enough leeway.

Eve took off her backpack and fumbled at the zip with shaking fingers. She rummaged through the pack, looking for her penknife, spilling her flask, map, and a glove out onto the grass before remembering that the knife was in the side-pocket.

It took an infuriatingly long time for her panicking hands to gain possession of the tiny metal tool and to open the four-centimetre blade. She put the knife under the rope and sawed with the tiny blade.

'Stop fidgeting. You're making it harder,' Eve hissed.

The sack stopped struggling but breathed hard and made occasional sounds conveying desperate urgency.

The blunt little penknife struggled to cut through the rope fibres. Eve grimaced, realising it would take a minute or more to saw through the thin rope. Finally, she was able to pull the blade through the last few strands of rope.

The person in the sack struggled and twisted as Eve uncoiled the rope. Once the rope was cast aside, she helped the person to stand, then pulled the top of the sack, dragging it off its prisoner.

Eve gasped. A young man in his mid-twenties stood before her – completely naked. He shielded his groin with bound hands. A rag had been used as a gag and tied so tightly around his mouth that it pinned the corners of his mouth back in a freakish grin. The man's black hair clung to his scalp and forehead in sweaty clumps. His body was flecked with scratches and grazes. Eve looked away, embarrassed.

'Sorry, Guy. I'm gonna have to cut those bonds. You'll need to hold out your wrists.'

The man tried to speak but the gag transmuted the words into incomprehensible mumblings.

'Wait: I'll get the gag first.'

185

The knot of the gag was a tight ball inside the man's mouth. It was wet with saliva and looked tricky to unpick. She managed to hook a finger under the gag behind the man's ear, but it was tied so tightly that when she tried to move it the man grimaced and bucked his head away from her, hurting her finger which was snagged under the rag.

Eve muttered a curse. 'Ok, I'm gonna do the wrists first then you can do the gag yourself. Hold out your hands.' She looked around, trying to remember where she put the penknife after cutting the rope, then finding it in one of her pockets.

'You know, in movies when they rescue a captive that's been tied up, they always take the gag off first – as if it's more important that they can speak than make a quick escape. I always thought that was dumb, and there I go trying your gag before freeing your hands.'

The man held out his cupped hands. His eyes fixed on hers, unblinking.

Eve gulped. She gripped his arm to hold it steady as she sawed through the binding. She kept her eyes on the task but felt her cheeks burning at the proximity of the stranger's nakedness. After a minutes' work, she was able to pull the knife up through the last few strands. The rope snapped and she staggered back, almost falling down the mound.

The man pulled at his gag. He winced at the effort before gesturing for Eve to hand him the knife. He spent a few minutes doubled over as he tried to saw through the soggy material, looking every bit like he was trying to extract a tooth. Finally, the dirty rag came away in his hand and he threw it to the floor.

'Bet that feels better,' Eve said, immediately feeling stupid for saying it.

The man groaned, rubbing his cheeks. He worked his jaw a few times as if to check that it still operated correctly, then his eyes fell on Eve again.

They stared at each other for a few seconds before Eve averted her gaze.

'I don't suppose you know where your clothes are at?' Eve said, blushing.

'Gone. I'll have to use some of yours.'

'What?' Eve gasped, blinking. 'Oh, you mean spare clothes. Sorry, thought we were having a *Terminator* moment there. Hang on.'

Eve emptied out the contents of her pack, producing a spare pair of socks, a fleece, and a raincoat. She turned away while the naked man dressed himself. It felt like a silly gesture: she'd already seen him naked despite her best attempts not to.

Eve turned back when it sounded like the young man had finished dressing. The socks were clearly tight and pinched his skin above the ankles. The fleece just about fit, but was almost skin-tight and the sleeves were a couple of inches short. He wore the raincoat like a kilt. He looked ridiculous, but his modesty was covered.

'You can keep the coat,' Eve said.

'We need to get away from here.' The man had a local accent. He looked about, seemingly checking the tree line.

'Why? What is it? Who tied you up and left you there?'

'I need to get out of here before they come back,' the young man said. His gaze fell on the water bottle among the upended contents of the backpack. He snatched it up, quickly unscrewed it and gulped the contents down, drinking the entire measure before dropping the empty bottle.

'Um, do you want food? I've got…'

'No. Let's go. Now.' The man started off toward the tree line.

Eve hurriedly stuffed her belongings back into her pack and went after him. The man slowed once he was out of the clearing, taking an effort to pick out a route through the tangled brush and uneven ground.

'Maybe I should lead, I've got shoes and a navigation app,'

The man span about.

'You got a phone signal?'

'Oh…' Eve picked the phone out of her pocket and moved it about. 'No. The map is downloaded so I don't need phone coverage. I can stand on the mound in the clearing and see if I get any bars.'

'No. We can't stay. It's too dangerous.'

The man moved on. Eve followed in his footsteps, looking about for any signs of movement among the trees.

'Who are you getting away from? The wood cutter guy?'

'What guy?' the man turned abruptly, facing Eve.

'Uh, I saw a lumberjack... well, ranger he said, marking trees. He was down on the road below here. Was it him that did this to you?'

The man grunted and moved off again, fixating on picking out his route. 'Bloody socks!' he snarled. He sat on a rock and pulled the socks off. Dirt and twigs covered the sky-blue wool. He threw the socks into the undergrowth and moved off, barefoot.

'You're welcome, by the way,' Eve mumbled.

It felt like a long time before the track was in view. The man ducked behind the nearest clump of bracken. Eve knelt beside him.

'What is it?' she said.

'That ranger you spoke of – where was he?'

Eve checked the navigation app, noticing that they'd come down about halfway between where she turned off the track and where the yellow tape was.

'Not far. Just over that way a bit,' she pointed. 'So, it *was* him?'

'I don't know,' the man said. 'I never saw their faces.'

'Their? How many...'

'Shhh!' The guy looked about urgently. He licked his lips and looked Eve in the eyes. 'This lumberjack: he saw you and let you go?'

'Yeah,' Eve shrugged. 'He was a bit *The Hills Have Eyes* though. Told me not to come up here.'

'Ok, but he saw you and let you go. That means he's probably not one of them, or if he is, they aren't interested in you.'

'Why would they be interested in *me*?' Eve's voice rose in pitch higher than she intended, causing the guy to crane his neck

188

above the bracken and check that the sound hadn't alerted any concealed foe.

'Ok, look… what's your name?'

'Eve. What's your…'

'Ok, look Eve: you can go on down to the path. Check the coast is clear. If the guy is there, greet him loudly so I can hear. If he's not there, I'll come on down.'

'Are you kidding?' Eve hissed.

'They're after me, not you. Besides, I don't have shoes.'

Eve grimaced and closed her eyes. The guy's plan sounded logical; it was the best idea, even if she was taking all the risk.

'Fine,' she said. 'Just answer me first: Who are you and why are they after you?'

'My name is Paul. I don't know why they want me. I was camping near the forest when they pulled me out of the tent and dragged me up here. Satanists or something.'

'Satanists? Christ! You said you didn't see their faces?'

'Yeah. They wore masks with antlers on their heads.' Paul spoke quickly, sounding almost irritated.

'How long have you been held up here?'

'I don't know. Look, let's just get going. The longer we hang about the more likely they'll catch us.'

'Ok,' Eve said, rising slowly on unsteady feet, squinting through the trees and straining to listen for any unusual sound. The snap of a twig somewhere startled her. She had to force herself to accept that she'd been hearing twigs snap all day and that it was a common woodland sound.

'Are you going or what?' Paul seethed.

'And they say chivalry is dead,' Eve snapped. She moved off without another word, staying alert for signs of life even as she concentrated on picking a route through the undergrowth. Caution made the descent agonizingly slow. A horrible shape in her peripheral vision startled her. She ducked down into a ball, hugging her hands around her knees, realising when she focused on the shape that it was a splintered tree trunk, which at a glimpse resembled a figure with terrible horns coming out of its head.

Eve waited while her pulse returned to its normal rate. She wondered if she had cried out in her momentary panic. She looked up toward where Paul was concealed, but couldn't see him and wasn't sure exactly which clump of foliage he was hidden behind. She imagined him glaring down at her, silently berating her for stopping.

The navigation app showed that the path was only another ten or so metres away. Eve forced herself to get up and move, holding her breath between each step and only releasing it when the foot was landed firmly on the ground. She remained tense – careful to avoid kicking a stone or snapping a twig. It was impossible to move in complete silence, but such noise as she made was no greater than that of the birdsong and the wind through the firs.

Finally, her boot landed on the track with a clump. The yellow tape across the path was just ten or twelve metres away, swaying lightly with the breeze. There was no sign of the ranger.

Eve made sure to look about carefully, even walking to the tape and looking down the path for sight of the ranger. Finding nothing of note, she returned the point where she'd stepped onto the track and waved up the hill, hoping Paul could see her.

Eve checked her phone. There was no signal, but an email had come through, so she must have picked up a fleeting signal during the descent. She paced the path, holding the phone up at arm's length to no avail. She saw Paul, picking his way through the trees, following her line of descent. She willed him to hurry; the character of the woods felt much more sinister since finding a naked man bound in a sack. She felt exposed on the path: as if all manner of concealed wildlife silently observed her, along with things more sinister lurking behind the rocks. Eve shuddered, trying to dispel notions of Devil-worshipers, demons, and Bigfoot.

'Shouldn't watch stupid old films,' Eve muttered to herself.

'Is it clear?' Paul said, standing on the verge of the path, craning to look each way along the track.

'Well, yeah.' Eve gestured along the empty track.

Paul descended to the path with cautious steps, hunched over as if ready to hide or flee at a moment's notice.

'My car is down at the main car park. Should take like an hour if we go the most direct route and don't stop. Are you ok walking on bare feet that long?'

Paul glanced at his dirt covered feet and snorted. 'Yes. Fine. Let's go.' He strode on ahead.

Eve jogged a few steps to catch up. She took to watching the woods to the left of the path while Paul kept an eye on the right.

'We should clear off the path immediately if we see or hear anything,' Eve said.

Paul grunted in acknowledgement.

Eve checked her phone again. There was no signal. The GPS app kept repositioning their location as it struggled to triangulate their bearings among the tall trees. The phone battery was at half charge: enough to last the trek to the car park.

'You still trying to get a call through for help?' Paul said, his tone disapproving.

'Yeah. Why wouldn't I?'

Paul shrugged. 'How long do you think it'll take the police to send someone out and find us among this maze? We'll be back at your car and out of here long before.'

'Well, I'd rather there *was* someone looking for us, and for people to know we are in trouble in case some psychos catch us before we get back to the car. Is there something you're afraid of? Don't you want me to call the police? Did you do something to those people to make them mad at you?'

'I told you I was camping. I was asleep when they attacked my tent.'

'That's it? Did you have a run in with them? Maybe pitched your tent inside their stone circle or something?'

'No. You said it yourself: They're psychos. They don't need a reason.' Paul didn't meet her gaze but watched the path and the undergrowth to the side of the track as they walked.

Eve scrutinised him through narrowed eyes. It felt like there was something he wasn't disclosing. His expression was more stern than traumatised. She wondered if the whole thing was a

stag trick gone wrong and Paul was protecting his friends'
identities, or perhaps the assailants were vigilantes and Paul was
some kind of molester. Vigilante groups had done worse. She
shuddered, drawing a scowl from Paul.

'Maybe I should run on ahead to the car,' Eve said. 'I've got
shoes and can get there faster. There's a phone signal there: I
spoke to my friend before I came up here. Hopefully, by the
time you get there the police will have arrived.'

Paul shook his head. 'I don't know the way. Might get lost.'

'Oh.' Eve hoped she didn't sound too disheartened.

Paul halted and slapped his hand on her chest, stopping her.
She swallowed a cry of alarm, noting that Paul was looking off
into the trees, peering into the depths of the forest.

'Did you hear something?' Eve whispered.

'Shut up.'

They listened. Male crickets made their rattling mating
sounds. A wood pigeon cooed. Paul kept his hand on her for the
best part of a minute before releasing her. They walked on in
silence, wincing into the growing gloom.

Eve felt a rising panic at the realisation that it was growing
darker. Grey clouds slowly drifted beneath a navy-blue sky.
Although Eve could see as far as the curvature of the land
allowed along the track, the canopy to the sides of the path the
woods were almost black beyond ten or fifteen metres. Eve
checked the time: it was another hour and half to dusk. They
should be at the car before then.

They came to a divide in the track. Eve recognised the steep
downward path as the one with the blood trail. She stopped and
shuddered at the memory.

'What?' Paul said, his tone inflected with worry.

'Nothing. I… it's just… there was a trail of blood along here
on my way up. I thought it was an injured animal or something.'

'Stag's blood. It leads up through the trees to the cairn
circle.'

'How could you know that?'

'They dragged me up here this way along with a freshly
killed stag. Before you ask, I could see it because they didn't put

me in the sack until they finished their ritual,' Paul said. 'Come on: blood drops won't hurt you. If *they* catch us, *they* sure will.'

Eve followed him down the trail, noting with a frown that Paul's assessment of the threat to her had changed dramatically from when he wanted her to scout ahead for him.

Paul suddenly halted again. His sight fixed at the end of the track is it curved around a bend near the bottom of the hill. A figure stood on the path. A woman or girl with red hair and grey overalls. She just stood in the centre of the path, staring up at them.

Paul cursed. He turned around, looking back the way they came. Eve followed his gaze, gasping when she noticed a man some twenty metres behind them, standing where she'd stopped just moments ago. He stared at them with a dispassionate, vacant expression.

'Run!' Paul cried, darting off the path into the woods.

Eve scrambled after him with arms flailing out to her sides to aid balance as she rushed among the boulders, tree stumps, and roots. She saw Paul trip. She paused, intending to help him up, but fear compelled her to abandon the attempt. She ran on, fleeing blindly without consideration for direction or terrain. The pack on her back lurched from side to side; the contents rattled noisily. Someone tore through the undergrowth close behind. Eve let out a startled cry and tried to veer right, hoping the downhill momentum might gain her some advantage so long as she didn't trip.

The footfalls rushed closer. As they neared, Eve dared a glance – relieved to see it was Paul, who even barefoot was able to manoeuvre with speed and agility among the many obstacles. His arms pumped like those of an athlete on the track. Eve suddenly felt in competition with him: that somehow, he was trying to outdistance her so she would be the one caught. She pushed on. Willing herself to move faster. Something snagged her foot.

Eve tumbled. The fall seemed to happen in slow motion, allowing time to release a curse and twist sideways to avoid landing on a piece of splintered stump. Dirt, bark, and decaying vegetation sprayed up around her as she rolled through the earth. Stones and twigs snagged at her clothing, but her momentum and the downward gradient caried her onward until her shoulder and ribs slammed into a green covered rock.

Eve winced from the pain of numerous scratches. It took a second to register that everything felt ok: she could breathe, nothing was broken. She scrambled to get up. Someone was running through the undergrowth close behind. Was it Paul? She imagined he was ahead now. The backpack put her off-balance as Eve stood on shaking legs. She stumbled a step then tripped on another rock but managed to catch hold of a branch to stop herself falling.

Her senses were overwhelmed; her heart thudded so loudly that she could hear and feel each pump of blood. Eve sucked in deep breaths and prepared to move off again. She couldn't focus on the terrain as she ran and dared not slow; the need for caution being outweighed by the desperate urgency for speed. A flurry of violent footfalls from behind sent her into a panic; she tried to make a sharp turn, releasing a cry of alarm upon realising that the pursuer was too close to evade.

Eve was propelled forward by an impact from behind. Hands grabbed her in a tackle as she fell. She landed face-first among mud, moss, and flakes of bark. A weight pressed down on her back, pinning her face-down. Eve kicked, striking nothing but the ground. She tore at the rocks and dirt with her fingers – the uselessness of the effort only exacerbating the panic. Something slammed into the side of her head, hard. She knew without looking it was a rock. A second later the pain came, spreading across the side of her skull. She felt her bladder empty. She was being stoned to death and there was nothing she could do about it. Her head jerked to the side from the force of another blow – then she lost consciousness.

***

Eve's head felt heavy. She tried to part her eyelids, but the light hurt. She groaned. Voices conversed in low tones. Footsteps paced on what sounded like laminate floor. She wondered where she was – a hospital? She jolted with the sudden recollection of the ordeal and forced her eyes open despite the optical overload. She blinked away bright light. Her vision was blurry. Someone in blue trousers was standing nearby – a doctor? Her head hurt, she felt dizzy.

'Where am I?' she said. Her voice sounded slow and inarticulate.

'Drink this.' A hand offered something close to her face: a plastic cup.

Eve accepted it with both hands, taking a sip of room-temperature water. Only then realising how dry her throat had been. She downed the rest of the beverage. Still-blurry vision could make out the profile of the man before her. She gingerly felt the side of her head: it still hurt, but it was a dull pain. She had expected to feel bandages, but there was just a swelling under the hair. Eve realised she was sitting in a plastic patio chair – not a hospital bed.

'Where am I?'

'You're in the kitchen of a Woodland Commission portacabin. Do you remember what happened?'

Eve focused on the man, recognising the ranger who had refused her entry to the grove. She groaned and looked around but could see nobody else. She seemed to be in a small room: a break room of sorts. She rubbed her temple.

'You attacked me,' Eve said.

'No. I carried you back here after you hit your head.'

'*You* hit my head,' Eve slurred. She tried to stand, to make her escape, but felt dizzy as soon as she began to rise and flopped back into the chair.

'You might have concussion. You were unconscious for a minute or so and groggy all the way back here. You were passed out when I put you down in the chair. I'll get you more water. Just relax – nobody is going to hurt you while you're in this cabin. You got my word on that.'

The ranger took the cup and walked away. She heard a tap running.

'If you didn't hit me, who did?' Eve said, feeling her senses returning. The light seemed to glare less, although it strained her eyes to try to focus on anything for long.

'The best thing right now is not to cause yourself any stress. I know the guy who chased you down: he works for me. I'll deal with it.'

'What about Paul?'

The ranger offered the cup. Eve gladly took it and drank half of it in one go.

'Paul? He's in the next room. Dressed in his own clothes and drinking tea.'

Eve stared into the cup as she gathered her thoughts. She had a vague memory of being carried over someone's shoulder through the woods. She downed the rest of the water. The seat of her shorts felt wet, she wrinkled her nose on realising it was her own urine.

'What's your name?' Eve said, deciding to play for time while figuring out what to do.

'Fid.'

'Fid? What kind of name is that?'

'An old one. Pre-Roman. It's actually shortened. Fid is easier to pronounce.'

Eve noticed her pack on a square canteen table. The bag was open and the contents spread over the tabletop. A window displayed black trees against a dimming sky. She tried to focus on a wall clock, but her vision wasn't clear enough to make out the time.

'It's a quarter past five if you were wondering,' Fid said, 'and it's still the same day. You were dozing in the chair there for like thirty minutes.'

'I think I remember you carrying me. I thought it was a dream. How long have you known Paul?'

Fid flinched at the question. He swallowed and dragged a chair over, placing it in front of Eve. He sat on it back-to-front, cowboy style. 'What makes you think I know him?'

'I asked after him and you knew who he was right away.'

196

'Uh-huh. Guess your head wound isn't that bad if you're thinking that clearly. However, isn't it likely that I asked his name when I brought you guys back here?'

'You had his clothes.' Eve looked down at the empty cup. She wondered if Fid would let her leave, assuming he probably wouldn't.

'Good point. He's my cousin. Works up here with us.'

Eve slowly lifted her head.

Fid smiled a friendly, rogue-like grin.

Eve didn't return the smile. She glanced at the door then back to Fid, calculating the chances of reaching the door as very low. Fid would probably reach out and grab her without even getting up.

Fid looked over his shoulder at the doorway.

'You wondering if Paul is ok? Hey, Paul! Haul your ass in here!'

A piece of furniture creaked in the next room. Footsteps sounded on hard flooring and the door squeaked open. Paul stood there, wearing a chequered workshirt and blue jeans. He looked like he had showered. He leaned against the doorframe. Behind him Eve could make out the red-haired woman in her grey overalls.

'Hey,' Paul said.

Eve blinked. 'What the hell's going on, Paul? You said you were jumped by these guys while camping. Now I hear you work with them?'

'Both are true. They caught me camping – years ago, admittedly. I've been here ever since.' Paul shrugged and smiled apologetically.

'Eve, I think we all owe you an apology,' Fid said with a dramatic sigh and an overly friendly grin. 'Most of us work up here all the time. We keep to ourselves. We don't have TV's, telephones, computers, or any of that. Some of the boys drink for entertainment. Sometimes a bit more than they should.' Fid cast a sideways look at Paul. 'When that happens, things get out of hand. I didn't want you dragged into it. I'm sorry that Paul got you involved. So is Paul – aren't you?'

'Yeah. Sorry.' Paul sniffed and examined his nails.

'Are you guys freaking kidding me?' Eve seethed. 'This was all a drinking game gone wrong? What is the problem with you lot? And why would one of you hit me with a rock? It's psychopathy, not drink-related boredom!'

The two men looked at each other. Fid shrugged.

'What do you want, Eve? Money?'

Eve swallowed hard, realising she had made a mistake. She should have just agreed with everything they said: whatever would make them decide to let her go. If they thought she'd go straight to the police they might finish what they started with the rock.

'Guys... I'm a Uni student. I know what dudes are like when they get a few drinks in them. I'll chalk this one up to experience. Honestly, I've seen worse on campus. You Devonshire guys sure are wild, right?'

Fid raised an eyebrow. His smile wilted somewhat. Paul just stared at her.

'I told you,' said the woman from the next room. 'Once she found Paul it was already too late. We'll have to finish her.'

The walls seemed to shrink in on Eve. She shivered, feeling suddenly freezing cold. The faces looking at her seemed to pulsate. Her breathing became rapid. She dropped the cup and gripped hold of her chair. There was no room to flee, nothing to defend herself with: she was at their mercy. She wavered, feeling feint.

Paul moved from the doorway, taking a step toward Eve. The woman advanced behind him. A third man – the one who had ambushed them along with the woman – appeared in the doorway.

'No!' It was all Eve could think to say.

Fid held up his hand and waved the would-be assailants down. 'Wait. This ain't right. I promised the lady she was safe in here.'

'What?' Paul spat. 'What matter is a promise to *her*?'

'A promise made in Pan's forest is a promise, Paul. Let's consult the crone. See what she thinks.'

Eve doubled over and threw up between her knees. Foul smelling, lumpy vomit spattered her calves and the floor.

'That's the concussion,' Fid said. 'Paul, go get the crone. And fetch the mop. Aoife, you and Rhys go back in the other room. Give Eve some space.'

There were footsteps then the door closed. Eve panted, catching her breath. She flinched as Fid patted her shoulder.

'Relax. I told you nobody's gonna hurt you in here and I meant it.'

'Why are you with these psychos?' Eve said, resting her forehead between her knees, she clutched her calves. She became aware of the weight of her smartphone in her pocket but dared not make any movement to retrieve it.

'Psychos?' Fid laughed. 'They're family. They're just protective.'

'Who protected Paul when they stuck him in a grave? Did you know they did that?'

'That needed doing.'

Eve looked up. 'Why? What did Paul do? Why are you doing this to me?'

Fid scratched his stubble, seeming to think for a moment.

'Well, there's no harm in telling you at this point. You see, our bloodline is very old. We've lived in these parts for scores of generations. Always as outcasts. We've been here since what you would call the Bronze Age. My ancestors worked as farmers on nearby hillsides. Later generations lived in the tinners' huts, then worked as quarrymen. When the Woodland Commission planted the trees here ninety years ago, my grandparents moved from a valley a mile away to these hills where we have remained since.'

'What are you talking about? Nobody can trace their family history back to the Bronze Age. What does that even have to do with any of this?'

'I'm getting to that. More water?'

Eve nodded. Fid picked up the cup and walked over to the sink. Eve looked at the doorway and held her breath for a second, contemplating making a rush for it, then remembering there were two others in the next room.

'We worship Pan: one of the oldest gods. We believe in nature. Our beliefs have always kept us outcast. You saw our stone circle. Those stones were recumbent until eighty years ago. I cut back the trees and created the grove last year to increase the power to the circle. Now the stones are aligned with the heavens again and painted afresh with symbols of devotion and power.'

Eve groaned inwardly, realising she'd stumbled into some sort of cult commune. Did the Woodland Commission know this was going on? She doubted it, and guessed the reason Fid rarely left the hilltop was to guard it from hikers stumbling into their religious domain.

Fid seemed to recognise the realisation reflected in her face. He nodded, smiling. 'You understand, I think.'

'Doesn't explain why you guys tied up one of your own and left him there.'

Fid exhaled and tapped a rhythm on the back of his chair. 'That was regretful, but necessary.'

'Why? What did Paul do? He told me a tale about...'

Fid laughed.

'Sorry, Eve. Paul was a sacrifice. Pan requires sacrifice: a stag, a hare, a bird. Depending on the interpretations of the crone. On unfortunate occasions we have had to sacrifice a lone camper or hiker – like Paul's pa back when Paul was a kid. We took care of Paul ever since. This time Pan demanded one of us. We were all sorry to have to sacrifice him, but you must understand that is our way.'

Eve shook her head. 'That's not even what cairn circles are for. They're just burials.'

Fid sighed again. 'Yes. As I said: our beliefs differ. Even thousands of years ago we were outcasts, but when the seasons grew harsh and the farmers left the moorlands for the coastal regions, we stayed and Pan looked after us.'

'You said Paul was a sacrifice. He was alive. Were you just going to let him starve to death?'

Fid sucked his lip before replying. 'Live offerings are much more powerful. If we offer up a body which the soul has already departed, then Pan is deprived of the soul. With a living offering, nature reclaims it bit by bit. Pan receives sustenance through nature. Do you understand?'

Eve closed her eyes. She had dared to hope that Fid was less of a psycho than the others.

A door creaked open. Footsteps.

'Mother,' a male and female voice said in union in the next room.

'Ah,' Fid said, 'that'll be the crone.'

Eve shuddered. Her eyes searched the room for a weapon or something she could use to escape, but the small space offered no solace or hope. She was completely at their mercy.

The door opened. An old woman shuffled in, followed by Paul, the red-haired woman, and the man who had ambushed them on the trail. Eve saw that the crone epithet was apt: hunched over and frail, greasy hair hung in knots, sagging skin almost grey in colour, and her eyes little more than two sunken black dots. She wore a ragged dress with a tattered shoal over her shoulders and carried a staff with beads, bones, and ribbons hanging from it. Eve was unsure if the staff was a talisman, walking aid, or both. The base of the staff clunked against the floor as the crone shambled nearer with beady eyes unblinkingly focused on Eve.

The crone stopped close enough that Eve could feel the hem of the old bat's dress brush against her knees. Eve pushed her chair back the few inches she could until it met the wall behind.

A withered and bony hand emerged from the folds of the crone's dress, reaching slowly toward Eve.

Eve leaned back, grimacing, but the hand clasped her forehead. Yellowed nails pressed against her skull.

'Please,' Eve whimpered.

The crone babbled. Saliva poured from her lower lip in a long shoelace. She leant forward. Her breathing came as a phlegmy rattle and stank like rotting meat.

Eve's eyes flicked to Fid. He watched with a frown, ignoring Eve's pleading sob.

The crone snatched her hand back from Eve's skull. The withered limb disappeared back into her dirty dress.

'Well? What should we do with her?' the red-haired woman said.

The crone pivoted toward Fid and made a guttural sound that might have been speech or perhaps just a result of clogged lungs. She waved a sign in the air with one of her yellowed talons.

'The crone demands a test,' Fid said. 'For both of them.'

'No!' Paul cried out, turning as if to make a run for it. The red-haired woman and the other man grappled with him, pinning his arms.

'Please!' Eve cried. 'Let me go. I'm sorry. I didn't know what I was doing…'

'I was freed by Pan's will!' Paul cried, 'I'm one of you! It should be her that goes to the circle.'

Fid held his hand up for silence. 'It may have been Pan's will, but you tried to flee with the outsider, Paul.'

'I wasn't thinking. I was afraid you'd drag me back to the circle. I should've come to you and not run when I saw Aoife and Rhys on the trail.'

'Yes, you should. We will let the woods decide who goes to the circle and who gets to live.'

The crone's tiny black eyes fixed Eve's with a malevolent stare. She hissed something unintelligible, then turned to the door and shuffled back into the next room. Aoife and Rhys followed the old woman, taking Paul with them.

Fid brought Eve another cup of water which she accepted with shaking hands, spilling much of it.

'What will you do with me?'

'Nothing. The woods will decide your fate. Go back to your car. If you can reach it, then it's Pan's will that you live.' Fid nodded and smiled like he was delivering good news.

'So, I can just… go?' Eve searched Fid's face for signs of deception.

'Yes, but remember: One of you two has to go to the circle. Paul isn't about to let it be him. If he catches you then you will have the honour of going to Pan.'

Eve dropped the cup. She struggled to control her breathing. The room seemed to roll from left to right like a boat floundering upon a rough sea.

Fid clutched her shoulders. He stared into her eyes with what looked like concern. 'Can you run?'

'My head throbs. It's getting dark outside. I can't... can't do it!' Eve sobbed.

'You must run if you are to live. Not only that, but Aoife and Rhys are Paul's friends. They are likely to aid him. Aoife mentored him in the ways since he was a lad. If the forest allows you escape from the three of them then you are truly blessed.'

Eve groaned. She felt that she might collapse from the chair if not for Fid holding her steady. She squeezed her eyes closed and the spinning sensation subsided a little.

'You should ready yourself,' Fid said.

'How?' Eve snapped, almost laughing at the absurdity of preparing herself to flee for her life.

'I'll fill your water bottle. You have your car keys and your telephone?'

Eve jolted. Her mouth dropped open.

'Don't worry: I'm not going to take it off you. The trees block transmission, right? Pan will not let you call for aid, but perhaps he will let you use the navigation aid on the way out as you used it on the way in.'

Eve shuddered. She pushed herself up from the chair, waving Fid off as he moved to help. She walked to the table, feet unsteady at first, packing the things back into her pack and handed her drinking bottle to Fid for refilling.

'Can I go now?'

'If you feel ready. They will be preparing Paul. I will ensure you have a fair head start, but perhaps it is best to go now if you're able.'

Eve snatched the replenished bottle form Fid and stuffed it nto her pack. Her fingers trembled as she tried to fasten the zip.

203

She muttered a curse under her breath and pushed her arms through the pack straps. She looked at the time on her phone for a few seconds until her eyes focused sufficiently to read it: about twenty minutes before dusk. She would have to cover some of the distance in the dark.

'I'm ready,' Eve said, looking pointedly at the door but hesitant to venture into the next room where the others had begun to make what sounded like low murmuring incantations.

Fid shrugged and walked through to the next room, holding the door open. Eve followed with slow, cautious steps.

The room seemed to be the restroom for the forestry workers. Empty tins, bottles and boxes littered a coffee table and the floor around a threadbare sofa. An old tv with its white plastic yellowed with age sat unplugged next to a pile of old newspapers.

Paul stood in the far corner, glaring at Eve as she entered the room. He was shirtless. Aoife painted his chest with a brown pigment, creating swirling symbols while repeating a phrase in an unintelligible language. Rhys and the crone stood nearby, making low humming sounds and watching Paul's preparation; they didn't even glance in Eve's direction.

Eve stepped toward the door, looking at Fid to make sure he hadn't changed his mind about releasing her. He gestured to the door. Eve hurried toward it, pulled on the handle, grimacing as she realised that it opened outwards, then pushed through and into the evening air.

A dirt track led away from the portacabin flanked by stacks of trunks and gloomy forest. Eve began to run, stopping when she noticed a battered pick-up truck parked on the far side of the cabin. The windows were covered in grime and the bodywork was flecked with rust, but the back was full of freshly felled logs, suggesting that the vehicle was still operational. Eve dashed to it, trying the doorhandle: locked. She ran around the other side and found that one locked too. She cursed and glanced at the cabin before running back to the track.

The side of Eve's head pulsated with a warm pain where she had been struck. Running made it worse. Each time her feet hit the ground the wound throbbed. She gritted her teeth against the pain and pushed on. The throbbing steadily grew until it began to blur the vision in her left eye. Eve refused to slow, even when her lungs ached for air, denying herself respite until her legs became dangerously weak and she felt she might trip at any moment. Eve finally stopped, fearing that if she fell, she might not rise. Bending over, she braced herself with hands on her knees, refusing to sit in case the foes should catch up to her. Eve took long breaths, regulating her breathing as the heart rate gradually returned to normal. She looked back the way she had come; the cabin was out of sight. She wondered how far she had run, figuring it to be just a few hundred metres – albeit all uphill. If Paul and his cohorts were to use the truck, they could cover that ground in seconds.

Eve dug the phone out of her pocket and, seeing straight away there was no signal, she opened the navigation app with fumbling thumbs. The app blinked as it tried to triangulate her location. She shook the phone in frustration, noting that the battery was down to less than a third of its power. Finally, the display showed her position: about two hundred metres from the junction where they'd been ambushed by Rhys and Aoife.

A howl broke the evening silence. A long, mournful cry like a wolf's, followed by three loud hoots. Eve tensed, bristling at the sound. She knew it was human – no doubt Paul's, signalling the start of his hunt.

Eve stuffed the phone back into her pocket and jogged up the path, deciding to keep moving until she could hear the pursuers' approach – then she would move off the trail and hide until they passed.

The incline levelled out as she reached the junction at the top of the steep path. Eve stopped, looking down the long, curving trail. The bottom of the track disappeared into darkness. Eve chewed her lip; the pursuers would be sure to check that path first as it was the most direct route to the car park. She took a few steps along the higher track when she reflected that Paul and the others might well split up and take both routes.

Eve looked off into the undergrowth. It was dark: the trunks, boulders and undergrowth showed as little more than shapes of dark green, brown, and grey, fading gradually into near blackness. *It's ok*, she thought, *I won't have to go far into the woods. Just far enough to be out of sight and see where they go.*

Eve stepped off into the undergrowth. She looked around at the sound of running feet. It was still a little way off, but she knew there wasn't much time. She took a few daring steps, unsure if the footfalls among the shin-high foliage would land on solid earth or on some hidden hazard. She grimaced as the ground crunched underfoot. The haphazard patter of several pursuing feet grew louder. Eve ducked into a clump of particularly dense undergrowth that was tall enough to conceal her. It was only six or seven steps off the track, but she reasoned that if she kept her head down, she would be all but invisible. Eve made a gap in the shrub to peer through, gasping at the sight her footprints on a mucky patch at the edge of the track.

Eve sucked in her breath. In the next instant the pursuers came into view, slowing as they reached the crossroads. The dusty floor was littered with partial footprints and tyre tracks that criss-crossed in a confused pattern. Eve's stomach knotted. She willed her chasers not to examine the prints.

The pursuers wore animal masks and antler headdresses. The strange guises were hand painted with demonic, goat-like faces and blazing eyes. Paul's painted bare chest heaved as he recovered from the exertion of running. The trio looked down the hill as Eve had done moments before, and then along the other path. Paul's masked head pivoted as he searched the treeline, then stopped, staring in her direction.

Eve dared not duck for fear that the movement would reveal herself. She held her breath, scared that even that would alert her enemies.

'Down?' said Rhys, walking to Paul's side.

Paul looked back down the track and shook his head. 'Split up. You two go down; I'll go along.'

'Wait,' Rhys said, examining at the ground. He paced, hunched over, examining the dirt.

Eve squeezed her eyes shut and ducked.

'These are our prints from earlier,' Aoife said. 'Look: this one is my shoeprint.'

'It's not easy to see which prints are hers,' Rhys said, 'but if I can figure it out, we might get an idea of which way she went.'

'What's the point?' Paul snapped. 'We all came this way earlier, and who knows where she was plodding before that. We could end up following old footprints for hours.'

'That'd be real bad for you,' Rhys snickered.

Eve heard a scuffle and grunt, sounding like Paul had shoved Rhys in retaliation for his jibe.

'This is my hunt. You two go down. I'm going along.'

Eve heard them depart. She listened for minutes after they had left. The songs of birds had given way to that of crickets. Wind gently teased the treetops, causing the trunks to creak.

I've got to go, Eve told herself. She rose, checking the path to ensure it was clear. She shivered upon noticing that the light had further dimmed and even the track was becoming difficult to clearly discern. She realised with a rising panic that she was running out of time. It would be a beacon to her pursuers to use light from the phone to navigate by, and as the cultists had split and taken both tracks, she either had to follow them or navigate off-trail though steep hills with very treacherous terrain.

'Please help me, God,' Eve whispered. She checked the phone again: still no signal. She pressed *999* regardless. The phone emitted static sounds for several long seconds before the call ended, the display dispassionately declaring 'No Network Signal'.

Eve looked down the precipitous hillside full of silhouettes and swathes of blackness which might have been ravines, deciding there was no way she could make it through such undergrowth. Even if she didn't twist an ankle or fall from some unseen drop, the noise of her progress would likely alert the others. Besides, she reflected, it would probably take more than the whole night to get to the car if she kept off the tracks.

'Maybe I don't need to get to the road,' Eve whispered to herself. 'People know I'm here. I only need to make it until I'm missed.' She wondered how long after her eight o'clock arrangement it might be before Greer raised the alarm. Would Greer call the emergency services when Eve was overdue, or would she go out to the party alone, get drunk, sleep in late and only worry about the absence when Greer woke find Eve's room still empty sometime the following afternoon? Eve decided that she had to press on. She opened the navigation app on the phone and studied it; if she followed Paul's route along the level track there were three different turn-offs, but only one led to the car park. If she followed Rhys and Aoife, she would need to follow the long winding path which she had already been ambushed on once. Neither route was favourable.

'No,' Eve muttered. 'I'm not going to outrun them: I need to outthink them.' She realised that if she followed Paul's path for a short distance, it was possible to turn off uphill instead of taking the obvious downward track. It would take her the opposite way she wanted to go but would ultimately wind around the hill and down to a narrow access road and out of the forest to the nearby main road. It was twice the distance of going to the car, but by the time Paul and company figured it out, she would be long gone – and with night fast drawing in, they wouldn't likely be able to follow her tracks. With a growing, desperate hope, Eve took off in the direction Paul had gone, trying her best to ignore the throbbing from her head.

Eve walked quickly, deciding that speed was more urgent than silence. Her steps sounded overloud, as did the swish of material from her shorts rubbing as she hurried along, but she consoled herself that the sound wasn't likely to be audible beyond a short distance. The turn-off soon came into view; a sharp right bend up a steep incline. Eve increased her pace, wincing when she kicked a stone which clattered across the track. She stopped, holding her breath and listening: nothing stirred, so she started on up the hill.

Something snagged above Eve's ankle only a few paces up the new path. She heard a tiny snap off to her left. She breathed a curse, shaking her leg to release a thin length of string which had caught on her boot. She knelt and picked up the broken length of string and pulled it; the line trailed off to the right side of the path where it was tied off around a trunk. Eve gasped as she realised the significance: Paul had used it to mark the path so that when he backtracked, he would know which way she had gone.

Eve swore. She walked to the edge of the path with the broken end, looking for a place to tie it off so that it would appear untouched. She wound it around a branch from a low shrub, hoping it would remain fixed. She gave the string a gentle tug to test that it wouldn't come unattached with a gust of wind. Attentive to her task, she only noticed the soft footsteps when they were within a few metres.

Eve spun about. She glimpsed the half-naked form of Paul stalking near, hands poised to grab. He launched into a sprint. Eve took off, sprinting blindly uphill. The gradient of the incline seemed intent on dragging her back into the grasping arms of her stalker. She had no idea if she was getting away from Paul or if he was gaining on her; his thunderous footfalls sounded a breath behind. She dared not look back. Eve ran off the trail without thought of direction. Twigs and thorns tore at her calves. Twice she stumbled, but managed to keep going, knowing that to fall would see her into Paul's hands.

Eve weaved around trunks and vaulted over a boulder – barely keeping her balance. A cascade of noise followed: rocks knocking together, wood snapping, and the ragged breathing of the pursuer. Paul cried out. Eve didn't even look around. She was running downhill, having unintentionally circled back through the woods. She emerged from the dense patch of woodland back onto the level track. Eve glanced behind, finding no foe, and ran as fast as she could, taking the next downhill branch in the trail, immediately regretting the choice: the first turning seemed the most obvious, but to go back would be to head back toward Paul. She continued down, hoping that Paul had broken a leg. Or a neck.

It was almost dark. The earthy path took on a grey hue under the failing light. The woods to each side were blanketed with blackness beyond the first trunks. Eve resolved to run all the

209

way back to the car: hiding in the dark woods was an unsavoury option. She kept running until she came to a diversion in the track; neither route continued downhill. She slowed on approach, daring to look around, gathering her thoughts. Adrenaline wore off and the throbbing returned. She dug the phone from her pocket. The app stalled as it tried to triangulate her position. Footsteps sounded nearby.

Eve darted off the track into the black. Bushes swished around her knees. She ducked down, out of sight from the road, and switched off the phone screen. At first, she only heard the wind and the occasional sounds of tiny detritus dropping from the trees – then she heard the steps again.

'I know you came this way!' Paul shouted. 'I only trip-wired two turnings before I heard you approach, and guess what: you broke the string at both! Pan is on my side, bitch. You're going to the circle!'

Paul's footsteps came closer. Eve drew herself into a ball, screwing her eyes shut. The steps passed on by. She wanted to stay hidden, curled up and safe, but needed to know which of the two paths Paul took. Eve uncurled herself and slowly stood, moving to the edge of the treeline with cautious steps, holding onto the nearest tree trunk for support. She watched Paul disappear from view at the left-hand path but knew he could double back at any moment. She chewed her lower lip.

'Go now,' Eve whispered and stepped out of concealment, holding her breath, walking at a brisk pace to the right-hand turn-off. All senses were alert to the sounds and fading sights of the forest: the incessant sound of crickets and the occasional crack of a twig and rush of air through branches. Eve decided if she couldn't hear Paul's steps, he couldn't hear hers, and so moved with greater speed than caution – spurred on by a feeling of urgency which silently screamed to run, always run.

Eve followed the route for about a minute before ducking to the side of the path to check the phone, cupping her hands around the screen to cover the light. The app showed that the left-hand path circled around some rocks and back toward the right-hand route where the two tracks ran parallel before meeting at another junction. She put the phone away and blinked away the ghost-lights from the screen that danced in her vision. She determined to only open the app when necessary: as well as giving away her position it ruined her night vision.

Footsteps sounded. Eve instinctively knew they were Paul's. It sounded like they were on the parallel path, but as only fifteen or twenty metres separated the tracks it wouldn't take Paul much time to cut from one path to the other. Eve remained still and silent: If she could hear Paul's movements, he would hear hers.

The footfalls faded into the distance – he was backtracking. Eve moved into the undergrowth, just a metre into the dark to lessen the chance of tripping over something or creating undue noise. She sunk down behind a tree trunk, deciding to wait until Paul passed by, then she could go back uphill and choose another path out of the forest.

A few minutes passed before Paul's steps returned. He was jogging, his breath coming in sharp puffs. Eve didn't even peek but waited until he had passed and his footfalls had dissipated into the darkening wilderness. She counted to twenty, then rose from her hiding place, heading back the way she had come.

Eve kept to a brisk walk. She held onto the straps of her backpack, the sensation of gripping hold of something seemed to offer some tactile comfort and stopped her hands from shaking. The cloudless sky had gone from dark blue to black, casting everything beyond the track into varying pitches of sable.

Eve walked past two branches in the track, turning off on the third one. It sloped gently downwards, which Eve took as a good sign; anything that led nearer to the base of the valley and the carpark was good.

Her mouth was dry. A dull pain behind her eye pulsated with each step, but she dared not rest. A sound of running water came from somewhere nearby. She halted, tilting her head to listen, remembering there was a stream that ran downhill near where she had found the blood trail. She held her breath as she listened, knowing that if she had come back to the blood trail it meant she'd doubled back to the route Aoife and Rhys had taken.

211

A sharp digitised beep blared from somewhere close. Eve jolted, gasping with fright before realising it was her own phone: the sound of an incoming email. She snatched the phone from her pocket. Her desperate hands struggled to unlock the screen. She swore twice. There was a signal: one bar.

'Thank God,' Eve breathed.

'This way!' a man's voice cried out.

Eve shut off the screen and plunged off the track into the woods. She dropped to the ground, falling among brambles which stung her legs and arms. She pressed her cheek to the ground, resolving to create as flat a profile as possible so that if Rhys searched the woods, he might still look past her.

Hurried steps and huffing breath drew closer.

'Are you sure?' said Aoife.

'I heard something.'

'Could it have been a fox or deer?'

'No. It was her. I know it.'

Torchlight swept through the trees and across the undergrowth. Eve watched the beam move on up the path before it disappeared. She waited for a few moments, making sure that the light hadn't affected her night vision, then rose, brushing down her arms and legs before taking careful steps from the nettles onto the path. She looked up the track the way the torchlight had gone, thinking she glimpsed it flicker between some trees further up the hill. Eve turned to the downward path, but something, a hint of movement, made her look back.

A black shape emerged from the far side of the track, as if a shadow taken humanoid form, stepping out from the silhouette of a tree trunk like a dryad. The black form was human, female, with angular antlers stabbing out from her demon head.

'Here!' Aoife screamed.

Eve sprinted downhill. The backpack jostled from left to right, threatening to unbalance her. She wished it off her but dare not pause the seconds it would take to remove it. Aoife's footfalls were mere metres away. Rhys wouldn't be far behind.

Eve ran as fast as she could but could hear Aoife gaining. She felt a swipe of air near her shoulder as Aoife tried a

212

desperate grab. Eve knew another attempt would follow in moments and would likely catch her. She turned off the path, leaping over the foot-high verge that separated path from the foliage beyond it. She landed awkwardly and tumbled sideways, pitching through shrubs before slamming into a tree trunk. She struggled to get up and was on her knees when Aoife lunged, tackling Eve to the ground.

Eve fell back with Aoife on top of her. Aoife's hair dangled from behind the mask, tickling Eve's face. Aoife gripped Eve's left wrist, pinning it to the ground as her right grasped for Eve's free hand.

'Here!' Aoife screamed.

Eve clawed at Aoife's neck. Her nails were short, but long enough to rake scratches across the flesh.

Aoife hissed. She released her grip on Eve's wrist to slap Eve hard across the face, then grabbed the front of Eve's tee-shirt and raised her hand for another strike.

Eve punched upwards. She felt her knuckles connect with skin. Aoife toppled backwards with a strangled cry. Eve kicked free of her entanglement with the assailant, struggling to stand just as Aoife had rose to her knees, coughing; it sounded like she was choking. Eve figured her punch had struck Aoife's throat.

Eve swung a wild kick. In the dark she couldn't see where it landed, but the wooden mask flew off into the bushes and Aoife collapsed onto her side.

Eve hesitated; she was about to run but knew that any head start would be fleeting. She had to stop Aoife now. She kicked at the shadowy woman on the floor. Her attack was met with a grunt. Eve fell upon the red-haired woman. She found a stubby piece of branch in her hands – unsure where she had grabbed it from – and used it to bludgeon the groaning silhouette. The short stick wasn't long enough to land solid strikes with, so she stabbed the splintered end into the writhing shadow. Aoife spasmed. Eve struck again. Then again. She couldn't withdraw the stick from her last strike – the stump was slick and stuck into the black crumpled shape.

Footfalls came rushing down the path accompanied by torchlight swinging in haphazard movements. Eve plunged through the nearest bush. The terrain on the far side sloped steeply downward – too steep to run down. She crouched and slid down the hillside, pushing herself on with her hands, sliding some distance before the ground become too rocky and she was forced to clamber down as best she could. Creaking tree trunks loomed like giant, jagged shadows. Large granite lumps with their light grey surfaces seemed to catch a little of the moonlight, standing out like tiny islands from the blanket of blackness. With some difficulty, Eve was able to navigate from one rock to another until she could see the glint of water streaming down the hillside.

'Nooooo!' Rhys roared from uphill. He repeated the cry again and again.

The beam of torchlight flashed through the trees like a lighthouse. Eve guessed that she had gained a good hundred metres from her pursuer. She thought of Aoife with a shudder – had she killed the woman? Eve's hand was sticky where it was wet: it was surely blood.

'It was self-defence,' Eve whispered to the trees.

She dared to produce the mobile phone. The signal had dropped off. She typed in '999' again, smudging the screen with red, and received the same negatory signal response. There wasn't time to consult the navigation app. Eve moved down to the stream, finding that it wasn't wide and could be crossed in a good jump. The path was just on the other side of the water and Eve figured that her head start was good enough to allow her to follow the track awhile, using the easier ground to gain greater distance from the hunters.

Eve jumped the stream. She dared to use the torch on her phone to find her way to the path, turning the light off again before proceeding at a jog. The path was just visible enough to follow without the aid of artificial light.

Dark shapes jutted out of the woods. Sharp, angular forms that might be tree, bush, or man. Eve slowed her pace when the path levelled out and branched off left and right. She turned to the right and froze. Something stood in the path. Its large black head turned toward her; piercing antlers stabbed out from its inhuman head. Eve cried out and stumbled back, tripping and landing on her backside. The four-legged creature bounded off the path and through the trees.

'Oh, Jesus. Thank God. Stupid stag. Jesus!' Eve panted, with her hand on her chest. She flinched as she was drenched in brilliant light. She put her hand up to shield her eyes, squinting through her fingers.

'He won't save you from me,' Rhys snarled.

Eve blinked, momentarily disbelieving that her pursuer had caught up so quickly, then realising the rush of the nearby stream had probably masked the sound of his pursuit. She scrambled to get up as Rhys charged. He was ten or fifteen metres away, but Eve knew there was little chance to outrun him. She had to fight.

Eve swung her pack off her shoulders and arced it at her attacker as he closed in. The bag struck the torch, knocking it from his grasp and sending it clattering to the ground, the light spinning around to illuminate the devilishly horned assailant.

Eve kicked at his knee. Rhys grabbed her by the throat with both hands, lifting her off the ground. Her feet scrambled for purchase as Rhys squeezed. Her eyes teared up. She coughed a dry bark and gasped but could swallow no air. Her throat burned. She clawed at Rhys's wrists to no avail.

The demonic painted red eyes of the mask seemed to burn through the blackness at her. Rhys shook her as if to try to shake the very life from her. She kicked at him, but the impacts made no impression. A rasp escaped her throat. Colours and flashes of light danced in her peripheral vision. Then the pressure around her throat suddenly released, accompanied with a heavy thumping sound.

Eve crumpled to the ground. Rhys collapsed on top of her, groaning. Eve cradled her throat with both hands, gulping at the air. She sobbed, only dimly aware of a figure standing over her.

'She has to go back alive,' Paul growled. 'If she dies, Fid will put me back in the hole instead of her.'

Rhys lifted his weight off Eve. She rolled onto her side, coughing.

'She killed Aoife. I'm going to snatch the life out of her.'

'*She* killed Aoife?' Paul said in high-pitched surprise. 'Well, it matters not. I need her alive.'

Eve heard what sounded like the two men struggling, grappling with each other, grunting and swearing. She turned over to see flashes of their struggle as they moved too and fro across the beam of lamplight and then rolled about in the dirt, each trying to pin the other down.

Eve struggled to stand. She took a step and winced, realising her knee must have twisted when Rhys dropped her. She limped away from the pair as best she could. The knee pulsated with a shock of pain each time weight was put on the leg. She gritted her teeth against the hurt and pressed on, lurching and waving her arms to aid balance.

The sounds of struggle from behind ended. Someone panted in recovery of their effort. Eve looked about for a hiding place and staggered to the side of the path, putting a hand on a tree for support. She walked a few more steps and fell over something. She crawled a short distance – although doing so hurt the knee more than walking did. She moved between two boulders and, exhausted and in agony, decided to stay there, awaiting whatever fate befell her.

'Eve! Where are yoooooou?' Paul called out. He stalked nearer, laughing. The torch beam swept along the path and through the undergrowth on both sides of the track. 'Come on out, Eve. I won't hurt you. We can still be friends. I just want to bury you alive!'

Notes from a pop tune blared out, jolting Eve into a cry of fright. It took a couple of seconds to realise the sound was coming from her phone, then another second to recognise it as her ringtone announcing an incoming phone call. She frantically dug the phone out of her pocket, trembling fingers almost dropping it.

The screen showed an incoming call from Greer. Eve slid the lock off the phone and put the phone to her ear.

'Eve!' Greer said in a scolding voice the moment the call connected. 'We're supposed to be going out and you're not even back yet, where the hell-'

'Greer, help! I'm in trouble!' Eve hissed.

Torchlight fell upon her, flooding Eve with blinding brilliance.

'What?' Greer snapped. 'Where are you? Are you still coming out?'

'I'm being chased... I can't run anymore-'

Paul's foot connected with Eve's knuckles, sending the phone spinning off into the bushes. Eve looked longingly after it. The dim light of the display vanished among black foliage. She desperately reached after it with fingers that were numb from the kick.

'No, you don't,' Paul said. Grabbing hold of Eve's hair, he pulled her up to her knees. He looked down on her through his horned mask. His body stank of stale sweat. 'You're coming back with me.'

'Let me go!' Eve begged. 'I rescued you, damn it! I saved you. You owe me!'

'Yeah, you rescued me. Now you'll rescue me again.'

Paul grunted as he picked her up and put her over his shoulder, holding Eve by her legs. He waded through the undergrowth back to the path. Eve scratched at his back. Paul squeezed her injured knee in response, making her cry out.

'Conscious or unconscious is your choice, Eve. Struggle again – I dare you.'

Eve took a deep breath, opened her mouth as wide as she could and bit into Paul's back. Sinking her teeth deep; determined to rip a mouthful of flesh from his body.

Paul screamed and hurled Eve off his shoulder. Eve flailed for purchase as she sailed through the air. Her fingers coiled around something, but it didn't stop her fall. She slammed into the dirt. All air was pounded from her lungs. The taste of blood was thick in her mouth.

'Bitch!' Paul seethed. He twisted and turned, shining the torch at his ribs as he struggled to see the bleeding oval wound on his back.

Eve caught her breath. Her hand hurt: she looked at it and found she was holding the antlers from Paul's hideous costume; the points of the horns had been sharpened and one of them pierced her palm with the point protruding an inch from the back of her hand.

'You damned bitch!' Paul roared. He stomped on her leg, snarling, reaching for her.

Eve screamed and swung the antlers at his face with all the force she could summon.

Paul stopped. His mouth dropped open. He collapsed sideways into a heap. The torch clattered to the ground at his feet.

Eve lunged for the torch, snatching it and then scrambling back away from Paul. She shone the light on him. He gulped. Half of his face was bathed in red. One of the antler horns protruded from just under his jaw. Blood poured freely from the wound. Paul gripped the horns with one hand and reached out to Eve with his other. He mouthed *please*.

Eve stood on shaking legs and gave Paul the finger. Dusting herself off with her good hand, she turned away and stumbled to the path, examining the injured hand in the torchlight: it pulsated and dripped red. The flesh had closed around the hole where the antlers had penetrated, but the entire hand looked swollen and the fingers quivered, hurting too much to test if the digits still functioned. She gave fleeting thought to searching for her phone but didn't want to waste time looking for it. Greer should have called the police by now, so she just needed to get back to the car.

Eve limped on. She hurt everywhere. She moved at a steady, lurching pace. She didn't feel the need to hurry: she had defeated all three hunters.

It took more than an hour to reach the car park. The reverse side of the information board came into view first. Finding encouragement in the proximity of safety, Eve forced herself to increase her gait, grunting with the effort and from the pain from her knee. The torch blinked three times. She shook it and slapped it against her thigh; the beam became constant again, if dimmed. The right palm still seared with pain, but with some pain she had managed to wiggle the fingers, reassuring that all could be mended.

The car came into view. Alone, at the far end of the empty car park. Eve cast the light about as she neared the vehicle – not fully trusting that Fid truly intended to let her go.

Eve felt her pockets for the keys, momentarily worried that she had lost them in one of her struggles, relieved to find them in her right pocket. She clicked the button. The lights on the car flashed, the doors clicked. Eve dropped the torch and swung the car door open, falling into the seat and slumping over the steering wheel.

Eve sobbed and clawed at the dashboard, crying in frustration, relief, and fear. She finally sat up, leaving a trail of mucus and tears on the steering wheel. She reached for the door handle, gingerly pulling the door closed with the injured hand.

Something caught the doorframe, jerking the door wide open.

Eve cried out, fumbling with the keys. She dropped them into her lap and desperately reached for the doorhandle again. Fid's cruelly smiling face lunged filled the gap in the door.

'You are truly blessed, Eve!'

'Get away from me! Get away! We had a deal!'

Fid nodded. 'We do, we do. Worry not: I mean you no harm, Eve. The opposite in fact.'

'You'll let me go?' Eve leaned away from the intruder and fumbled to slot the key into the ignition with weak and throbbing fingers as she looked into Fid's eyes, hoping to keep his attention on her face while she started the car.

Fid glanced at the jangling keys and back to Eve. He put his hand over hers but made no move to wrestle the keys from her. 'That wasn't part of the deal, Eve. I said you could live – and live you shall: as a welcome initiate of Pan.'

219

'No!' Eve screamed. 'People know I'm here. The police are coming!'

'It's okay, Eve. They can come. They won't find you. Pan won't let them.'

She kicked at Fid, but strong arms dragged her from the vehicle.

***

They stood inside atop the burial mound inside the circle. It was daytime and the sky was clear of cloud. The crone held Eve's bandaged hand and Fid held the other. Eve felt light-headed. She wasn't sure how long she'd been staying in the woodcutters' cabin, but it felt like days. She knew they had been putting something into the gruel they fed her; she was having trouble remembering simple things about her past and the outside world and was seeing strange sights. In glimpses she could see what looked like strange bipedal creatures, peering at her from the trees or bushes, but when she looked again, they would be gone.

Paul stood in the burial chamber, head bowed in submission, naked other than a bloodied bandage around his neck. His hands and feet were bound.

Fid finished an incantation and released Eve's hand. He picked up the hessian sack by his feet and put it over Paul's head. Paul didn't resist but looked at Eve in the moment before the sack was pulled down over his face and dragged down to his feet. Fid wrapped a rope around Paul, and once he'd tied it off, he helped Paul to lay down in the tomb.

Fid stood back from the grave and raised his hands to the sky. He looked upwards, chanting something in a strange language that sounded similar to Welsh.

The bodies of Rhys and Aoife lay at the bottom of the mound, presented to Pan as excarnations. Naked, with their limbs splayed out. Eve looked off to the treeline, thinking she saw movement. She squinted. A horned head looked back at her; the face too dark to see.

Afterword and author's notes on the stories

It is hoped that you have enjoyed the thirteen tales that make up *Darkest Dartmoor* and that they have left an impression – although perhaps not to the extent of causing sleepless nights! The author always welcomes any feedback on his writing and can be contacted through andrewmcauleyauthor.com – which will make a pleasant change from the countless spam emails offering to build a better website!

Many of the stories in this book don't have specific locations while some have had placenames changed for various reasons – well done if you've identified these locations. If not – read on and all shall be revealed!

The White is based on the true story of Soldier's Pond; in 1853 three fusiliers were returning from Dousland to their barracks at Princetown Prison. They were warned not to venture out into the blizzard, but they pressed on and sadly all died. The two privates were found not far from Dousland. presumably having turned back, while the corporal was found not far from Princetown in a snowdrift now known as Soldier's Pond. The Church of St. Michael in Princetown has a memorial plaque for the three soldiers. Of course, none of the men were really murderers, and so the names of the soldiers have been changed in *The White* and only the initial of the surname has been retained. There is also another slightly longer version of this story in existence in the form of a short play in which Corporal Parsons is the subject of bullying from his comrades at Princetown and his obsession with Mary is given more attention – it is however unlikely that this version will ever see the light of day.

Cursed Earth has no specific location in mind: it is reflective of the often harsh landscape and weather throughout the moor and the historically difficult farming conditions. The story is however inspired by the local legend surrounding Snaily House, the ruin of which is located on the East Dart River near Bellever Forest. The old Dartmoor tale tells of two sisters who ate nothing but snails – although the house is also said to have gotten its name from a French prisoner of war who supposedly built the house while on parole during the Napoleonic Wars and was known for his fondness for consuming snails. To be honest, this second version sounds more true to me in an age when the French soldiers used to refer to their English enemies as 'Roast Beefs' in respect of British culinary leanings.

Wolf at the Door is very loosely based on a Dartmoor legend of the Devil and his Wisht hounds which were fond of hunting unbaptised children. There is no specific location for this story but, if it matters, I had one of the farms near Combestone in the back of my mind.

Ordeal has its origins in a local legend in which wives from Gidleigh who were accused of being unfaithful would have to wash at Cranmere Pool, crawl through the Tolmen Stone (a good few miles from Cranmere Pool), and then pray for forgiveness in Scorhill Stone Circle. It might be that this superstitious rite was carried out at some point: some say that the circle has a female energy, and it has been said that some men feel uncomfortable entering the circle. All these things were used to inspire *Ordeal*, although the part about the Tolmen Stone was left out in order to move the story along more smoothly.

Devil's Cauldron is set at the place of the same name at Lydford Gorge which, as with many Dartmoor places, has mythical links with Satan. This story has also been inspired by the true story of the Gubbins gang which operated around Lydford in the 17th century.

No prizes for guessing the source of the *Legend of Vixana*. Vixen Tor has been off-limits to visitors since 2003 when the new landowner decided to block access to the tor. The pub in the story has been invented – unless there was once an inn somewhere in the vicinity of Yellowmead Farm.

The Whaler is based on The Highwayman Inn. Readers who may be unfamiliar with this unique pub are missing a treat. The Inn is reputedly haunted (it wouldn't be a Dartmoor Inn if it wasn't!). The old Tavistock-Launceston coach has been built into the porch of the pub and parts of the interior resemble a smugglers' cave. There is plenty to explore in the strangest of inns, and it is without doubt one of the best Dartmoor pubs.

The Grey is not attached to any particular legend or place, although I came up with the idea while walking on Cox Tor and seeing someone come out of the fog. The many times I slipped, or nearly slipped, off wet granite more than likely contributed to the story too.

Beast is set near Cranmere Pool, among the very boggy ground that characterizes the whole area. In reality, it is unlikely that someone could become as firmly stuck in a bog as Mel does, but I have spoken to people who have sunk past their waist in bog and spent a good deal of time trying to free themselves. There are areas of bog covered by sphagnum moss which is very bright green. The moss soaks up a lot of rainwater and the surface of the bog can be very springy to stand on and one can very easily fall through just as Mel does – it is also exceedingly fun to run across, despite the risk of submersion in stinking bogwater. It would also be difficult to compose a collection of dark tales on Dartmoor without including at least one big cat story. There have been alleged sightings of pumas, black leopards, lynx, and even a lion. Benjamin Smee, the owner of Dartmoor Zoo, once saw a black leopard late at night near his zoo, which he suggested was attracted to the sounds of his big cats. I have also been told that big cat prints were found around the zoo sparking an escaped animal alarm, only for it to be found that all the cats were secure. It is quite probable that big cats were released onto Dartmoor with the introduction of the Dangerous Wild Animals Act in 1976, but whether there are any on Dartmoor now is often debated, yet each year there are sightings of varying credibility.

Every Abbey has a legend about some secret passage connecting it to a nearby castle or church. I was told of such a thing many years ago while on a primary school visit to a Dartmoor church – I think it was probably St. Andrew's in Buckland Monachorum but the passage of years has clouded memory. I do, however, recall nine-year-old me spending time trying to search out this supposed secret tunnel to Buckland Abbey and was vexed when the tour guide didn't pay any attention to my declarations that it sounded hollow under certain flagstones. This memory is what became the foundation of the story *Passage*.

There is no mystery of the location of the story *Crazywell Pool* (or Cressywell as some prefer to call it). The story encompasses two legends: that it is bottomless (it is in fact only about five metres at the deepest point), and that the pool calls out the name of next resident of Walkhampton Parish to die. The story is also slightly inspired by superstition around the death of two bikers who died in a crash after visiting the pool.

Heathfield House is based on an old manor house on southern Dartmoor which I am fortunate to reside in. The name and many other details of the property have been changed as it is a private residence which I don't suppose the family that own it might necessarily want associated with ghost stories. The house itself is not particularly spooky, although I have never ventured to peer through the hatch to the loft. The ghost in this case in inspired from an old tale of a man who died in the Warren House Inn and his pickled remains were left in a room over winter so he might be taken for burial in the spring.

The Circle in the Woods is set in Fernworthy Forest. The name has been changed to Ferntor Forest and the name of the Forestry Commission (Or, I think, it's Forestry England now) has also been changed so as to not malign their workers – none of which, I'm sure, are members of an ancient cult. The inspiration for the story came from when I was walking up a steep trail near Assycombe Brook and found a trail of blood which I followed, much as Eve does in the story, until it disappeared into the woods. It was a cold winter day and I was seemingly alone in the forest, providing excellent inspiration for storytelling. Anyone visiting Fernworthy Forest outside of the summer months and venturing along the tangle of lonely trails is sure to feel like they are being watched; peering into the thick forest is likely to produce glimpses of things which at first glance might resemble Herne the Hunter, or some beastly shape, but on second look are mere oddly shaped tree stumps. In the right season it is a truly spooky place and I encourage everyone who can visit to do so. The stone circle in the story does not exist (there is of course a well-known circle in Fernworthy at Froggymead), however as recently as 2007 a stone circle was discovered near Sittaford Tor, a short hike from Fernworthy.Who knows what archaeological remains lay undiscovered under the thick undergrowth of Fernworthy Forest?

I hope you have enjoyed reading these stories. It would be very much appreciated if you could leave an honest review at Goodreads.com or on Amazon; few readers review books and as readers we look for reviews when browsing for possible purchases, so taking a minute to leave a review (or even just a rating) helps make further books possible. For updates on future works or just to chat about Dartmoor please check in with me at Andrewmcauleyauthor.com.

Also available from the author:
The March of the Dragons
The Sampford Slaying

Non-fiction:
Conflict in Medieval Devon, 614 – 1497

Printed in Great Britain
by Amazon

39622605R00128